Take My Hand

Marguerite Mooers

Copyright © 2014 **Marguerite Mooers**
All rights reserved.

ISBN: 0990444805
ISBN 13: **9780990444800**
Library of Congress Control Number: **9780990444800**
LCCN Imprint Name: **Potsdam, New York**

To Dick, my supporter, cheerleader, first reader and wise critic. I could not have done any of this without you.

Come away, O human child!

To the waters and the wild

With a faery, hand in hand,

For the world's more full of weeping than you can understand.

W. B. Yeats, The Stolen Child

Table of Contents

Acknowledgements: 11
Chapter One 1
    Chris Bellini 1
Chapter Two 11
Chapter Three 16
Chapter Four 23
Chapter Five 32
Chapter Six 45
Chapter Seven 62
Chapter Eight 69
Chapter Nine 73
Chapter Ten 85
Chapter Eleven 94
Chapter Twelve 98
Chapter Thirteen 106
Chapter Fourteen 115
Chapter Fifteen 120
Chapter Sixteen 126
Chapter Seventeen 134
Chapter Eighteen 141
Chapter Nineteen 146
Chapter Twenty 157
    Lorna Smith Watson 157
Chapter Twenty One 165
    Lorna Smith Watson 165
Chapter Twenty Two 172
    Chris 172
Chapter Twenty Three 179
Chapter Twenty Four 191

Chapter Twenty Five 199
    Lorna Smith Watson 199
Chapter Twenty Six 204
    Chris 204
Chapter Twenty Seven 213
    Lorna Smith Watson 213
Chapter Twenty Eight 220
    Chris 220
Chapter Twenty Nine 226
Chapter Thirty 240
Chapter Thirty One 256
Chapter Thirty Two 269
Chapter Thirty Three 280
Chapter Thirty Four 298
Chapter Thirty Five 304
Chapter Thirty Six 317
Chapter Thirty-Seven 328

Acknowledgements:

Each writer composes a first draft alone. Whether he is working at a computer, or scratching words on paper, writing a first draft is like hacking your way through a dense jungle using only a butter knife. You may have a general idea where your story is going, but the way ahead is clogged with foliage, thick with roots underfoot and blocked by a bird sitting on your shoulder crying that this is never going to work and you're crazy to try.

This is why writers create acknowledgement pages. I would like to thank those friends who said I could do it when I was full of doubt about my own ability, who read and critiqued my work, who suggested changes, said nice things about my writing, and kept me going.

To my first readers: Barbara Briody, Pat Holt, Dick Mooers, Pat Mueller, and Aileen Vincent-Barwood. You have helped to bring this book out of the file drawer and made it real.

To my writing friends: Ruth Asher, Toni Somers, Sue Rourke-Calnek and Maggie Noble, and all others who have shown the way. Thank you for your encouragement.

Last, but certainly not least, my family. To my stepchildren, John and Sarah, their partners, Christine and Tim and my grandchildren, Ben, Caitlyn, Hannah and Rebeccah; thank you for being there. If I have forgotten anyone else, my sincere apologies.

One note: This book is a work of fiction. However, the lawn posters demanding "Justice for Ethan" are based on a real event, the murder of a boy in my home town. Though the real child was older than Ethan LeBrun, and the circumstances of his death were different, I choose to show in my novel the way a close community can come together in dealing with the death of a child.

To my readers: Obviously without a readership, no writer can succeed. I am grateful to you for buying, borrowing, stealing or otherwise acquiring this book. (Actually I hope you didn't steal the book.) I am very interested in what you thought, pro or con. I've got a pretty tough skin. Please give me your feedback. My e-mail is: funstories043@gmail.com.

Take My Hand is available through Amazon either as a paperback or Kindle e-book. It is also available on Smashwords for other e-readers

Take My Hand

Chapter One

Chris Bellini

Friday afternoon, at the end of shift, is the worst time for a cop. I am eager to get home, pop a cold one and put my feet up, but those citizens without a regular nine to five have already got a head start on the weekend and are looking for trouble. I'm Chris Bellini and I'm a cop and it was Friday afternoon, just before the end of shift, when we got the call. I recognized the address immediately. The Battling Bickertons. Their name was actually Barstow and at least once a month we were called to their place on a domestic. We would arrive at the scene. She would complain that he struck her with (your choice: vase, skillet, kid's plastic baseball bat) and he would be drunk, hardly able to understand what was happening.

"Wish the hell they'd just divorce," my partner, Larry Grindon said. He and I have been together for little more than a year and we work together well. Larry's a good cop, even if he's a little untried. We pulled into the driveway of the Barstow's. The front door stood open and I could hear shouting from inside. I called the station to say where we were, in case something happened. Then we got out of the car.

As the senior officer, it was my job to walk up the steps first. Even though we'd been here before, I could feel my heart racing and my palms sweating. The walk to the front door seemed like miles.

I rapped loudly on the door. Silence.

"Mrs. Barstow," I called. "It's the police."

"You god-damned bitch," someone yelled. I think it was the husband. "You called the fucking cops."

"Jimmy," she wailed. "You were hurting me."

"Mrs. Barstow," I called again.

At that moment the door opened and Emma Barstow appeared. She was barely five feet and weighed about two fifty. Her hair was in curlers, her face blotchy and tear stained and she was wearing a dirty housedress and bunny slippers.

"Thanks for coming," she said. "But we don't need you anymore."

"We're here to help you, Mrs. Barstow. You need to come to the station and file an order of protection against your husband."

She shook her head, and leaned toward me. "Just go," she said. "He's got a gun."

Damn. I turned to Larry who was standing behind me. "Call for backup."

In the darkened hallway behind Mrs. Barstow I could see someone's bulk.

"Mr. Barstow," I called. "Drop your weapon and come out."

"Yeah right," he said.

"Barstow, this is your last call. Throw down the gun and come out."

Larry was behind me fumbling for his gun. He was new to the job, and seemed to panic easily. "Let me handle this, Larry," I hissed.

Barstow appeared in the doorway his hand on his revolver. Before I had time to draw my own weapon, he raised the gun and pointed it directly at my chest. "Back off cop," he said.

I moved slightly trying to avoid the gun barrel. "Mr. Barstow," I said. "Let's rethink this. Just put the wea..."

Barstow fired.

The bullet hit my shoulder and I stumbled backward, landing in the bushes beside the concrete steps. It's as if I've been hit by dynamite.

"Jesus, Jimmy. You shot a cop," Emma Barstow screamed.

Take My Hand

I was struggling to rise, but the body/brain connection had been cut off and all I could do was thrash helplessly in the bushes. I must have passed out, because when I came to, there were cops all over the place and paramedics were lifting me onto a stretcher. Inside the ambulance, I was given drugs for the pain and then slipped into blessed sleep.

Most of the first six hours in the hospital happened without my conscious participation. I was taken to surgery where the bullet was removed. Then to the ICU where I drifted in and out on a blissful sea of painkillers, until I woke in a hospital room with my shoulder heavily bandaged and tubes running from an IV into my arm. When I was finally fully conscious, I saw Amelia sitting in a chair, watching me with Mrs. Gentile, the babysitter close by.

Amelia is my six year old granddaughter whom I am raising because her mother is a drug addict. Since my wife died of cancer, I've been a single parent. I don't mind the job; in fact sharing my life with a six year old has made life interesting, but my work as a cop is dangerous, and I worry that Amelia may end up alone. Six months ago, I took the exam for detective. That job is not without its dangers, but there's less chance I could be shot. What am I thinking? I have been shot.

"Poppi, Poppi, you're awake," Amelia bellowed. She rushed toward me and tried to hug me.

I point to my bandaged shoulder and the arm which is bound against my chest. "Careful, sweetie. It's still sore."

"Can I see it?"

"Maybe later, when it's healed." I look toward Mrs. Gentile, who as her name suggests, is grey-haired, soft spoken and very kind. "Thank you for bringing her."

"We were worried, Mr. Bellini. When they said you'd been shot, all I could think of was what would Amelia do without you."

I could have reminded Mrs. Gentile that Amelia has a mother, though where my daughter is, and whether she is free of her drug habit is anyone's guess. I hadn't seen or heard from Cecile for three years, and our last meeting was far from cordial with Cecile shouting at me that I had no right to keep her daughter from her, and my shouting back that I had legal custody and she wouldn't see Amelia until she was clean. Amelia's father isn't even in the picture. He never married my daughter, and the last I heard he was doing time for armed robbery.

"When are you coming home, Poppi?" Amelia asked. She had tucked herself close to me and was clutching my good hand.

"A few days. I have to learn to do everything with my other hand." I mimed using my uninjured hand to bring food to my mouth and missing it completely. Amelia laughed.

"Nice to see you're awake," a doctor said from the doorway. He looked at Mrs. Gentile and Amelia. "Would you two wait in the hallway, please? I'd like to speak to Mr. Bellini alone."

"Are you going to give him a shot?" Amelia asked.

"No, we're just going to talk."

"That's good, 'cause Poppi don't like shots."

The doctor watched them go. "Your daughter?"

"Granddaughter," I said. "It's a long story."

He nodded and then sat back in the chair. "You were very lucky Mr. Bellini. The bullet could have hit an artery and you might have bled to death on the way to the hospital. As it is, you will not have the use of that arm for about six weeks, and you'll have to do stretching exercises to get back full mobility."

"Six weeks," I echoed.

He nodded." You won't be able to drive a car or shoot a gun I'm afraid. You'll have to get used to dressing, eating and writing with your left hand. Do you have someone at home to help you?"

"Just my granddaughter. She's six but she can do some things. Mrs. Gentile can help with the cooking."

Take My Hand

He nodded. "I think we can release you the day after tomorrow. You might need to hire a nurse's aide just to get you through the first few days, but you are strong and I think you'll make a good recovery."

When the doctor had left, I settled back on the pillows, but I couldn't relax. What would I do if I couldn't go back to patrolman? My father had been a cop and from the time I was a teen and the police force was the only job I wanted. And now, at forty two, I might be facing the end of my career. I was too young to collect my full pension and too old to start something new. I might be able to grab a job working night security, but I would probably die of boredom before I could retire. At that moment Tom O'Malley, the Police Chief poked his head in the door. Tom is slightly overweight, with piercing blue eyes and salt and pepper hair. He looks like someone selling life insurance on late night television. Three years ago, when the old Chief retired I'd been offered the job, but I've never wanted to be desk jockey and turned it down. Now I wonder if I made a mistake. If I'd taken the job of Chief, my future would be secure, even if I couldn't carry a gun.

"You don't look too bad Chris," the Chief said, sitting in the chair against the wall. "How you feeling?"

"Like I've been shot. How's Larry doing?"

"Not too well. You'd think he was the one that took the bullet. His wife, Sally says he isn't sleeping, and he sits around all day just staring into space. I'm sure he's dealing with guilt and wondering how his family would make it, if he were shot. Of course, you have the same issues."

I nodded. "You're not thinking of letting me go, are you Chief?"

"Hell no. You're just about the best man I got. What I'm trying to do is find something where you can get paid, and you're not in the line of fire."

"And Larry?"

"He'll be OK. We'll give him a little vacation and hope he can snap out of it. I've seen this before. In Maine we had a man who came out of the

Academy with great shooting skills, and the first time he was in a firefight, he just froze. He ended up working security for Wal-Mart."

"I was hoping not to do that." We were quiet for a moment. I was running through all the things a cop with a broken wing could do and still be on the payroll. I could lecture school kids about the dangers of recreational pharmaceuticals, or stand in front of old ladies and enumerate the ways they could get scammed. It would be a living, but not much. I waited, hoping O'Malley had something better in mind.

"You remember the LeBrun case?" he asked.

"Sure."

Ten years ago, it had been major news. On a cool spring day, eight year old Ethan LeBrun, was walking home from school when he disappeared. A ransom note was found on the kitchen counter of the house, but when the father went to meet the kidnappers, no one was there. Later that evening, police dogs found the boy's body in the woods behind the LeBrun home. Ethan's hands had been tied, and duct tape put over his mouth. The boy was wearing a light cotton sweatshirt, not much protection against the fifty degree temperature of that April night. Some children might have survived the ordeal, but Ethan LeBrun had severe asthma and when police found him, he was dead.

Sandy LeBrun, Ethan's father had been a famous plastic surgeon who moved his family from New York City to Euclid because he saw country life as safer. After the kidnapping, TV and print media descended on the town, clogging the Save-A-Lot parking lot and trolling through the citizenry for stories. In spite of the work of two local detectives, after several years there was still no closure. Ten years later, there was still none.

A fund was established and lawn posters sprang up demanding "Justice for Ethan." The unsolved case festered under the surface of the town's public image. How could any place promote itself as family friendly when the kidnapping and death of a kid remained unsolved?

"Harner, the new D.A. wants to re-open the case. Want to take it on, Chris?"

I shook my head. I had Amelia to raise. I didn't think I could bear to think about another child's death for the length of time it would take to solve the case. I looked at my boss. "You've been thinking about this for a while, haven't you, Chief?"

He nodded. "Harner came to me right after he was elected, said he wanted to do something to restore the town's image."

"And burnish his own image as D.A?"

"Yeah, I guess. Anyway, we threw around some names and yours came up. You did better than anyone else on the detective exam; you're the logical choice. And the grant funding came through last week. Think about it, Chris. You can do this from home. You won't have to carry a weapon and it will be a chance to see if you like detective work."

"You'd promote me?"

"We need a detective in the department. I'd rather it be you than some hot shot from out of town."

"You're serious?"

"Yup." he reached forward to slap me on the shoulder and then remembering my wound, pulled his hand back. "Think about it, Chris."

I lay back against the pillows, weighing the pros and cons of the offer. On the plus side, I had been waiting for such a chance. On the minus side, it would mean living day by day with the death of a child only a little bit older than my granddaughter. It's one thing to confront evil from a distance. We all do it when we watch the evening news, but this was a child who had died in my home town. This was a child who'd been kidnapped by someone familiar. It could have been someone I went to church with, or ate meals with, or sat beside during concerts in the park. Those thoughts twisted in my gut and made me want to walk as far away as I could from this case.

It had been ten years and in spite of the hard work of two good local detectives, the case was still unsolved. If I could find Ethan's killer, it wouldn't be to bring the good name of the town back, or even to burnish Chief O' Malley's image. I would do it for a little boy who had no voice of his own. I would do it for a child dying alone in a place where no one could find him. I would take the case to bring justice for Ethan.

Chapter Two

A week later two burly cops arrived at my door and started carrying cardboard boxes down to the basement, plunking them onto the old pool table. I had been home for less than a week now and was still getting used to doing everything with my left hand. I could feed myself, but dressing was a different matter. Through some intricate contortions, I could get my pants on with one hand but buttoning a shirt was beyond my ability. I was too embarrassed to ask the very proper Mrs. Gentile to dress me. In consequence I often went around wearing sweatpants and a sweater.

When the cops left, I stood looking at the five cartons of material that weighed down the elderly pool table. Pulling off the cover of one box, I glanced inside. The files were stuffed into the box in no order, and jammed on top were tabloids. I pulled out one called *The Star*. On the cover was a photograph of Mr. and Mrs. LeBrun, their hands covering their faces fleeing from the photographer. Above them was the headline. "Who really killed Ethan?"

Poor folks, I thought. *To have lost a child and then be hounded by media.*

I pulled several files from the box and laid them out on the table. They were interviews with major witnesses, photographs, a piece of duct tape in a plastic bag. It was going to take me weeks to sort this stuff out. I needed help sifting through evidence, interviewing witnesses, even driving. The Chief had not specifically forbidden me to recruit a partner, so I dialed up a man I thought could help.

"Larry, it's Chris. Listen, I need a favor. The Chief has put me on this cold case. You remember the LeBrun kidnapping? That one. Are you still on leave? Good. I can't pay you any extra, but I could sure use another hand. You can? Thanks."

In twenty minutes Larry was standing in my basement, surveying the piles. Since I had last seen him he'd grown a beard and had dark circles under his eyes.

"Sure you want to do this?" I asked.

"We need an evidence board," he said.

"Lowes has bulletin boards," I said. "That will do us for now."

We drove to Lowes and bought the biggest honking bulletin board we could find and lots of push pins. Larry had to muscle the thing down to the cellar by himself, but then I offered him a beer, one of the perks of working in your own house. We propped the board up in the corner and got to work sorting. By three o'clock, we'd got photos up of all the major players. I even had the names of the two detectives that had worked the case, although I'd heard that one was dead and the other retired to Florida.

"I didn't mean to keep you here all day Larry," I said when we were sitting on the sofa, surveying our handiwork.

"Hell Chris. This is the most fun I've had all week. Seriously, I've been moping around the house, getting underfoot and making Sally anxious. If you're willing to take me on, I'd like to work this case with you."

"I'll have to run it by the Chief," I said. "I don't think there's any extra money for you."

"I'm getting vacation pay, and when that runs out---well, then we'll decide."

Just at that moment, Amelia came running down the stairs. Amelia never walks when she can sprint, prance, jump, spin or do cartwheels. She threw herself onto the sofa beside us.

"Hiya Mr. Grindon," she said to Larry. "Did you get shot too?"

Larry shook his head.

"But you aren't wearing your uniform."

"Nope," he said. "I'm on vacation."

"Poppi's on vacation because he got shot," she announced proudly. She looked over at the pool table. "What's all that stuff?"

"Mr. Grindon and I are working on a case together."

"Can I help?"

"Not right now, sweetie. Maybe some other time."

"You always say that," she said, getting up from the sofa. She stood in the doorway, one hand on her hip, pouting. "I'm big enough to help, you know. I'm six." And then she flounced out.

Larry stood up. "Got to get home, Chris. What time tomorrow?"

"Nine," I said. "I want to see where the kid was taken." I picked up two of the interview files from the pool table and handed them over. "Bedtime reading."

When I got upstairs, I could smell the supper Mrs. Gentile was heating up. After the shooting, I'd become a minor celebrity, and a whole army of concerned neighbors had descended on the house with casseroles. There was enough food in the refrigerator to keep me stocked for months. I went to the cupboard and pulled out a wine bottle.

"Would you open it for me?" I asked Mrs. Gentile and she graciously did the job. I poured two glasses, handing her one. "Why don't you stay for supper." I knew she lived alone. Her husband died before my wife got cancer, and her only daughter lived ninety miles away.

"I don't think so," she said.

"I couldn't do any of this without your help, Mrs. Gentile. You know that. When you came to us, I was trying to hold down a job, care for a dying wife and wrangle a lively three year old."

"Claire was a lovely woman. I remember how much she helped me when Doug was sick." She took a sip of wine gazing fondly at Amelia who had just come into the kitchen.

"Can I have some of that?" Amelia asked.

"No," I said. "It's a drink for grownups."

"Someday I'll be old enough for grown up drinks," she declared. "And I'm gonna wear a uniform and carry a gun, just like Poppi."

"In the meantime, you can help set the table," I said.

Chapter Three

The next morning after walking Amelia to the bus stop and kissing her good-bye, Larry and I drove to the elementary school and parked the car. School had been in session for an hour, and though I knew which classroom was Amelia's, I resisted the urge to sneak past her room and wave through the window as being undignified for a police detective

Instead, we took out a small map of Euclid and consulted it. "Ethan's house was that way," I pointed. "So he would have set off in this direction. I wonder what time he left?"

"Three ten," Larry said. "I read the interview with the mother last night. Ethan always did things at the same time. He was a little compulsive."

"What else was he?"

"What do you mean?"

"When you read the interview, did you get a picture of the kid? Was he outgoing, introverted, smart, dumb, a suck-up or know it all?"

We were walking away from the school grounds, heading past a row of small houses that would give way to tiny businesses, the sort of casual zoning that happens in small towns.

"I think he was an anxious kid, eager to do well, bright, but not very strong. He had chronic asthma, which probably marked him as a wimp. And he was rich in a community of mostly poor and middle class families. One teacher said he was frequently picked on." Larry stopped to study the map. "How far is the house?"

"Half a mile more. So the mother was supposed to pick him up at three ten, but didn't?"

"According to the interview, she was at a meeting and couldn't get away. She called her husband at work, and he rushed over to the school to walk Ethan home."

"This boy was eight, couldn't he walk himself home?"

Larry shrugged. "He might have been a tad overprotected."

"Or maybe he'd often been set upon by bullies and his parents wanted to prevent that. What time did the father get there?"

"Three twenty. He parked the car at the school and began looking for Ethan. Went into the school, but everyone had left. He walked down the street, but there was no sign of the boy."

We stopped walking and I looked around. We'd come to an area of small shops. A tiny grocery store, stood next to a dry cleaner, a coffee shop, a resale store and a tailor. Between the coffee shop and the resale store was a miniscule alley that led to a small parking area. An ancient Volvo was parked there. Behind it, were woods.

"What if someone were able to get the boy past the coffee shop, through the parking area and take him into the woods. Wasn't he found bound and gagged there?"

Larry gave me a look that said I should have done my homework. "He was found in the woods behind his house, not here in the village."

"But the woods here in the village could be connected to those behind the LeBrun house. If the kidnappers could get the kid off the street, away from anyone who would hear him cry out..." I looked at the coffee shop. Could they have hustled Ethan past the coffee shop, and through the parking lot without anyone seeing or hearing him?

As if reading my mind, Larry said. "What if they took him *through* the coffee shop. Maybe there's a back door to the parking lot."

I nodded. There was only one thing wrong with that theory. Eight year olds don't generally drink coffee.

We went in. The smell of coffee was wonderful, reminding me that breakfast had been a good two hours ago. I went up to the counter and ordered two black coffees. Larry pointed to a blueberry muffin. "And one of those," he said.

Take My Hand

Fortunately we were the only patrons in the place. A sign in the corner pointed to the toilets, and when I walked in that direction, I noticed the door. I pulled the handle and saw that the distance from the back door of the coffee shop to a dense line of trees was about eight feet. Enough room to park a car but small enough to hustle a kid across without anyone knowing. If this was how Ethan had been taken, no one on the street would have heard him cry out.

I returned to the service area and stood in front of the barista, a twenty-something kid with long dark hair, face tats, and three studs in each ear. I could see him spending his evenings smoking pot. "How long has this place been in business?" I asked.

"I think they opened four years ago, but don't ask me, I just work here."

"Who is the owner?"

He looked at me sharply. "You guys just inspected us three weeks ago," he said. "And we passed. OK, I know I'm supposed to wear a hair net…"

"We're not health inspectors," I said. "I'm looking for information about the building. I'd like the phone number of the owner." Reluctantly, the kid grabbed a piece of paper, scribbled a number on it and handed it over.

When I dialed the number, a woman answered. Yes, she was one of the owners, was there a problem? I gave her the short answer about the investigation, trying not to go into too much detail, and she said they'd bought the building five years ago after it had sat unused for a while. She had no idea what the business had been before she bought it, or who the former owner was, but guessed if I went to the County courthouse, I could research the deed.

I chugged the rest of my coffee and gestured toward my partner. "We're going for a walk, Larry," I said.

We exited through the back of the building, down a short flight of steps, across the tiny parking lot, squeezed through the dense line of white spruce and we were in a forest.

"I didn't know this was here," Larry said.

"Euclid has these little pocket woods throughout the village. That's why the deer population has exploded." As if to prove my point, a doe walked casually past us, not more than a hundred feet away.

"Here's the path," Larry said. "And I know what kids do for recreation." The area around us was littered with cigarette butts, used condoms and once in a while, a needle. These woods were the perfect place for all sorts of mischief. We headed off in the direction of the LeBrun house, the path winding past a small brook, clogged with pizza boxes, chip bags and empty water bottles. I came across a rusted bicycle and an old mattress. And then we could see in the distance a chain link fence and beyond that the backs of houses that comprised the gated community where Ethan LeBrun had lived.

Larry stopped and sat down on a fallen log, wiping the sweat from his forehead. It was still early September, which in this part of northern New York fluctuates between sunny sixties and chilly forties. I could hear birds calling and smell leaves underfoot. If Larry and I had been in better shape, it would have been a great day for a walk in the woods.

We sat for a minute. In the distance a dog barked and somewhere, nearby, I could smell manure being spread. It was almost eleven, and I could hear very faintly the sound of kids laughing, so the school must be in the middle of recess or having an outdoor gym class. I wondered if Ethan had heard those sounds when he was being taken down this path.

I shook off the image and stood up. "Come on, Larry. We're almost there."

We were in luck. As we got closer to the fence, we could see a break in the chain link. Neither Larry nor I are young or fit enough to wriggle under a fence, but this was almost a doorway, a place where the fence had been muscled away from its connecting post and was hanging open invitingly.

We stepped through the opening into a grassy lawn, beyond which we could see the back yards of the houses. I was a law abiding man, a cop and here I was trespassing. And yet this part of the gated community seemed to be public land. I moved toward the back yards, feeling slightly guilty, but every house seemed to be empty.

"Which house was it?"

"Number two thirty seven. I think it's over there." Larry said, and without another word he started off across the field.

"Stop right there," a voice said. "or I'll shoot." I turned to see a man standing behind me, his shotgun pointed at my head.

Chapter Four

The man with the gun was eighty if he was a day, and wore an old plaid jacket and blue jeans that made him look like something out of the Beverly Hillbillies. His hand was shaking so hard, I was sure that he would plug one of us just by sneezing.

"Mr...." I began.

"Hofstetter. Folks call me Red. You guys are trespassing, you know that."

"Mr. Hofstetter, we're police officers investigating the death of Ethan LeBrun. Do you remember the case? Happened right here ten years ago."

He looked at me and slowly lowered the gun. "Sure do," he said. "Was working at the Hardware then. All them people running around taking pitchers and giving out money. You never heard such lies as people told about that doctor. Made things up just so they could share in the loot."

"Did you know the LeBruns?"

"Knowed the mister. He was some fancy plastic surgeon in New York City, but when he come into the Hardware, he was just like everyone else. 'What paints do you recommend, Mr. Hofstetter? How can I get the tile to stick, Mr. Hofstetter?' I felt real sorry for him when his little boy was kilt. In those days there was no fence back here. They had a guard at the front gate, thinking that was all they needed. If I'd a been back here, I'd a plugged that kidnapper for sure."

I looked at Hofstetter. Maybe the old man hadn't had a tremor ten years ago, but I bet now he couldn't hit the side of a tractor trailer parked two feet in front of him. Now that Red and I were on friendlier terms, I called out to Larry who was a hundred yards ahead, and oblivious. He turned and seeing the old man with the gun, came loping back.

Take My Hand

When Larry got within speaking distance, he held out his hand to the old man. "Larry Grindon," he said. "And you've met Chris Bellini, my partner."

I could see now that the old man was sweating. Even though it was September, it was too warm for that wool jacket. He was beginning to wobble on his feet too, and I wondered if we would have to call the ambulance and take the security guard at this gated community to the hospital.

"Is there somewhere we can go and sit down?"

"Sure, I got a little shack right up the way here. It ain't much, but it keeps me out of the weather. But don't you two try nothing. I got an eagle eye and very good hearing."

I promised that we would be good and we followed Mr. Hofstetter across the grass and up the road to a small structure painted red. It was clear that not much money had been spent on amenities here. The walls of the guard shack had only a single layer of siding with the studs visible on the inside. There was no insulation against what would be, in another two months, real cold. A tiny space heater in one corner was doing its best to warm the area around a chair and beside the chair was a rickety table on which was a hot plate, an ancient tea kettle, two cups, a jar of instant coffee, some sugar and a box of donuts.

"I come on duty at six and leave by three thirty," our host said. "The night guy, he's the one really gets the cold."

"Can we ask you some questions about the LeBruns?"

"Sure, fire away. I'm gonna tell you up front, that I never said nothing to them reporters, even though they was flashing money around like it was Christmas."

"We're not publishing anything, Mr. Hofstetter."

"I told ya call me Red. Everyone does excepting my wife who calls me things I daren't repeat."

"OK, Red. Larry and I are trying to play catch up on the LeBrun case. If we can get some answers we might be able to bring some criminals to justice. Your answers can help."

He straightened in his chair, imagining himself as the defender of the rights of the downtrodden.

"Were Mr. and Mrs. LeBrun happy in their marriage?"

Without answering he walked to the teapot and began filling it with water from a gallon jug. Then he put the teapot on the hot plate and fired the thing up.

"Folks has different ways of showing togetherness," he said. "My parents fought like two cats thrown into a bag, and yet they was together for seventy years, and when he went she never stopped talking about him. The LeBruns, they was city folks. I never saw him hug her, or even smile at her much, but then maybe that's how people act when they come from New York."

"What was their relationship to Ethan? To both their boys? Did you ever see them together as a family?"

"Once. In the summer the town has these concerts in the park and the four of them came together. The doctor acted like he was real bored, and I think she was mad at him. She kept fussing over the younger boy, Ethan, and the doc didn't want her to do that. I could hear them arguing about it. But you know, lots 'a people argue about lots 'a things. Don't mean they hate each other."

I remembered the arguments I'd had with Claire, mostly about how we should deal with our increasingly difficult teenage daughter. If she were alive today, would I take back any of those words?

"Red," Larry said. "Do you know that little shop that's close to the elementary school, the one that sells coffee?"

Red nodded. "Was a comic book store for a while, and then the owner retired. No one wanted to buy it, so it just went downhill. Heard it's a real nice place now."

Take My Hand

"They sold comic books?"

"Din't I just say that? Yeah. Old ones, new ones. I don't know how that man could make money selling things that most folks just throw away, but he did."

"Do you know who the owner was? The man who sold comic books?"

The water in the kettle had reached full boil and was screeching to be removed. Red got up and began putting instant coffee into two cups. He turned toward me. "Black or white?"

I absolutely hate instant coffee. "Black," I said."

He turned toward Larry. "How about you, mister?"

Larry was less fussy. He watched as Red added 'whitener' to the coffee. Then Red gave us both our drinks.

"Man's name was something beginning with an A. Ambrose? Andrews? Arrow? No, it was like 'arrow'. Archer. That's it. Giles Archer. It was Archer Comics, I remember because the store had a picture of a man shooting an arrow beside the front door."

Larry had taken out his notebook and was scribbling in it. I had finished my coffee in one gulp, giving it the absolute minimum time to ruin my taste buds. Red took the cup, rinsed it out with water from the jug and then poured more instant coffee into it, adding water.

"No more for me, thanks," I said.

"This ain't for you," he said. "I only got two cups so we have to drink in shifts." He poured a liberal amount of whitener and sugar into the cup, possibly to kill the taste of the instant coffee and sat down. "Anything else I can help you gents with?"

I pulled my card out and handed it over. "We may have more questions. Do you have a number where we can reach you?"

Red tore a corner off the donut box and scribbled a number on it.

"Thanks for your time," Larry said. "If you think of something that might be important, please call us."

"Will do," Red said. He finished his coffee in quick order. "I'd better get out there so they can see I'm working. You gents can find your way out." He pointed. "Front entrance is that way."

We walked dutifully toward the front entrance, where a man was ensconced in a warm little building beside a gate. He gave us a strange look. He was used to people entering and exiting by car, not on foot, but he let us out.

We headed back toward town. By now it was about noon and some of the high schoolers who had only a half day were crowding the sidewalks. I watched them as they laughed and joked with each other. One boy was walking by himself, his head down, isolated in his own world. Suddenly another student came up behind him and pushed him hard, nearly knocking the kid over. I expected the boy to retaliate, punch his attacker or yell something, but he said nothing, only moved off the sidewalk. A second kid did the same, pushing the boy hard, knocking the books out of his arms. I knew that bullying was a problem, but I'd never seen it up close.

"Hey" I yelled to the second boy. I started after him, but he was soon beyond my reach, laughing at me.

I moved to the boy who had been bullied. Tears were running down his cheeks and he was rubbing his eyes, walking fast.

"Does that happen every day?" I asked.

He nodded.

"Have you talked to someone about it? Your parents? A teacher?"

"My dad says to fight back. 'Be a man,' he says. But if I fight back, it'll just be worse."

I fished in my pocket, pulled out my cards and handed the kid two. "I'm a police officer," I said. "I'd like you to come to my house and give me the names of the kids who are bullying you. They won't know who ratted them out, but I will do everything I can to make them stop."

He looked at me like I was crazy. A man with his arm in a sling who was going to fight bullies? "Put your name on the back of one card and give it back." He did and it was only then that I saw the faint smile.

"You can really call them off?"

"I'll try," I said.

"What was that all about?" Larry asked as the kid ambled off. He'd been following some distance behind, distracted by the pubescent girls in their scanty tops and belly-revealing skirts.

"I wonder if Ethan LeBrun was bullied, and tried to fight his attackers?"

"And they took their revenge?"

I nodded. "Ethan's kidnapping feels like a prank gone wrong. I don't think whoever kidnapped him intended for him to die, they just wanted to teach him a lesson. What they didn't realize was that you can't cut off the air supply of a person with asthma."

"There was a ransom note, Chris. It had to be pre-planned."

"We need to go through the files. I'm going crazy trying to sort out what's important and what's junk. I need a secretary."

"I've got a teenage daughter, Myra. She's not much for school but she loves computers. We might be able to get her to come over one or two afternoons a week."

"It would help," I said.

"I'm trying to get her to save money for college, but she thinks she's gonna be the next Bill Gates, and make a million before she's nineteen. I tell her the real world doesn't work that way."

"Ethan must have known the person who took him into the comic book store. I don't think he would willingly go with a stranger. So if he went with someone he knew, who were they? And why would he go off with a friend when he expected his mother to pick him up at school? It doesn't make sense."

"We could talk to some of his teachers," Larry said. We had reached the parking lot where Larry's car was parked. Larry got into the driver's seat and I got in beside him.

"Let's go have lunch," I said.

"On the department," Larry said.

Chapter Five

We had our lunch at Katie's Kountry Kitchen, a place where at noon you can meet everyone from dog-catcher to mayor. A lot of these people had read about the shooting but hadn't seen me until today, so I had to spend some time reassuring them that I was OK, and thanks for the good wishes and the casseroles.

When I finally got to sit, Larry had already ordered and was half-way through a huge Pastrami sandwich.

"You could have waited," I said.

"You sound like my wife," he said. "Just give her your order. You're a celebrity here; she'll get it chop chop."

He was right. I ordered a turkey sandwich, with cranberry sauce and mayo, something called a Pilgrim's Progress, and got the sandwich before Larry had started on the second half of his.

I took out a piece of paper and drew Ethan's name in the center. "We need to learn the names of the kids who knew Ethan. If he was being bullied, there should be evidence."

"There'll be something in the notes won't there?"

I hoped so. I thought of the kid we'd seen that morning. If I hadn't stepped in and promised to help him, would he have confided in anyone? Apparently he'd told his father and got no help from that quarter. We needed to find out more about Ethan, who were his friends, who were his enemies. what he was like?

"What was Ethan's older brother's name? Gavin?"

"Greg. He was five years older, so he'll be twenty-three. College student? Working? I've no idea."

"We're close to the elementary school. There might be a teacher there who knew Ethan."

"And knew Greg."

"Did you find any teacher interviews with the other material?" Larry asked.

"To tell you the truth, I haven't got that far. But we're close to the school now. Let's just go ask."

As it turned out, when we talked to the principal there was one teacher who'd had Ethan LeBrun as a student, and who was still teaching. Her name was Helena Bledsoe, and after eighteen years in the school system, she was due to retire. Since it was quarter to two, we had to wait for a while until school was dismissed. I had an urge to run down to Amelia's classroom and say hi, but I knew that would be disruptive. We spent the forty five minutes chatting up the principal, who'd been an elementary school student in this very school and even remembered my father, who'd been the cop that gave safety lectures here.

We stayed in the principal's office until the swell of children's voices had died and then we went down to Mrs. Bledsoe's room. Mrs. Bledsoe was a tiny woman with short white hair who was gathering up papers in piles.

"These are detectives Bellini and Grindon. They're looking into the death of Ethan LeBrun," the principal said.

Mrs. Bledsoe sat down suddenly, and I could see sadness cross her face, as though the tragedy had happened yesterday, not ten years ago. "You were his teacher, weren't you?" I asked.

She nodded, and then turned the principal. "I'll be all right, John. It just took me by surprise. That poor little boy. I've never gotten over his death."

Larry and I went into the classroom and sat at two of the child sized desks.

"You're Amelia's father, aren't you?" she asked looking at me. "I thought I recognized the name."

"Actually, I'm her grandfather. Amelia's grandmother and I were raising her, but..."

"Amelia told me," Mrs. Bledsoe interrupted. "I am so sorry."

I nodded. We weren't here to talk about my loss, but about the child she'd known.

"How long was Ethan LeBrun in your class?"

"About eight months. His family moved to Euclid the year he started first grade. He was in my second grade class from September until he died in early April."

"Would you characterize him as hard working or lazy, smart or not so smart, stingy or generous?"

"You have a lot of black or whites, don't you detective?"

"Sorry, I don't mean to push you in any direction. It's hard for us to get a feel for him from the documents we have. Tell me how you saw him."

"Ethan came to this small town from the big city. Not just that, but he came from wealth. He'd had the benefit of a private pre-school, so he was much farther ahead than most of the kids in his class. He wasn't a mean kid, just young. In the circles he'd grown up in, families went to the museums on Saturday, spent Christmas in the Bahamas, or summered in Paris. Most of the kids who grow up here have never been out of the county, and the big event of the year is the Demolition Derby at the County Fair. When you have a kid coming in who knows a lot more than anyone else, and who's been to a lot more places, he's a foreigner. Ethan was as much a foreigner as if he'd been born in Russia or Tibet. He didn't speak the language."

"You said he was smart," Larry said.

"Very. And well educated. But he was also small for his age, and had asthma."

"Making him a target for bullying?"

"I'm afraid so."

"Did you see any of the bullying directly?" Larry asked.

Mrs. Bledsoe shook her head. "Most of it happens before and after classes, on the bus or when the kids are walking to school. Sometimes it happens in the school yard at recess, but it rarely takes place in the classroom."

"But you knew he was unhappy."

"He was quiet, withdrawn, almost apathetic. In March, I tried to get his parents to find a therapist for him. The next month he was dead."

"Do you have any idea who his tormentors might have been?"

She shook her head.

"Did he ever talk about his home life?" I asked.

"He admired his brother, but Greg was five years older, so he must have seemed like another adult. His father worked long hours and his mother was studying to be a lawyer. I remember his talking about the gardener, a Mr. Shevchenko, whom he was close to. He wasn't completely without adult support, but I think he spent a lot of his life alone."

The three of us sat silently for a moment, thinking of the sad life of a child who should have had everything, but had very little.

"Did you know Ethan's older brother, Greg?" Larry asked.

"He was never in my class, but my friend Mary Rowling taught sixth grade that year. She said Greg was kind of a wild child. He had his own cell phone, and free use of his mother's charge card. Some of the kids said he smoked and drank in the woods behind the house."

"In the same woods where Ethan died?"

Take My Hand

"I think so."

"He was doing those things at thirteen?"

She nodded. "It happens. Kids are more sophisticated now than when we were growing up."

"Can you give us Mary Rowling's number?" Larry asked.

She scribbled a number on a piece of paper and handed it to Larry.

We stood up. I reached out and shook her hand. "Thank you for your time, Mrs. Bledsoe."

"You're welcome. Give my best to Amelia. She's a wonderful child."

We had reached the door of the classroom, when Mrs. Bledsoe said. "One more thing. I don't remember Ethan ever talking about anyone who was bullying him. But he did have one friend."

"An adult?"

"No, a seventh grader. Ethan said he'd met this boy at Archer Comics, you know where the coffee shop is today. It seemed an unusual friendship to me. Why would a fourteen year old kid want to spend time with an eight year old? But Ethan liked him."

"You don't happen to remember the kid's name, do you?"

"Nope, sorry."

We stood and shook hands. It was now almost three. My injured shoulder was beginning to ache and it was time to head for home. Larry drove me to my house, and we agreed to meet here the next day.

Amelia was home when Larry and I got there, as was Mrs. Gentile. They were in the kitchen making cookies and helping them was a pale, thin child that Amelia introduced as Carey.

"We're in the same class, Poppi. And we're going to be in a play."

"A play?"

"Apparently the school is putting on a combined Thanksgiving and Christmas play which is going to involve a cast of thousands," Mrs. Gentile said.

Amelia left the room and came running back with a crumpled piece of paper which she shoved at me. The paper said that tryouts for the play called Welcoming the Holidays would be held the following Wednesday at three-thirty p.m. Everyone in grades one through six was invited to try out. There would be singing and dancing so kids should come prepared to do one or both. Suggestions for sewing costumes would be provided once the cast had been chosen.

"This says you have to try out, Amelia," I said. I looked over at the pale child who had not said anything throughout the whole interchange. "Are you hoping to be in the play, too, Carey?"

She nodded solemnly.

"Let me tell you something," I said, drawing both girls close as I crouched before them. "A tryout means that you have to either sing or dance to show the director how good you are. Then after everyone has a chance to do that, the director chooses the person who will be in the play."

Amelia's face fell. "I thought *everyone* was going to be in the play. That's what the teacher said."

"Everyone who is *chosen* after the tryouts will be in the play. I'm afraid not everyone will get in."

"I don't have to be in the play," Carey said. She looked at Amelia." I just wanted to be in it 'cause of you."

"We'll both be in it," Amelia declared stoutly. I admired her loyalty but I suspected that after tryouts, there would be a few broken hearts.

"You should think of a song you want to sing, and practice it. If you want to dance, you have to practice that too." Just then the doorbell rang. Mrs. Gentile went to answer it. When she came back into the kitchen, she was being followed by a stunning redhead nearly as tall as I was.

"Mommy," Carey cried and hugged the woman around the waist. The woman looked at me and held out her hand. "I'm Willi DeGrasse. Sorry, I should have asked ahead of time if Carey could come back with Amelia. This play has everyone in a tizzy."

"It's fine," I said. "Mrs. Gentile is always here."

"What happened to your arm?"

"Poppi got shot by a bad man," Amelia declared. "He's a cop, only he's on vacation because he got hurt."

"Actually I'm working on a cold case, one that I hope to solve single handed." I waved the fingers of my broken wing.

Willi looked at her daughter. "We really should be going."

"I'd offer you a glass of wine," I said. "But I expect your husband may be waiting for his supper."

"Daddy died," Carey said.

"I'd love some wine," Willi said.

"We could give you supper, too," I said. "I have a freezer full of donated casseroles. Amelia, why don't you take Carey out to the garden and see if there are any tomatoes still ripe out there."

"I've got to leave early tonight," Mrs. Gentile said. "My sister's coming to visit tomorrow and I'm getting the house ready."

When we were alone in the kitchen, Willi looked around. Maybe she was trying to guess where I'd stashed my wife, if indeed I had one.

"My wife, Claire died of cancer," I said.

"I'm so sorry."

"How did your husband die, Mrs. DeGrasse?"

"Please call me Willi." She took a sip of wine. "The truck he was driving ran into an IED in Afghanistan, two years ago. The irony of the whole thing was that he joined the reserves so we could save for a house. It was only going to be a one year deployment. Two weeks after he went over, he was killed. I was going to school full time, getting my master's degree in teaching. After Jim died, I decided to leave the Ohio town where we had lived and move back here to be near my parents. We moved here in June and I got a job teaching seventh grade English. But then my Dad died, and my Mom moved to Florida. The people who were going to be my support system vanished."

"I'm sorry about your husband," I said. I watched anger and sorrow flicker across her face. I knew how she felt.

"This is an awful hard place to meet people," Willi said.

"Male or female?"

"Both. I didn't realize how 'small townish' it was."

I've lived here most of my life, so to me the small town works, but I know how hard it is to be single. To change the subject, I asked. "What do you know about the play?"

"It's a mishmash of all the holidays: Halloween, Thanksgiving, Hanukah and Christmas. I think they've even thrown in Duwali and Kwanzaa. There are almost forty kids who will be on stage at one time or another. Stanley Mann, who teaches eighth grade English is a saint to take it on, mainly because he's got a third grade boy who is mad for the theatre. I have agreed to help, but I vowed I would not co-direct."

"I think Amelia and Carey will need some help planning an audition routine."

Just at that moment the two little girls bounced into the room. They had taken up a tomato plant by the roots, and there were three ripe tomatoes hanging off the end.

"I told you to pick the tomatoes not the whole plant," I scolded.

"We tried, Poppi, but they wouldn't come off."

"OK," I said. It really wasn't a problem because in another few weeks we'd be pulling up the garden anyway.

"Willi, do you mind taking a casserole from the refrigerator and putting it in the oven?"

She opened the freezer. "It's pretty frozen, Chris. Why don't we send out for a pizza."

"Yeah, pizza," Carey said, jumping up and down.

"Sure," I said. I picked up the phone and ordered the pizza.

It arrived fifteen minutes later. With Willi's help, I managed to make a small green salad and then we sat down to eat.

"We make pizza in our back yard," Amelia declared. Willi and Carey both looked at me, imagining pizza dough stuck in the trees.

"We have a brick oven," I said. "We make the pizza in the kitchen and cook it out back."

I saw the color rise faintly in Willi's face. She looked down at the meal she was eating, realizing that I must consider this very inferior to the pizza I could make myself.

"This is fine," I said. "Considering I only have one good arm, it's much better than what I could have made." To change the subject, I turned to the girls. "What are you going to be in the play?"

"I'm going to be a dancing pumpkin," Amelia said. "Josh Waters is going to be Santa Claus. He already told me."

"We get to sing and dance," Carey said.

"And wear costumes."

I could sew as easily as I could assemble a fighter plane. I looked at Willi. "I may need some help with costumes."

"Not a problem." She looked at her watch. "Carey. It's time to go." She turned toward me. "Can I help you with the dishes?"

"Thanks, I can manage."

She and Carey left. I was a little sorry to see them go. Besides the fact that she was a good looking woman, and I hadn't had many of those in my life recently, it was nice to have a conversation with a grownup that didn't involve police work. Amelia and I loaded the dishwasher, did a half hour of homework and then it was her bedtime.

Chapter Six

It took me a long time to get to sleep that night. When Claire was alive, we'd often spend our evenings talking about the day. It was my chance to de-stress and share what had happened. Not having a partner to bounce things off of, was only one of the ways I missed Claire.

Claire Baxter had been the prettiest girl in my junior class, bar none. She had dark hair that shone in the sun, and bright blue eyes. Her father owned a major department store downtown, and they lived in a big house on Hillcrest, with a swimming pool and flower garden. Compared to my house which was a modest bungalow, bursting with six children, Claire lived in a palace.

You'd have thought that living in the upper echelons of Euclid society Claire wouldn't want anything to do with the rest of us, but she got dirty playing soccer just like the rest of us, was yearbook editor, sang in the chorus, worked at the food kitchen downtown on Saturday and had already been accepted to Princeton. It took all my courage just to say hi when we passed in the hallway.

I don't remember when she started to notice me. I played football pretty well, but I wasn't a star and she seemed to have lots of admirers. It might have been when I accidentally dropped my lunch tray at her feet, and then slipped in the mess to the amusement of the whole cafeteria that she finally saw me. After that we started talking, doing homework together, and, incredibly, she found me attractive. We married right after our high school graduation and Claire enrolled in nursing school. I went to a two year college and then the police academy. Cecile was born the year both of us graduated.

I turned over, feeling the empty pillow beside me. "I miss you sweetheart," I said.

The next morning I had a doctor's appointment. It had been almost two weeks since the shooting and I was doing the prescribed exercises and trying to wean myself off the pain meds. The doctor took the arm out of the sling and gently moved it upward. I yelped. He patted me genially on the shoulder and said he'd see me in two weeks.

"Can I get my arm out of the sling yet?"

"Sorry, no. You've got to let this thing heal," he said.

When I was walking home I got a call from Tony Aarondson, the fifth grader I'd seen being bullied yesterday. He spent ten minutes berating me about not answering his three text messages, and his two phone calls. I kept my cool, reminding him that I was the one helping him, so he'd better be nice.

He calmed down, and gave me the names of his tormentors, all seventh graders, saying that he'd already texted me that information. As much as I wanted to help him, I had no idea how I would get rid of his bullies. We talked for a while, when Tony asked. "What about YouTube? You could take a picture of the bullies and put it on the net."

I grew up in the nineties when the internet was still in diapers. "OK," I said. "If I get pictures, you post the video."

"No prob," Tony said.

I spent the next hour at home, practicing using the video on my cell phone. The camera was OK, but in order to see a person's face, I was going to have to get real close. Reluctantly I called Larry. On the one hand I didn't want to involve him in anything not department business. On the other hand, he had two hands. We agreed that the next day, Friday, we would post ourselves near the sidewalk and try to take videos of the bullying. I could identify Tony as one of the victims and if we got other victims of the same bullies, all the better.

On Friday, Larry and I got up early, and positioned ourselves along the route that the middle kids took to school. We found a handy bench and tried to look like two geezers enjoying the air. The kids came in tiny groups, first graders with their mommies holding their hands, second and third graders by twos or threes, fourth graders, among them a few bullies who grabbed at the younger kids' hats, throwing them onto the ground. I think Larry got a good shot of their faces. My job was to distract the kids, especially those who saw Larry's cell and might figure out what was going on.

After the fourth and fifth graders came the sixth, seventh and eighth graders. High schoolers went to a different school. Lots of girls walking together in groups, boys joking and laughing. I noticed two boys positioning themselves near a tree where they were partly hidden. I leaned toward Larry. "Get their faces." Then I saw Tony, head down, shuffling. He probably knew he was being filmed. He would certainly recognize me. The bigger of the two boys grabbed for his books, scattering them on the leaf-covered ground. The other boy stepped on them with his dirty boots. When Tony bent down to retrieve his papers, one of the boys struck him hard on the back, and Tony fell. It took everything for me not to jump up and grab the boy. I was just here to document the abuse, I told myself. Tony said something. The other boy looked over and made a move toward me.

When he got closer, I saw how young he was, probably only fourteen. Just a kid, but picking on kids smaller than he was.

"I wouldn't try anything," I said. "Or it will go badly for you."

He looked over at Larry, who had tucked the phone in his pocket. Then the two boys marched away.

Tony came over to where we were sitting. "Did you get it?"

Larry and I nodded. "What next?"

He thought for a moment. "If I take the phone with me now, those goons will figure out what I'm doing. Let me get it from you this afternoon and I'll download the video to the internet."

I wrote down my address.

"Thanks," he said. He walked away. Maybe it was just my imagination, but he seemed to stand straighter and taller.

We had the rest of the day to work on the case, so we went to Katie's Kountry Kitchen and had a sandwich and a cup of coffee. My shoulder ached, so I took a pain pill. Then I ordered a sandwich, and when it came, I put half aside.

"You on a diet?"

"Just trying to cut back a bit." I didn't have the huge gut that a lot of men have, but I was starting to think I could lose a few pounds.

"What brought this on?"

"I met a woman, Willi DeGrasse. Her daughter is a friend of Amelia's."

"Single, good looking, searching for the right man?"

"Two out of three. I'm not sure she's searching. I think her husband's death made her cautious."

He took a bite of food and looked at me thoughtfully. "You're a great guy, Chris. If I weren't married, I'd think of hooking up with you myself."

I gave him a look and then said, "Seriously, Larry. I don't know what women want these days. The last time I asked a girl out on a date, I was sixteen. What is today's courtship ritual? Tweeting, bleeting, skeeting? Do you sleep together on the first date or get tested for a venereal disease before that happens?"

"I saw this program last night on the Australian Bowerbird," Larry said. "The bird builds an elaborate hut in the woods, roof and all and then he decorates it with shiny beetles, oak nuts, leaves and flowers."

"Shiny beetles, huh? You think that will work?"

"Nah. but something shiny with carats might."

"We're not at that stage yet. I just want to catch her attention. What do you do when you want to treat Sally to a night out?"

"My wife might not be a good example. Last Christmas all she wanted was a belt sander so she could do some craft project. A great night out for her is the two of us camping in the wilderness."

"Decorated with shiny beetles, and oak nuts?"

"The beetles drive her crazy. She becomes an animal."

I took a bite of my sandwich. "I'm a good cook," I said. "I could feed her."

"Birds do that. Take the food in your mouth and gently put it in hers."

"Jesus, Larry, you're no help at all."

I finished my sandwich and took out my notebook. "Who've we got to talk to?"

"The parents, April and Sanford LeBrun. The brother, Greg. The maid who was absent when the note was left in the kitchen. The gardener. The old man who ran the comic book shop. What was his name?" I took out my notebook and flipped through it. "Giles Archer. Think he's still alive?"

"It's possible."

"Mrs. Bledsoe said Ethan had a friend, an older kid."

"Who would now be in his early twenties."

"We need to talk to…" I consulted the notebook again. "Mary Rowling who was Greg's teacher. Maybe she knows Ethan's friend."

"Let's go back to the house; there might be last known addresses in the files."

We spent an hour sorting through old files. The two detectives who'd originally worked the case, Blake Gunther and Gerald Besom had done a pretty good job of documenting everything. Sandy LeBrun's call about his missing son had come into the police station at four fifteen in the afternoon and two cops had arrived at the house at four thirty.

They'd found two distraught parents who kept saying that their son had asthma and needed his medication. They'd talked to the older brother and Evangeline Swindon, the maid. Neither had seen the boy all day. That night, the dogs were called in, and they found the kid in the woods.

"What about the ransom note on the counter?" Larry asked. "Did they match it for fingerprints?"

"They did," I said. "They got nada."

"What about tracks around the house? Signs of a break in?"

"Double nada."

"So someone with access to the house put the note there."

"According to her testimony, the maid was there but saw nothing."

"I'd like to get into that house," Larry said. I nodded. This time we'd go to the gated community the right way, by car.

"Are the parents still around?"

"April LeBrun moved to Vermont, shortly after Ethan died, and Sanford LeBrun is in the Adirondacks."

"A whole day's trip to both places."

"I need a cup of coffee," I said. We went upstairs and with some help I brewed two cups. We found a number for Giles Archer who said he would be willing to talk with us. He gave us the name of an assisted living facility on the edge of town, about ten minutes away.

Giles Archer was a small man, with thinning hair and a pinched face. He was sitting in a wheel chair in a corner. When we told him we were re-investigating the death of Ethan LeBrun, his face clouded over.

"That poor kid," he said. "Used to be a good customer. Loved the comic books."

"Do you remember him coming into the store, the day he died?" I asked.

"Yup. Come in with two older boys."

"What time was that?"

"Three fifteen, thereabouts. I told this to the cops before."

"What did the boys look like?"

"One was short, with dark hair and glasses. The other was bigger, older, wore a T shirt advertising one of them rock groups."

"You said they were older. How much older?"

"Ethan was eight, so I guess one was twelve or thirteen. I think the other was eighteen or even nineteen."

"Had you ever seen them before?"

"I seen the younger one before 'cause he come into the store with Ethan. It was Ethan paid for the books, but the other kid told him what to buy."

"Can you describe the older boy?"

"Blonde hair down around his shoulders, black leather jacket, mean looking. When he came in with the other two, I thought he was there to rob me. Sometimes my daughter would come to help me out, but that day it was just me."

"What did the three boys do when they came in the store?"

"I don't know, whatever kids do. They walk around, look at the comics, talk about which ones they like and which they don't like."

"Did Ethan seem particularly nervous around the two boys?"

"I don't remember. He and the younger boy were friends; they got along all right."

"What about the older boy. Did he look at the comic books too?"

"No, he had this electronic game he kept trying to show me. Made me nervous, I tell you."

"The three boys came into the store about three fifteen. Was there anyone else here at the time?"

"Nope, just me."

"So Ethan and his friend walked around, looking at comic books and talking about them, while the older boy tried to get you to look at his electronic game. Did any of the kids buy a comic?"

"Nope."

"What time did they leave the store?"

For a moment, something flickered in the old man's eyes. "Quarter to four," he said. "I looked at my watch,'cause my daughter usually came in at four. Quarter to four, it was."

We thanked the man and left. When we were outside, I said.

"Something's fishy here. If Ethan were really being abducted by the two boys, wouldn't he be agitated?"

"He knew the younger kid. They'd been there before."

"What about the older one? If the eighteen year old made Archer nervous, why wouldn't he make Ethan nervous?"

"Did you see his expression when we asked him what time the kids left?" Larry asked.

"Either he's deliberately lying, or he doesn't remember and can't admit it. I'd like to talk with the daughter." We went back into the nursing home and got the name of Archer's daughter from the nursing staff. We dialed the number but no one answered. It was mid-afternoon, giving us a few more hours to work. "Let's go to the LeBrun house," I said.

Take My Hand

This time we drove. When we gave the house number to the man at the gatehouse, he told us that no one lived there and in order to see it, we'd have to call the Realtor. We called the agent who said she'd be happy to show us the house, and she would be there in fifteen minutes. I guess things are slow in September. We weren't there as legitimate purchasers, and when the young woman arrived at the gatehouse looking hopeful, I felt I had to level with her.

"The house is in really great shape," she began, when we were standing outside her car. "The current owners have come down in their price twice now and are willing to negotiate again."

Reading off her name tag, I said. "Ms. Swan, I'm afraid we've got you here under false pretenses. We're not looking to buy a house; we're detectives investigating the death of Ethan LeBrun."

"The little boy who was kidnapped? That case was all over the news."

"We'd like to see the house where he lived," Larry said.

She stared at us both seeing the bright image of a sale dissolving like smoke in the air.

"What the heck," she said finally. "I might as well go and take a look at it. No one has wanted to see that house for a month. People think it's haunted. "

"We'll be grateful for your help," I said, which is cop-speak for 'you'll be rewarded in heaven.'

"Yeah, I know," she said. "And I might win the lottery, but I'm not holding my breath."

She got back in her car and we followed her to the house, an enormous two story McMansion that, in spite of its value, showed signs of neglect. The walkway to the front door was fringed with weeds and dotted with dog poop. A window blind was askew, and decorative plants on either side of the mahogany door had expired long ago.

"Did you know the LeBruns?" I asked when we were out of the car.

"I was sixteen when it happened. Sure I knew *about* the case, but I didn't know them personally. I knew the Harrises who bought the house after the LeBruns moved out. They didn't seem to mind the notoriety, but they moved away six years ago, and since then the house has been stuck in limbo."

"Could be the economy?"

"Maybe. I told the Harrises their price was too high. Since then they've come down a third of what they paid, but still no nibbles."

"I'm sorry," I said.

"Yeah, me too. I've got a two year old and a four year old I'm trying to support on an agent's salary. If things don't pick up, I'm going to have to do something else." She unlocked the door and we were led into a large open foyer with marble floors and a dark wood stairway curving up to the second floor. It smelled of dust and mildew, but there was no hiding the fact that a lot of money had been spent building it.

"Can you show us the kitchen?" I asked.

"Sure," Ms. Swan said, leading us back to a large open room, with Corian counter tops and a restaurant-sized stainless steel refrigerator. One wall was taken up with two French doors that looked out on a weed-choked garden and an empty swimming pool. I went to the doors and tried them. They were locked tight. It was impossible to know whether those doors had been open or closed when the ransom note was left.

"Could we see upstairs?" I asked.

Ms. Swan nodded. We retraced our steps back to the foyer and went up the stairs. The master bedroom held a huge double bed, with an equally large bathroom attached. There were three other bedrooms on the floor, each one with its own bath. I guessed that two of the bedrooms had been for the boys, and the other room might have been used as an office or guest bedroom.

"Larry, will you do me a favor?" I asked. "I'm going to imagine that I'm the maid, Evangeline Swindon vacuuming up here. I want to know if she would have heard anyone coming into the house. Go down to the front door, open and close it. Don't slam it. Just close it normally."

Larry left. I heard him go down the stairs, and I could hear his footsteps faintly on the marble floor of the entrance. I moved to the master bedroom, where Mrs. Swindon said she'd been cleaning and looked out toward the back of the house where a weedy stretch of lawn met the fence and woods behind. I heard Larry's footsteps as he stepped across the foyer and climbed the stairs.

"So?" he asked when he'd returned to the bedroom.

"Nothing," I said. "If I were working a vacuum cleaner, I wouldn't have heard you come in." I turned toward the window. "But if I were looking out the window, I might have seen someone walking across the lawn from the woods." I looked at the Realtor. "Would you go down to the kitchen with Larry and open the back door to the outside?"

She nodded and I waited. All was silence. Suddenly there was a loud squeal, the sound that wood makes when it is scraping along a floor. A minute later, both of them were climbing the stairs.

"Has that noise always been there?"

Ms Swan shrugged. "I remember the Harrises telling me that when they bought the house, the door to the garden was warped. It's possible it was left open a lot."

"Evangeline Swindon testified that the back door was always locked," I said.

"Even when she was there?" Larry asked. We looked at each other. We needed to research the daytime temperature for the day Ethan LeBrun was killed.

We thanked Ms. Swan for her time, and stepped outside while she locked the front door.

"I really should get someone out here to do some cleaning," she said. She glanced at the lawn, which now in early fall was browning and covered with leaves. "I guess the realty company could pay for a landscaping service too."

We said our good-byes, got back into our car and drove back toward the house. On the way Larry said, "We need to look at that interview with Evangeline Swindon again."

"If the door to the garden was open, it would be easy for someone to get in and out of the kitchen without being noticed."

"Whoever left that ransom note knew the layout of the house."

"And knew when Evangeline Swindon was out of the kitchen."

"So whoever left the note."

"And kidnapped Ethan."

"Knew the family."

Chapter Seven

By four we were back at the house, digging into the notes. According to the interview with Evangeline Swindon, all the doors to the house were locked during the day. Greg had his own key and Ethan, always came home accompanied by his mother. Evangeline had been working upstairs on the afternoon of the kidnapping, and had never heard anyone enter, until Mr. LeBrun came in, calling for Ethan.

At that moment the phone rang. It was Tony Aarondson, out of breath, like he'd been running. "I'm coming to your house, Mr. B. I want to post those videos on YouTube."

I'd forgotten all about the videos Larry and I had taken that morning. "Sure," I said. I gave him the address.

"You got a computer, right?"

"I do," I said. In the kid's eyes, I might be nearing senility, but I had some grasp on modern technology.

Ten minutes later he was ringing the doorbell. I could hear Mrs. Gentile answer the door and then Amelia's voice. I went upstairs. The two females were standing in the hallway, looking at Tony.

"It's OK, ladies," I said. "He's here on a special assignment."

I ushered Tony downstairs to the basement and showed him the computer.

"I need the cell phone with the video," he said. I handed him the cell and watched mystified as he scrolled through screens. Suddenly, the video with the two bullies came up on the computer. "What shall we call this?" he asked.

I had no idea. "How about 'Is this your school?' That sounds catchy doesn't it?" Tony pressed a button. "There," he said. "Let's see who watches it."

"How many people will see this?"

He pointed to the screen. "There's a counter that records the hits. We'll know by tomorrow." He got up from the chair, slung his backpack over his shoulder. "Thanks Mr. B.," he said, and then he was gone.

My shoulder ached; my head ached. I would spend a few more hours tonight reading through the notes, but now I needed a beer. Larry and I went upstairs, and he said good-night. He had a stack of folders to pour through too, but he could do it at his leisure.

The next day was Fall Fest Saturday in Euclid which meant that the whole of Main Street had been blocked off allowing room for sidewalk sales, petting zoos, bounce houses, hot-dog and cotton candy vendors, and ear-splitting bands of various stripes. I was standing in line for the bounce house, when I heard Amelia's squeal of delight and looked around to see Carey DeGrasse and her mother.

"What a great day for the festival," Willi said.

"What?" I said, leaning toward her, my hand cupping my ear.

"It *is* a little noisy isn't it," she said moving closer. "But the kids are having a great time."

Inside the bounce house two little boys were jumping up and down their grins stretching across their faces. Amelia and Carey squeezed inside the structure and, started bouncing. "I'm glad she's found Amelia," Willi said. "Carey's a bit shy, and your daughter is so outgoing."

"My granddaughter," I said.

"That's right. I forgot." She looked at me. "You don't look like her grandfather."

I bent over in imitation of an old man. "Yeah, Ma'am, I'm really one hundred and seventy. Got these new teeth and can't do a thing with 'em."

She smiled, then taking my hand, pulled me toward a bench. "Chris," she said, suddenly serious. "Have you heard anything about a YouTube Video? It shows a kid from our school being bullied. Apparently it was made yesterday, and already it's gone viral. I got a call from a fellow teacher this morning. She said one of my students, Jason Hedgewick is in it."

I couldn't lie. "I made the video," I said. "Tony Aarondson posted it yesterday on the internet."

She looked at me. I couldn't tell whether she considered my complicity in this event a good thing or a bad thing.

"Let me explain," I began. "My partner, Larry Grindon and I are investigating the death of an eight year old boy, here in Euclid. His name was Ethan LeBrun; he died ten years ago. Larry and I had gone to talk to one of Ethan's teachers and on the way we saw two older kids beating up on a younger one. I got the bigger boys to leave the kid alone and then promised the kid we would do something to help."

She nodded. At least she was with me this far.

"The three of us, Tony, the kid who was being bullied, Larry and I came up with the idea to make a video of the bullying and put it on YouTube."

"Jason Hedgewick *is* a bully," Willi said. "Do you know who his father is?"

I shook my head.

"William Hedgewick. He owns that big Ford dealership on Maple Street. I met him the first week of class, and disliked him from the start. Be careful. He can be mean."

"The other kid was Grant Lakom. Do you know him?"

"His mother is a single parent who works as a hairdresser. I'm not sure she has much control over him."

"I hope this video doesn't make your job any harder."

She smiled. "Don't worry about it, Chris. It's certainly going to shake things up a bit, but I wouldn't mind seeing those boys taken down a peg. Especially Jason. Actually, I don't blame the boy for being who he is. His father is a loudmouth who thinks because he's wealthy he can do what he wants. And Grant follows Jason's lead." She leaned toward me, I could smell her perfume and for a moment I had the urge to kiss her. What was going on here? Willi was looking at me. Was she thinking the same thing? "You're doing a great job, Chris," she said. At that moment, Amelia and Carey bounced up to us and the moment vanished like a soap bubble.

"Poppi," Amelia said. "Can we get a hot dog?"

We got our food and then went and sat beside the river. The trees were turning a brilliant orange, their colors reflected in the blue of the river. A family of geese floated by, and a kayaker, lured by the warm fall day was paddling on the shiny surface.

"Have you lived here all your life?" Willi asked.

"Yeah," I said. "My father was a policeman and I went to the same school that Amelia's attending. I think some of my old teachers are still teaching."

"Not really."

"No, not really. But I do remember when the hardware was a drug store, with the prettiest red-headed girl serving sodas."

"You're not that old."

"Forty two," I said. "Some days it feels ancient."

"I grew up in California," Willi said. "I met Jim, my husband at a dance there. I was going to teach high school English and he was going to be a Sociology professor. His senior year he decided to take Engineering courses instead."

I looked over at the two little girls, who had finished their lunches and were running back and forth over the grass, giggling. "I want Amelia to grow up in a place where no one will bully her," I said.

"Amen to that," Willi said.

We picked up the papers from our lunch and deposited them in the trash can. Willi said she had some shopping to do, and I wanted to clean out the garden. We said goodbye and then Amelia and I walked home.

The garden chore was something we did every year. In the early spring we planted peas, tomatoes, cucumbers, broccoli, corn, carrots and Brussels sprouts. We harvested through the summer and then in the fall we pulled up all the dead plants and spread compost. I could pull pretty well with my left hand, but I had to leave carrying dead plants to the compost to Amelia. She was a good sport. By the end of the day, we'd got almost everything cleared. We were tired, dirty and ready for supper.

We ate. I read Amelia a chapter from *Little House on the Prairie*, and then she went to bed.

I called Larry to give him the news about the video, the two boys who were its stars, and their families.

"I'm not worried about Jason's father," he said. "I've met his type before. I think we did the right thing."

"I've been going through the notes on Evangeline Swindon," I said. "She lives in Caleb Corners, about forty miles from here. Let's talk with her on Monday."

"Have a good weekend, Chris."

Chapter Eight

Sunday is a day when I can sleep late, make a special breakfast for Amelia, and generally relax. I had planned to look at the notes from the investigation, or let Amelia show me her song and dance routine. All that was shot by a call from O'Malley. "Get over here now," he barked.

When Larry and I were sitting in front of him, like two pups at obedience school, he leaned toward me, his face red with anger.

"What the hell are you two doing?" he barked.

"Working on the case, like you wanted," Larry said.

"Like hell you are. You've been videotaping kids walking to school." He pushed himself up from behind the desk and stamped across the room to stare out the grimy window behind him. Then he turned toward us. "I just got call from a parent, William Hedgewick. He said that you took pictures of his son WITHOUT THE CHILD'S PERMISSION." These last words were said at top volume.

I started to speak and O'Malley held up his hand for silence.

"I don't want to hear it," he said. "This is a small department. I've got two guys out at training, and one fellow out sick. I've got break-ins at the Senior Center, kids drunk and falling into the river. There's cocaine being smuggled across the border, and I think there may be a meth lab starting up. I have a big area to cover, Bellini. I DON'T HAVE TIME FOR MY OFFICERS TO WANDER AROUND TAKING PICTURES OF KIDS WRESTLING EACH OTHER ON THE STREET.

"They weren't wrestling..." Larry began.

"Shut up, Grindon. You're on a tight wire here. I promised Bellini he could have you for six weeks, but once that's over, you're back on the street. One more word and you'll be back there now."

We sat chastised. After several minutes of silence, O'Malley said. "So why did you decide to take pictures of those boys? Don't you have enough to do with this investigation? Because if you have time to kill, I have plenty that will keep you busy."

We were silent.

"I'm waiting," O'Malley said. "Right now I need to say something to Hedgewick, who as you may guess, is really pissed. What shall I tell him when he calls again, complaining about you two?"

"His son, Jason, who is fourteen years old, five six and easily one sixty, was beating up on a boy who was eleven, barely five feet and about a hundred pounds. There were two of them. Grant Lakom, the other boy is the same age, and about the same size."

"How did you get their names?"

I hesitated. "Tony Aarondson, the boy who was being bullied told us," I said.

O'Malley leaned forward and glared at me. "Tell me how this dustup between two kids has any relation to the case you're working on."

"I thought that Ethan LeBrun might have been bullied. Maybe he was killed because he tried to stand up to his tormentors."

"Any evidence of that?"

"Not that we can find. But it doesn't mean it didn't happen," I said.

"OK," he said. "I'm making some changes. I'm not having two rogue cops running after every situation they think needs fixing. You are being paid to solve a crime. Starting tomorrow, all of the material pertaining to the case will be brought back here to the station. I don't know where I'll put you, but I'll find a spot even if I have to stick you in the toilet. You will keep me in the loop regarding everyone you talk to, every lead you follow, every clue you think is important. Understand?"

We nodded.

"Is that it, sir?" Larry asked.

"It is. You are dismissed."

As we walked back to my car, I said. "I'm sorry I got you into this, Larry. You're a good cop. You don't need this on your record."

"Hell Chris, this was fun. I haven't seen the old man so animated in a long time. I think it will be a good idea to play by the rules for a while, though."

Chapter Nine

It was still Sunday, but my rest day was becoming more restless than restful. Larry had driven us to the station in his old beater which sat wearily on the street. As we walked toward the car my cell phone rang, a number I didn't recognize. I have an aversion to robo-calls, but this one had a local area code, so I picked it up.

"Mr. Bellini?"

"Yes."

"Are you the person who videotaped the two boys bullying Tony Aarondson?"

"Yes, what's this all about?"

"I'm Helena Grant, a high school teacher and advisor to the Journalists Club. I hope you don't mind my calling you on Sunday, but I have a group of high school girls, who want to do something to help stop bullying in the school. Would you be willing to come and talk to our club this coming week?"

My first thought was to say 'How about never? Is never good for you?' but a cop is a public servant and my mother taught me to be polite. Instead I said. "I'm sorry, Mrs. Grant. But I'm working on an active case. My partner and I are very busy."

"It wouldn't take much of your time, Mr. Bellini. I can't tell you what this YouTube videotape has done for this school. A couple of students have already called me. They want to do something. They're energized."

Think of me as a pink bunny banging on a drum.

At my silence she continued. "They know that this has been going on for years, and now they have a way to fight it. All they can talk about is the YouTube video and of course, you."

"Me?"

"You're a local hero, Mr. Bellini."

"It was actually my partner, Larry Grindon who did the videotaping. I was wounded in a police incident a few weeks ago, and my arm is still in restraint." Larry was waving his arms and making 'don't- bring- me- into- this' noises.

"We would be deeply honored to meet you and Mr. Grindon. We're in Room 107 in the High School wing. How about Tuesday."

"Ok," I said. Larry was mouthing that I was on my own in this. When I hung up, he said, "You know I don't do public speaking, Chris."

"We won't have to say much. Think of it as PR for the department."

"The Chief does PR for the department. Getting into this bullying shit is what got us in deep doo-doo in the first place. I would strongly suggest we run it by O'Malley."

"I will. I will," I said. By now we were in the car. "How about we talk to Evangeline Swindon tomorrow."

"What about moving our stuff?" Larry asked. I had no idea where O'Malley would put us, but we were going to be on a short leash.

"If O'Malley wants us to move he can get his goons to carry files back to the station. I have a bad shoulder and you have..." I looked at Larry.

"A herniated hernia? A ruptured rectus femoris? A sagging sacroiliac?"

"That'll work." We pulled up to my house and I hopped out. "Have a nice rest of your day."

On Monday we called the E. Swindon listed in the telephone directory, and as soon as we identified ourselves as detectives, the woman hung up.

Take My Hand

"What's the address?" I asked.

Larry read it to me. It was eight thirty in the morning. "Let's hope she has a job that doesn't start until after nine." It would take us a while to drive the distance to her house. We hopped into Larry's car and headed toward Caleb Corners.

The address given was for a faded blue house on the edge of town sandwiched between two semi-abandoned modular buildings. We pulled into the driveway, just as a small, thin woman with grey hair bustled out the front door.

"You can't park there," she said. "I've got to leave."

"Mrs. Swindon, we want to talk with you."

Hand on her hip, she glared at us. "I told you to get your car out of my driveway. I ain't got time to talk. I'm already late."

"I'm Chris Bellini, we're investigating the death of Ethan LeBrun," I said.

That stopped her, but just for a moment. "I talked to them detectives ten years ago. I ain't got nothing more to say. Now move your damned car."

"Will you talk with us?"

"I done told ya no."

We were at a standstill, but I can be as stubborn as the next man, or woman. Mrs. Swindon got in and started her car. She tried maneuvering around our parked vehicle, but we were firmly in the way.

"Will you get your asses out of my driveway," she yelled from the open window.

"Mrs. Swindon," I said, moving toward her car, "We have the authority to take you to the station and ask you the questions there. I can call a trooper, who will be here in about ten minutes, and then it will be another twenty minutes to the station. You might have to call your boss and tell him you'll be late."

"God damn you boys," she said. "OK, follow me. I'll get the boss to give me some break time now, though he won't like it. Come on now, move."

Reluctantly Larry backed out of the driveway. I still didn't trust Evangeline to keep her promise, but I had no choice. Once we were out of her way, she peeled rapidly backward onto the street and sped off. Keeping her in our sights, Larry followed. We pulled up in front of a restaurant called Billy's Luncheonette, which still had a 'closed' sign hanging in the front.

Evangeline put a key in the lock and pushed open the door. Larry and I followed. Evangeline returned to lock the door. Then she flicked on lights and went back into the kitchen area where a man was rolling out dough on a table.

"Billy," she said to the cook, "These two men are detectives. They need to talk to me for ten minutes."

"Just when we open? Jesus, Vangie," he said.

"We'll try to be quick," I said.

Billy jerked his thumb toward the back. "In the break room," he said.

The break room was actually a storage closet, with boxes piled almost to the ceiling. The three of us squeezed ourselves onto metal folding chairs around a tiny card table. Vangie looked at her watch. "OK," she said.

I checked my notes and then said, "In your interview with Detectives Gunther and Besom, you said that when you came down to the kitchen from cleaning upstairs, the ransom note was on the table."

She nodded.

"Do you have any idea who might have put the note there?"

"No sir."

"You told the detectives that the front door was always locked, what about the back door?"

"The back door?"

"The door that led from the kitchen to the garden. Was that always locked too?"

"Of course it was."

"Mrs. Swindon, when we visited the house last week, that door had a terrible squeak, as though it were warped. If someone had opened that door, you would have heard it upstairs, wouldn't you?"

Something flickered in her face, but she pushed through. "I didn't hear nothin'. I was runnin' the vacuum."

"We have located a bill from a locksmith, dated two days after Ethan's death. It stated that the lock was replaced on 'the back door.' Are you still telling me that the door was firmly locked the day of the kidnapping?"

She looked at Larry and then at me. "The Mrs. liked to keep that door open during the day and sometimes it didn't close just right. But I am sure it was locked that day."

"All right," I said. "Tell me about your relationship to the LeBruns. Were they good people to work for?"

"They was OK," she said.

"Just OK? Were they fair to you? Did they complain about the work you did? Make you work long hours? Ask you to do things beyond your duties as a housekeeper?"

"She had a temper, she had. Sometimes, when the Doctor was late, she would throw things around. It scared little Ethan, made him cry. And the day the boy went missing, she was drunk. I could smell it on her when she came in."

"Was she the one who normally picked up Ethan at school?" Larry asked.

"Yup. The Doctor was always busy. Sometimes he didn't get home until after they ate supper. Ethan was the only one she picked up. Greg came home with his friends. After school the boys did homework, or played around the house."

"Did they ever play in the woods behind the house?"

"Sometimes."

"Did Mrs. LeBrun cook supper?"

"No, I done the supper and then I'd go home."

"What happened after the kidnapping?" I asked.

"You mean right after?"

"Sure."

"Doctor LeBrun comes home, says he's looking for Ethan. He calls all Ethan's friends and then they call the cops. After that, he tells me to go on home. The next day Doctor LeBrun calls me at home, says little Ethan has died in the woods behind the house. Don't come in to work, he says, the cops are all here, and the media is out front. So I waited a few days, and when I came in, the cops were there wanting to ask me the same questions you all are asking me. The Mrs. was a wreck, stayed in her room mostly. They planned the funeral. Then the Doctor says they're going to sell the house, move somewhere else, start again. I felt sorry for Greg, he was only thirteen, but he'd made friends in the town. By then the Doctor and Mrs. wasn't even talking to each other. And, of course, I'd lost my job."

"We understand that Dr. LeBrun went to the Adirondacks and Mrs. LeBrun went to Vermont. Do you know where?"

Take My Hand

"I think he went to Saranac Lake and she became a lawyer in Burlington. Greg went with her. I think he's in college there." She looked at her watch. "Your ten minutes is up."

I stood up. "Thank you for your time," I said.

As we drove back to Euclid, Larry asked, "Was she telling the truth about the door being locked?"

"I don't think so, but how can we prove otherwise?"

We went back to the house where we needed to start packing up so we could be moved back to the station tomorrow. The paper had been delivered, and over a cup of coffee I scanned the local news. This is a luxury I would not have when we changed venues. The coffee served up at the station was watered down cat pee which even liberal amounts of milk and sugar could not make palatable. It wasn't that Larry and I didn't work at my house, but it was a more leisurely work than we would be doing at the station. Here we could stop to drink coffee and as the day wore on, pop a beer. We hadn't moved yet, but already I missed our office away from the office.

"Look at this, Larry," I said. "Giles Archer died."

"We just talked to him, when was it? Five days ago?"

"The wake is tomorrow. Do you want to go?"

"Nope. I hate funerals, and I didn't know him that well."

"I'd like to go. But I can walk."

We spent the next few hours going through more of the materials. On the bottom of one carton was a whole file of old newspapers with names like *The Daily Word*, *Secrets,* and *World News Revealed*. The headlines of these tabloids seem to follow a predictable pattern. Popular are stories of homosexual celebrities, babies that resulted from animal and alien coupling and the real truth behind celebrity deaths (Elvis, JFK, Diana and Michael Jackson to name a few.)

This time though, the tabloids had jacked up readership by skewering the LeBruns. Over a photo of April and Sandy LeBrun (she with her hands over her face, he glaring at the photographer) was the headline, "What Are These Two Hiding?" Another cover featured Sandy LeBrun in a lab coat under the headline "What Dr. Death's Patients Are Saying." I was curious about this one since I had no idea what Sandy's patients thought of him, so I read on.

"Under a promise of confidentiality, two of the patients of Dr. Sanford LeBrun have disclosed that they felt Dr. LeBrun was slipshod in his surgery, leaving unnecessary scars and that his bedside manner was brisk to the point of rudeness." The article went on to enumerate what sounded like sour grapes, rather than serious complaints. I also reminded myself that people were being paid for their stories, firing up an active let's-get-those-rich-bastards mentality.

I pulled out another paper that featured Ethan, looking pale and thin under the headline "Are Ethan's Parents Hiding Abuse?" The article said that that Ethan had been to the doctor six times in the two months before he died, suggesting he was a victim of Munchausen by Proxy Syndrome, where the parent (usually the mother) creates illness in a child, so that she can get medical attention, and appear to be unusually caring. I would try and find Ethan's doctor so we could talk about his care.

Another paper showed Sandy LeBrun walking with his arm around a young woman. Sandy was looking toward the camera, but the woman's head was down, her long blonde hair obscuring her face. The headline read "Who Is this Woman?" The article alleged that Sandy had been seen with this woman two months before Ethan's death, but no one knew who she was. For all I knew she was a patient, or the relative of a patient. I rummaged through the previous interviews with Sandy, but there was no mention of this mysterious woman.

I put the papers with the articles, "Parents Hiding Abuse" and "Who Is This Woman?" aside. The others I didn't consider credible.

At four o'clock we called it quits. Tomorrow our files would be delivered to the police station. Larry and I had done our best to preserve the order, but who knew what we would find at the station when O'Malley's goons had finished moving things. I would go to Giles Archer's funeral and then speak to the budding Leslie Stahls and Gwen Ifils in Mrs. Grant's class. Larry had a dentist appointment and then he promised to try and locate Ethan's doctor. He would also try to get interviews with Sandy and April LeBrun.

Chapter Ten

At seven-thirty the next morning, I was finishing my coffee when two cops knocked at my door. I showed them to the basement, asking them to please, please try to keep everything together and then went to finish dressing. It had been eighteen days since the shooting, and getting dressed one-handed was becoming a bit easier. I still needed Larry to drive me around, but my shoulder was getting stronger. After the cops left, Larry arrived and drove us the station. When we arrived, we learned that they had set us up in a former conference room divided in half by an accordion 'wall.' The room lacked even the smallest amount of privacy, because anyone could walk through or be on the other side listening.

At nine the Chief came in and we explained everything we'd undertaken since we'd been given the case. We'd been careful to keep him in the loop, but it was the first time he'd seen pictures and notes, including the ransom note. Chief O'Malley had not been Chief when Ethan was killed, so he'd not been part of the original hoopla. Gunther and Besom, the original detectives, had both left the department before O'Malley came on board.

I handed him the ransom note, handwritten on ordinary paper. The note read:

"Someone you love is gone. You can get him back by bringing twenty thousand dollars in small bills to room 512 in the Morrissey Hotel and the person you care about will be released. Do not contact the police."

"Did LeBrun go to the hotel with the money?" O'Malley asked.

"He got the money, but the detectives discouraged him from meeting with the kidnapper."

"Did he?"

"I don't know. The notes don't say."

Take My Hand

"It's a relatively small amount of money from a man who was very wealthy. And why would the kidnapper ask him to come to the hotel, when the child was in the woods behind the house?"

"I can't figure that one out" I said. "Was the person who planned the whole thing, one of the two kids who brought Ethan into the comic book store, or was it someone else?" I looked at the note again. "This seems to be pretty sophisticated language for a teenager."

"So what's next?" O'Malley asked.

"The Morrissey Hotel is being torn down," I said. "I doubt that anyone who worked there ten years ago is still around. I know Gunther and Besom would have talked with the hotel staff, but I haven't read those interviews yet."

"Well, keep on working," O'Malley said, and strode out.

I glanced at my watch. It was about ten minutes to eleven, giving me just a few minutes to walk the couple of blocks to the funeral home. I went to the men's room, smoothed down my hair and splashed water on my face. Then I headed toward the funeral.

Attending someone else's funeral is always an invitation to consider my own mortality. Would I leave this earth when I was still young enough to be remembered, or like Mr. Archer, would I have outlived all my relatives and friends? There were just three people standing in line when I got to the door. Two of them were Archer's age, both female. The person standing, shaking hands was a grey-haired woman who appeared to be in her fifties and was, I guessed, his daughter.

"I'm Chris Bellini," I said, when it was my turn to shake hands. "I visited your father recently when we talked about the Ethan LeBrun case."

Her face fell. "What a terrible thing to happen to that poor child," she said. "Dad felt so guilty."

"Why would he feel guilty? He told me the three boys came in, looked around a bit and then left by the front door. Isn't that what happened?"

Just at that moment a man wearing a clerical collar appeared behind me. Archer's daughter brightened, and said. "Thank you for coming, Reverend. You are a good friend."

When we were alone again, I asked. "Do you know what happened the afternoon Ethan LeBrun was kidnapped?"

"I think so," she said. "But only a little part of it. When the detectives interviewed Dad ten years ago, he insisted that the boys came into the shop and then left. Later he told me in confidence that he didn't actually remember them leaving."

"Didn't remember them leaving? Had he left the shop before they did?"

"No. He was there, but my father suffered all his life from epilepsy. He was pretty good about taking his medicine, but once in a while he'd forget and then certain things could trigger an attack."

"Your father said that one of the boys had a game he was trying to show him. Do you suppose that could have done it?"

She nodded, then reached out and touched my hand. "I am so sorry that my father wasn't honest either with the first detectives or with you. He was a proud man who hated to admit his disability, but I think his failure to tell the truth haunted him."

I nodded. It was enough to have the truth now. The two young men had taken Ethan into the store, and when Giles Archer slipped into his seizure, they'd hustled him out the back door into the woods, confident that no one would hear the boy's cries for help.

It was almost noon. I was due to speak to the budding journalists at one o'clock, so I grabbed a sandwich at Levi's Deli with the idea of eating it at my desk. When I got back to the station, it was abnormally quiet. I ducked my head into the secretary's office, but no one was there. I went around the corner to the break room, and saw almost the whole force gathered there, glued to the television set.

"The mayor's speaking," Larry whispered. "She's talking about us."

"And I want to say again how proud I am of these two patrolmen, from our village, who had the courage to take a stand against children being bullied in schools. They have started a movement that is going to end this terrible practice. This is community policing at its very best."

There was applause on the screen and then the newsman came on. "That was Mayor Jane Whiting, speaking about a YouTube video showing a local boy being bullied. The video was made by Officers Chris Bellini and Larry Grindon, who were investigating an unsolved crime when they came across the bullying. Next week, we hope to bring you interviews with these fine officers."

"Like hell you will," I said aloud, but my voice was drowned out by men scraping back their chairs and leaving the room, some of them clapping me on the back as they left.

Rather than eat my lunch in the public space that was our office, I went outside and gulped it down, and then walked to the school where I was scheduled to speak. True to his word, Larry was not there, so I took a deep breath and went in, hoping that I'd not scattered bits of my lunch on my tie. In truth, I didn't want to be here, and I didn't want to be a local hero. All I wanted was to be left to solve a murder in peace.

I was greeted with applause when I walked in. I said a few words about truth, justice and police work and then I took questions. The kids were eager to talk about bullying and though I admired their zeal in doing something, I also cautioned them against trampling on the rights of others. When the session ended, it was three-thirty. Most of the students had left the school and I was eager to be done with my day.

At that moment, my phone rang and I recognized Willi's number.

"Chris," she said. "Can you come over for a minute? I just got home from school and there's something making a loud noise in the house. I can come and get you, if you want."

"No, I'll walk," I said. It would take me twenty minutes, but I needed to clear my head from all this other crap.

When I got to her house she was standing by the front door. Carey came bounding in from a room in the back but when she saw Amelia wasn't with me, her face fell.

"I hate to be such a wuss," Willi said. "But I can't stand things in the house. I don't know how to get rid of them and they make me feel helpless." She was walking away from me, wearing the same figure hugging jeans and sweater that I'd seen on her at the Fall Festival. For a moment I had an image of that luscious figure without the jeans and sweater, until I reminded myself that I was here for only one reason. We got to the kitchen where I could hear a loud knocking coming from under the sink. Fall is the time when creatures decide to move into warmer quarters, often our sheds and garages, and sometimes our kitchens.

"Do you have a big plastic bag? The heavy kind?"

She nodded and came back with a bag which she held out to me.

"I'd like you to stand there and hold it open for me." Her lower lip trembled, but she did as I asked.

I put on a pair of gloves. Wild animals bite and some of them can carry rabies. Then I opened the door to the storage area under the sink. Crashing around among the cleaning supplies was a squirrel with its head stuck in a peanut butter jar. I grabbed its tail and dropped it headfirst into the bag. The squirrel began to thrash wildly. In two steps I was out the front door, depositing the animal in the yard.

"Thank you so much," Willi said, throwing her arms around me. I held on for longer than was absolutely necessary, savoring the feeling of having her in my arms. Shiny beetles be damned. Squirrels in peanut butter jars might be the trick to get me noticed.

We went back into the house and I peered under her sink. A lot of trash had been dislodged from the can, which is probably where the squirrel had got the jar. I knelt down and saw at the base of the wall, a squirrel sized hole. "This is where he got in. I'll come back and patch this up, if

Take My Hand

you like. We should also look for a hole outside. Winter is coming. You might get more visitors.

She nodded, tears in her eyes. "One of the things about being alone is situations like these. I hated to call you, but I had no one else."

"I'm happy to be the superman of last resort," I said.

She reached forward and touched my hand. Her skin was cool and soft. I resisted the urge to bring it to my lips and kiss it.

"Would you like coffee?"

"Not instant, is it?"

"I can make brewed if you want. It's no problem."

When the coffee was ready we sat at her tiny kitchen table and she told me about her childhood in California. About being the only child of two ambitious parents, who barely had time for their child. "I swore that this would never happen to Carey," she said. "But that's what has happened. That's why I'm so grateful for Amelia's friendship." Again the touch, quick, soft. This time I couldn't resist. I took her hand in mine and brought it gently to my lips. The result was a widening of her eyes and a pulling away of her hand.

Had I just blown the whole game? Willi got up, took the coffee cups and put them both in the sink, then stood there watching me.

"What's wrong?"

"Nothing's wrong. You're a sweet man, Chris. I'm grateful to you for so many things but..."

"But what?" I went over to where she stood. Running my hand gently down the side of her face I looked her in the eye. "You're a beautiful woman, Willi. I want to go out with you."

"I think it's too soon."

"OK, I'll back off if you like, but I'm not giving up."

"The strong stubborn type?"

"Say you'll come out with me."

Reluctantly she nodded.

"How about Saturday night. Francisco's? Six o'clock?" When she nodded again, I leaned forward and kissed her.

Chapter Eleven

Francisco's on the Waterfront is a small stone building sitting with its back to the St. Lawrence River, so if you're lucky enough to get a table near the window, you can watch the ships working their way up or down river. At dusk it is magical, and I hoped that some of that magic would rub off on me.

"This is interesting," Willi said as we entered. "I've never been here before." She was looking at Francisco's collection of antiques which crowded every wall, every flat surface and even the floor. The first time I'd been to the restaurant I'd had the same reaction. This man was a collector, but could he cook?

I pointed to the Specials board which in fact, was the menu. "If you don't see something you like, he'll grill you a steak."

"I like to eat local foods when I can," she said, studying the board.

Just then Francisco himself appeared. He was a large man who, from his girth, enjoyed his own cooking.

"Hello Chris, and who is this vision of beauty."

"Willi DeGrasse," I said.

"Do you have fish?" Willi asked.

"Tilapia with crushed almonds and Parmesan cheese." He brought his fingers to his lips and kissed them. "With a nice white wine, *magnifico*."

"I'll have the steak," I said.

"You need to get more adventurous, Chris," Francisco said. He showed us to a table near the window and while he was bringing our wine and bread sticks, I ran through my personal attractiveness inventory. I had no food on my teeth, no stains on my tie, and my fly was zipped. I wasn't going to make some dorky move with a woman I liked. I'd done some homework on starter topics that I hoped would show me as being witty with a touch of warmth.

"What are your five greatest pet peeves?" I asked.

Willi looked at me with an 'Ok, I'll play this game' smile.

"Let's see. Number one, telemarketers at any time of day or night. Number two, people who drive very slowly and forget that their turn signal is on. Number three, TV ads aimed at children. Number four, parents who blame the teacher because their kid isn't getting all A's, or isn't polite and good looking. Hellooo. Number five, men who wear their hats in restaurants." She reached for a bread stick and crunched it. "How about you?"

"Once I got a phone call when I was in the shower. I left the shower, tripped on a toy Amelia had left on the floor, bashed my head against a table, and when I got to the phone it was someone trying to sell me home-accident insurance. It's probably a good thing Mrs. Gentile wasn't there. She'd have found me on the floor, bloody, half naked, and swearing at top volume." I took a sip of wine. "Let's see, my five. Number one, a person who parks so badly he's taking up two spaces. Number two, car alarms that blare for hours without anyone turning them off. Number three, dog owners who leave their animal tied up day and night. Number four, elected representatives who lie, cheat, commit adultery or perjury. and five, crooked cops who give the rest of us a bad name."

By this time our meal had come and over our excellent supper, we discussed our children. I told her about two-year old Amelia who came out to the living room one evening wearing one of my wife's bras and being devastated when I said she was too young to wear it. Willi told me about Carey jumping into the deep end of her sister's swimming pool, and herself jumping in right after the child, fully clothed. The ice had been broken.

When the meal was ended, she drove us back to my house where a babysitter had been taking care of Carey and Amelia. "Want to come in for a glass of wine?" I asked.

Take My Hand

She nodded and we went quietly in, tiptoeing around the babysitter sleeping on the couch. We went into the kitchen where she poured us the wine. I drank; she drank. I put my glass down and gently moved to kiss her. I had got to the point of kissing down the length of her neck to her lovely breasts when I heard a cough. The babysitter was standing there watching us.

"I didn't hear you come in, Mr. Bellini," she said. "Can I go home now?"

Willi hastily re-did her clothing while I paid the sitter. Then she retrieved her sleeping daughter and after a quick kiss she left. The babysitter was old enough to drive herself home, so I sat in the kitchen, finishing the wine and thinking about the date. Except for the ending, which I might have written differently, it had been a wonderful evening.

Chapter Twelve

On Monday I sat in my new office and threw myself into reading the transcripts of the interviews. Larry had come back with addresses for April LeBrun, Sandy LeBrun and a Doctor Klein, who had just retired from his pediatric practice in Watertown. Tomorrow I would interview Ethan's father, who after his son's death had moved to Saranac Lake, in the Adirondacks where he worked in a health clinic. Apparently, Sandy was able to live on much less money than he'd made as a New York plastic surgeon. But before I talked with Sandy, I needed to know what questions had already been asked.

I was almost finished with the file when the telephone rang. It was someone from the local television station KWTV, who wanted to talk to me. I was put on hold for several minutes while cheesy music played and then a smooth female introducing herself as Myra Johnson came on the line.

"Is this Mr. Bellini, the man who videotaped the bullying at the Euclid public school?"

I almost hung up. I was heartily sorry that I'd ever agreed to participate in this YouTube thing. It had got me in trouble with my boss, and now it was threatening to take up time I needed for the investigation. Reluctantly I said yes.

"Would you be willing to the station and be interviewed about your part in the YouTube video?"

I said nothing.

"How about tomorrow? Will that be convenient?"

The invitation was not a question, but rather a summons. "Look," I said. "I'm right in the middle of a criminal investigation. I'm happy the video did some good, but I'm really busy right now."

Take My Hand

"What about your partner, Larry Grindon? Do you think he would be available? We'd really like both of you to be there, but I understand your busy schedule."

"The person you should talk to is Chief Tom O'Malley. He's the spokesman for the department. I'm sure he'd be very happy to give you an interview."

"Was the videotaping Chief O'Malley's idea? In that case we do want him on the air."

Did I say I never lie? "He's a very modest man," I said. "And a great Chief. He always lets his people get the credit while he stays in the background. He saw this TV show on bullying and wondered if things like that were going on in our community, and well you know the rest of the story."

"I'll call him," she said. "Maybe it would be possible to have the three of you on together. I'll check back with you later."

"Later," I said. I hung up, not knowing whether to laugh or start packing. O'Malley was not immune to flattery, and if he thought something would make him look better in the public's eye, he would use it. On the other hand, if he thought I was manipulating him, he would be very, very angry.

I didn't have long to wait. Fifteen minutes later O'Malley strode into my office, looking like a man just elected Mardi Gras King. "They want to interview me on TV," he said. "Was this your idea, Chris?"

I nodded. "I hope you don't mind. This will be a chance to get some good publicity for the department, and I could mention the case we're working on. Maybe there's someone out there who's been keeping a secret all these years."

He lowered himself onto a folding chair, the only one available and nodded. Finally he said. "Good idea, Chris. Glad we thought of it. I'll tell Myra Johnson that we'll do the TV interview Wednesday afternoon. Get Grindon in on this too."

Ten minutes later, Larry came into the office. When I told him that he and I were going to be interviewed on television he was not happy.

"What the hell will I say?" he fumed. "In high school, if I was scheduled to speak in front of the class, I purposely got sick."

"Let O'Malley do the talking. We can brief him beforehand and he'll be happy to take all the credit."

After he'd settled down a little bit, we talked about the case. Was there anyone else on our list who might have known or worked for the LeBruns? The two boys who had taken Ethan through the comic book shop were primary suspects, but we had no idea who they were or where they were now. Maybe the TV show would shake some secrets out of closets. I hoped so.

At two o'clock, I put away the paper work and got my coat.

"Where you off to?" Larry asked.

"Amelia's in a play at school and tryouts are today," I said.

"You need a ride?"

"No thanks, I can walk." In fact, all the walking had been doing me good. I'd actually lost a little weight. "See you tomorrow," I said stepping out the door quickly, so I didn't get waylaid by the Chief.

The elementary school auditorium was a scene of chaos when I arrived. There were at least a dozen children of all ages, standing nervously with their parents or running up and down the corridors laughing. Finally a short, blonde man came on stage and said loudly, "Take a seat and we will begin. As I announce a name, each child will come up to the stage. The children are invited to recite a poem, sing or dance, whatever you feel you can do best."

A woman took her place at the piano, and then the man looked at the list he was holding and announced, "James Blakely." A little boy about Amelia's age walked slowly to the microphone and in a breathy voice began to recite a poem.

"This part is tough," someone whispered. I turned to see Willi DeGrasse standing in the aisle slightly behind me. She was wearing a pale blue sweater and dark pants and her reddish hair was drawn back in a pony tail. When I patted the seat beside me, she slid in and sat.

"Best seats in the house," she whispered. Her face was close to mine, and I could feel her breast pressed close to my arm. I was beginning to respond to her closeness. I took a deep breath to try and regain control of the situation. "Where's Carey?"

"An attack of nerves. She decided, in spite of her friendship with Amelia, that she could not be on stage in front of lots of people who might laugh if she did something wrong. She's going to work on the sets. Is Amelia here?"

I pointed to a line of children. "She's next."

"She'll get in. She's a natural."

"Will Carey be jealous if Amelia gets in the play and she doesn't?"

"I don't think so. She's pretty shy. I don't think public speaking is her thing."

I could have told her about my partner who felt the same way. As for me, I didn't mind saying what I thought in front of a lot of people, and Amelia had inherited some of that willingness to show off. We watched as she walked up on the stage, stepped up to the mike and belted out an off-key but enthusiastic version of "Sing" from the Muppets movie. I saw the director nod in approval. She was in.

To celebrate, we went out to supper at my favorite Italian restaurant, and while the two girls whispered secrets to each other I told Willi the story of Amelia's mother.

"When our daughter Cecile was fifteen, she started using cocaine. I should have known what was happening, hell, I'm a cop, but I was working long hours and the kid seemed to spend every minute in her room. Claire kept telling me Cecile had changed; she'd been a child who loved school and now she was sullen and withdrawn. I blame myself for not seeing what was going on."

Willi reached for my hand. "These things happen, Chris. You did the best you could"

It was having her hand in mine, more than the cheesy platitudes that touched my heart.

"At any rate," I continued, "we put Cecile into a detox facility. She was fine for a while, but then she met this boy, Zach, who was an alumni of the juvenile justice system. Claire and I tried to discourage the relationship, but you know how that goes. The more off limits something is for a teen, the more they want it. Cecile got pregnant by the asshole. I remember *that* family meeting. 'Mom and Dad, meet your grandchild's father. He's a scum bag with less than an eighth grade education and has done serious time in Juvie. But I'm sure he'll make a great Dad.' Claire was devastated. The father-to-be cared little for his offspring-to-be, so Cecile stayed at home until the baby was born. Then she announced that she and Zach were moving to California. That news was even harder on my wife than the unplanned pregnancy. When Cecile was in our home, Claire could keep an eye on Amelia, but in California, who knew what would happen."

"Poppi, Poppi," Amelia said, tugging at my arm and pointing.

On the other side of the plate glass window, a man was walking a small white dog. Having a dog had been a frequent topic of conversation between me and Amelia, and I was trying, without much success to discourage her interest.

"Can I go pat him, Poppi, please?"

"Dogs aren't always friendly," I said. "Especially little ones. They have 'the small dog complex,' you know like Napoleon. Have to prove themselves all the time."

"Whose Nap something?"

Take My Hand

"A French man." I said, standing up and taking Amelia by the hand. Outside, the dog owner was waiting while his dog defecated on the sidewalk. To his credit, the owner pulled out a plastic bag and picked up the poop. "Can my granddaughter pat your dog?" I asked. The man smiled.

"This is Spencer," he said. Amelia knelt down and timidly patted the dog. "You should always ask first," the man said. "Some dogs don't like to be patted by strangers."

"Like Mr. Nap something," Amelia said.

I led us back inside the restaurant, where I paid the bill, then we got into Willi DeGrasse's car and she drove us home.

When we'd reached home, I pulled a sleeping Amelia out of the back seat and carried her to the front door. Willi followed me. I unlocked the door and then turned to say good bye.

Silently, Willi reached forward and kissed me. Not one of those polite pecks on the cheek or the forehead. Not an air kiss, where you press cheeks together and smooch the ether, but a real kiss, a kiss with promise. A kiss with possibilities. A kiss with a future.

Chapter Thirteen

The next day I had arranged an interview with Sandy LeBrun. Larry would talk with Ethan's doctor if he could, and locate Gunther and Besom, the detectives who'd worked the case earlier.

Except for the interview with Sandy LeBrun and Ethan's doctor, most of this was telephone work. Larry could also go through the transcripts of other interviews and craft a set of questions. And since we were now being very careful to keep O'Malley in the loop, I popped into his secretary's office and told her where I would be. I reminded Larry that tomorrow was the TV interview.

"How can I forget?" Larry said gloomily. "Can't I just be the silent partner?"

"Larry," I said. "Think of that little boy, dying alone in the woods. We can't bring him back to life, but maybe if we can find his killer, we can bring peace to his parents. Someone out there knows who took him, I'm sure of it. If we go on TV, we might scare up information that no one's been willing to share."

Larry nodded. "You're right," he said. "We're doing this for Ethan."

"See you Friday," I said.

The next morning I took the early bus for the village of Saranac Lake. It would take me two and a half hours to travel south into the Adirondacks, a place that was a patchwork of public lands, and private towns. After his son's death, Dr. LeBrun had decided that he wanted solitude more than anything else. The man who'd treated international celebrities seemed to need very little in material comfort. He wasn't affiliated with any local hospitals and no one I talked to knew whether he was practicing medicine anywhere other than the clinic. It seemed to be a monumental comedown for a man who had previously had so much.

The bus deposited me in Saranac Lake which had a string of houses and businesses overlooking Lake Flower. It was one of those days when everything glowed. The sky was blue; the trees were changing into their gaudy fall threads, and geese making migratory practice runs, were calling overhead. I bought my lunch from a place overlooking the lake and sat on a bench watching the view. Saranac Lake had come to prominence in 1876 when Dr. Edward Trudeau opened a sanatorium for tuberculosis patients. You could still see 'cure porches' on the sunny side of many local houses, where tuberculosis patients were cared for.

I walked to the health clinic, which at eleven o'clock was bursting with patients.

"I'm here to meet with Dr. LeBrun," I said to the receptionist.

"Do you have an appointment?"

I shook my head. I hadn't phoned Sandy ahead of time, fearing that he would bolt.

"I'm afraid he's cancelled. If you can come back on Monday, you probably can see him."

"I need to see him today," I said. "It's a personal matter."

The receptionist, who was probably all of twenty one, looked at me for a moment and then made a decision. "We're not supposed to give out the physician's private numbers, but this is where he lives. It's way out in the woods, and I don't think you can get a car in there, but..." She scribbled an address on a piece of paper and handed it to me.

It took me another half hour to scare up a taxi that would take me the six miles to Sandy LeBrun's place. If I'd called ahead, I might have timed it for a day he was at the clinic, and saved myself the extra trip, but it was now too late to change. I'd come all this way to talk, and I would do it.

The taxi dropped me off at an opening in the trees lining the highway that, when I looked carefully, turned out to be a dirt road.

"This is it?" I asked.

The driver pointed. "A couple miles down there's where he lives."

Reluctantly I got out of the car. I paid the fare, tipping the driver generously, and asked if he would be willing to return in two hours to pick me up. He nodded. I waved goodbye and started up the road.

Autumn leaves crunched underfoot as I walked, sending up their distinctive yeasty smell and overhead I could hear bird song. If I'd been walking for pleasure, it might have been wonderful. As it was, after a half mile or so, my shoulder began to ache, and then itch, and I was sweating from the heat. I wasn't used to this kind of exercise, and because it had been cold this morning, I'd worn too many layers. I'd walked for a half hour more when the path widened out to a small clearing and I could hear a dog barking. I saw ahead of me a log building, almost hidden in the trees. In spite of its rusticity, there were solar panels on the roof and a windmill was set up in a clearing. I moved closer to the cabin unsure whether I would be a) shot as a trespasser or b) mauled by a vicious dog.

Neither happened. Instead, a large golden retriever came bounding around the corner, followed almost immediately by a bearded man, wearing a short-sleeved plaid shirt, blue jeans and work boots.

"Blakely," the man called. "Come here." He stopped when he saw me. "Who the hell are you?"

I held out my hand to show I'd come as a friend. "Chris Bellini," I said. "I phoned you last week. We're re-investigating the death of your..." I couldn't say the word 'son.' Instead I said "Ethan."

"Did I agree to talk with you?" LeBrun asked.

I shook my head. "I just need twenty minutes, Dr. LeBrun."

He turned without a word and walked away from me toward the house. I had no choice but to follow. The cabin I'd seen faced a small lake in which a pair of Canada geese were swimming. LeBrun walked up to a porch and sat in a rocking chair. I followed and sat beside him.

"I don't think there's a question you can ask, I haven't answered before," LeBrun said. I could see, now that I was closer, how much he'd aged from the earlier photos.

"Tell me what happened that night?"

He sighed heavily and ran his fingers through his hair. "April usually picked Ethan up at school. He'd had some problems with kids picking on him, so she would either drive him home or walk with him."

"Did Ethan ever walk home by himself? Your house wasn't far from the school."

He shrugged and looked out toward the pond. "I thought he should walk. Ethan had asthma, but he was still a tough little kid. I used to argue with April that she was coddling him too much, that she ought to let him work things out. She said I was never home, that I knew nothing about my son." He shrugged. "You know how those things go."

"But your wife didn't pick him up that day?"

"No, she called me and said she was with a group of friends and asked me to do it. And well, you know the rest of the story."

"Tell me about the ransom note. When did you find it?"

He sighed. "I think it was six thirty. I'd been driving up and down, looking for Ethan. We called the police and told them he was missing and they had sent an officer over. I don't know why I hadn't seen it before. The note said not to call the police, but by then we'd done it. I had a ferocious argument with the detectives. They didn't want me to pay the money, saying that once the kidnapper had the cash he wouldn't return Ethan. But I was desperate. All I could think of was my little boy, afraid and alone." He stopped for a moment, struggling to regain his composure while I waited.

"So you got the money and went to the hotel?"

"I did. I didn't have all of the money that they wanted, but I thought I could talk them into taking what I had. When I got to the hotel, there was no one there. I began to realize then that I would never see my son again."

I looked out at the pond. The geese had flown and a soft breeze ruffled the water. Somewhere a cardinal called, answered at a distance by another.

"Dr. LeBrun, let me ask another question."

He looked at me warily.

"When you were working as a surgeon, did you ever make any enemies?"

"Enemies?"

"Did you ever have anyone sue you for malpractice?"

"Do I look like a man who would kill his own son? Are you going to be like those other detectives who grilled April and me for hours on end? We were the ones who had lost a child, but to them, we were the enemy. If they had spent half as much time looking for the kidnapper, as they had spent questioning me, they would have found someone."

"One more question," I said. "And then I'll be gone." I held up the newspaper. "This is obviously you, but who is the woman?"

He looked quickly at the paper. "That garbage," he said. "I was well known in New York, so that made me fair game in the newspaper, but it was one lie after the other. Just to sell papers."

I looked at my notes. "Do you have an address for your wife and your son, Greg?"

"Sure," he said. He went into the house, got a pen and some paper and scribbled addresses on them. "I don't know what Greg is up to these days. When he was a kid, he was going to be an artist, but now I have no idea. I just pay the bills. His mother's in Burlington, where she's a lawyer. You can find her in the phone book." He stood up. "That's it, right?"

I was being dismissed. I stood up and held out my hand. His was slender, long fingered but strong. And then I was down the steps and back on the trail.

Walking back down the trail to where I hoped the taxi was waiting, I thought about my own family. I hadn't seen my daughter, Cecile for a while and it had been a contentious relationship even before that. When she was growing up, I'd not spent enough time with her, and I blamed myself for the way she turned out. But I could not forgive her for her treatment of Amelia. After Cecile and Zach took the baby to California, Claire and I tried to keep in touch, but when the phone calls became less frequent, we decided to visit. What we found shocked us both. Cecile and her boyfriend were living in a filthy apartment, the sink was full of unwashed dishes and dirty clothes lay strewn about. Zach had recently been fired from his job and Cecile seemed to spend her days, lying in bed reading movie magazines. But the most shocking was the baby. Amelia was wet and dirty and there didn't seem to be a single bit of baby food in the place. Claire burst into tears and sent me immediately to the store for diapers and baby food.

Claire and I went to court and got temporary custody of the baby. We told Cecile, that when she could prove that she was clean and sober, Amelia would be returned. But that had been more than five years ago and in the meantime, Amelia had become my child. What would I do if Cecile contacted me and said she wanted Amelia back? Could I give my child up to the woman who'd let her go hungry and unchanged in a dirty apartment? In spite of what the courts might rule, I knew I would fight Cecile for custody.

I had no idea where Cecile was now or how she was living. What would my reaction be if police called me saying that Cecile was dead from an overdose? Would I mourn her as Sandy LeBrun mourned his son, or would I be relieved that now Cecile would not fight me for Amelia?

I had reached the road and found to my immense relief that my faithful cabdriver was waiting for me. When we reached the bus station, I had just time to get to grab some snacks before the long trip home.

Chapter Fourteen

It was Wednesday, the day that we were due to go on television with Myra Johnson, but Larry and I still had time to catch up on what we'd found. It was Larry's turn first. He held up the tabloid with the picture of Sandy and the girl.

"Nobody knows who she is, but I did discover something interesting, " He handed me the paper. "Look in the lower left hand corner. Wait a minute you'll need this." He rummaged in the desk drawer and came up with a magnifying glass. I scoped the picture. In the lower corner was some kind of symbol, but it was so blurred it was hard to make out.

"That's the digital signature of the photographer, the person who sold the picture to the newspaper."

I studied the image again. It looked like a logo of some sort. I thought of all the ways that people 'sign' art work. The Chinese use a seal, the print from a stone or wood stamp. Wood carvers carve their name or just write it on the bottom. And visual art is worth much less without the name of the artist on the front. Whoever had taken the photo was confident of his/her skill and knew that the digital signature would make it valuable. We had only to decipher the signature.

"What did you learn about Gunther and Besom?"

"Gunther died six years ago of prostate cancer. Besom retired two years after the case was closed. He lives in a gated community in Boca Raton, Florida. Want to visit him?"

"I don't think we have the money."

"Skype is free."

"But not as much fun as sitting on the beach drinking Margaritas."

I took out my notes and paraphrased my visit with Sandy, ending with, "He denies knowing the woman in the photo."

"All we got now is dandelion fluff," Larry said.

I stood up and scribbled everything we'd learned on the board. LeBrun had given me a phone number for his wife. When I called, April picked up, agreeing to talk to me on Monday. Was her son still at college? He was. She gave me an address, though she couldn't guarantee that he would be there. He was very busy with his classes. When I called the number I got no answer. Larry and I would take our chances with the boy.

It was now twelve- thirty and we were due at the studio in five minutes. No time for a real lunch just crackers and rotgut coffee from the machines. As we were heading toward the car Larry said, "I'd rather have root canal without anesthesia than talk on television."

"Let the Chief do most of the talking. I've prepped him on everything and he's a quick study. You and I just need to talk about the case."

We got ourselves to the studio in plenty of time to be made up and have our hair coiffed. As we were standing in the corridor waiting to go on, the Chief joined us. He had a new suit, and a new haircut, and his aftershave enveloped us all in a sweet fog. Our hostess, Myra Johnson was polite and professional. This was an interview designed to showcase Euclid's public servants, and Chief O'Malley's remarks were sharp and to the point. He was doing his best to show the department in its best light. Then it was our turn. I gave an impassioned plea for anyone who might know something about the LeBrun case to come forward. The phone number of the department flashed on the screen. Myra Johnson thanked us, and we were done. It was now three thirty in the afternoon. I was ready to go home, and have a little bit of private time, but the Chief wanted to go out for drinks and celebrate our fifteen minutes of fame. I normally don't drink in bars, but O'Malley was our boss, and I couldn't very well tell him I wasn't interested.

We spent an hour and a half bringing the Chief up to date on the case. I told him about our planned trip to Burlington the next morning, but he seemed to be more interested in guessing what the impact of 'his' interview would be, imagining his next campaign for Police Chief. I watched the clock tick slowly toward four thirty, and then guessing that

Take My Hand

I'd spent enough time schmoozing, I excused myself and walked toward the door.

Someone bumped into me, deliberately and hard. I turned and was facing a stranger who glared at me as though I'd just incinerated his mother.

"Sorry," I mumbled.

"Not sorry enough, asshole."

My back was up. "Look mister, I'm just trying to get out of here," I said. First rule of conflict, try to defuse the situation.

But the stranger wasn't on that page. Instead he pushed me hard against the brick wall and shoved his face into mine. I could smell sweat and too much beer. "Listen fuckwad." he said. "You may like these little media games you're playing, but I've got you in my radar."

I wanted to turn him around and grind his face into the wall, but I managed to remember rule number one. I pushed myself away from him, but the man wasn't done. He grabbed me by the arm and popped me one hard. OK, if he wanted to play that way, I was ready, even with an almost-healed shoulder. I popped him back awkwardly with my left arm, stomped on his foot and got my knee up into his groin. The last maneuver managed to get him on the ground where I kicked him hard in the side.

We had drawn a crowd. Mr. Macho heaved himself up from the floor and was going for me again when the Chief weighed in and grabbed the man by the arms. "Hedgewick," he said, "This isn't solving anything."

Hedgewick? The father of the bully I'd made famous? Now I understood what made the kid who he was.

Slowly O'Malley released Hedgewick. At least my boss wasn't making us shake hands and apologize. Hedgewick shot me a murderous glance and stomped out of the bar.

"He calls me at least once a week," O'Malley said. "Tells me he's losing business because of the notoriety."

"He needs serious anger management," I said.

O' Malley nodded. I don't think he had any idea what was going on in that family, and I was only starting to get an inkling. These were truly frightening people.

I straightened myself up. My jaw hurt where Hedgewick had popped me. My hand hurt where I'd popped him. Mustering all the dignity I could, I strolled out of the bar.

Take My Hand

Chapter Fifteen

On Thursday Larry and I drove the two and a half hours to Burlington, to a large glass and steel building that housed the law firm where April LeBrun was a partner. I was ushered into an office that was dwarfed by a huge cherry desk behind which floor to ceiling windows displayed a panorama of Lake Champlain. It was a beautiful day, sunny and unseasonably warm and a few sailboats were tacking their way up and down the lake.

April LeBrun had one of those anorexic figures that only look good on twelve year old models, blonde hair that fell to her shoulders and blue eyes, partially hidden by tinted glasses. She shook hands, then she picked up the phone, said something and a young woman entered. "Gwen," she said. "Would you bring us three coffees?" I almost said no, remembering the god-awful stuff Red Hofstetter had offered us. As though reading my mind, April said. "Don't worry, this is Vermont's best. You'll like it."

She sat back in the chair observing us. I couldn't detect any nervousness, and I wondered how she'd prepped herself for the interview. Meditation? Alcohol? Drugs?

"Mrs. LeBrun, why did you and your husband decide to leave New York City?"

It was obviously not the question she had expected. Her eyes narrowed and she clenched her jaw.

"Sandy read this article that talked about the simple rural life, and decided that was what he wanted. He decided without asking any of us, mind you._" These last words were said with some fire. "Greg was in a wonderful private school for the arts; Ethan had a tutor who was fantastic. We had an apartment right on the edge of Central Park, where on weekends we could take a cab to the ballet, the opera, or the museums. We had great friends that we'd been close to since Sandy was an intern. And he wanted to throw all of that away so he could enjoy the _natural_ life. We had great plans for our sons, Mr. Bellini.

Greg was going to be a great artist, and Ethan, even though he was young, had a natural bent for science. With their educations, we knew both boys would get into very good schools."

"I argued with Sandy, telling him that this move wasn't just depriving us of the cultural riches of New York, but it was depriving our children of their future. You know what he said? He said New York City was dangerous. Dangerous. So we come to a small town in upstate New York and now my son is dead." Her voice broke and she grabbed a tissue from her desk and wiped at her eyes.

I waited for her to compose herself. "Do you know anyone who might have had a grudge against your husband? Someone who might have died or been injured during an operation? Anyone who wanted revenge on your family?"

She was thoughtful for a moment, then she said. "It wasn't his fault, really. The woman had a heart condition that no one knew about. Before the surgery, the hospital did blood work and took a history, but no one knew..." Her voice trailed off for a moment. "After the woman died, there was an investigation, and Sandy was declared innocent. Is that the sort of thing you're looking for?"

I nodded. "What was the woman's name?"

April shook her head. 'Norris? Nordland? I can't remember it clearly. It was more than twelve years ago."

"Did you notice any changes in your husband after the death of his patient?"

"He was quieter. He used to enjoy being a surgeon, but the death of that patient scared him. He said he wanted to do other kinds of medicine."

I looked down at my notes. "Mrs. LeBrun, I'm sure you read the tabloids that were circulating at the time of the original investigation. One suggested that Ethan was the victim of Munchausen by Proxy Syndrome. What is your reaction?"

She stood up and marched stiffly to the window, her fists clenched at her side. "Those god-damned papers," she said finally. "They were free to print any fucking lie they wanted. It made us, the grieving parents seem like monsters. What parent would do that to a child? My son had asthma, and he had frequent visits to his asthma doctor. In fact when we came to Euclid, we had a hard time finding anyone who was as qualified as our physician in the city. For a couple of months we would drive the five hours just to see the doctor that he knew. Yes, he saw the doctor often. No, I was not abusing him."

I pulled out the tabloid showing Sandy LeBrun and the young woman, and held it up. "You've seen this too, I guess."

"You believe those lies too? she said sharply. "If that's what this is about, the interview is over."

At that moment, the coffee arrived, giving us all a chance to calm down. I put the newspaper to one side and said, "Tell me about Evangeline Swindon. How long did she work for you before you moved to upstate New York?"

"Vangie came from Louisiana originally. She was an unwed mother with an eleven year old daughter. At that time, we only had Greg. Then Ethan was born and I decided to go back to school. Vangie was invaluable and she really loved our boys."

"Did you have a disagreement with her before Ethan's death?"

"No, of course not. Why would I?"

"She doesn't think very highly of you."

"I expect not. After Sandy and I divorced, we didn't need Evangeline any more. We were generous in our compensation, but she was angry about losing a job she'd had for many years. I don't even know where she is any more."

"She's waitressing in a diner," I said. "Tell me about your gardener, Konstantyn Shevchenko. Where did you find him and what was his relationship with your sons?"

"I found him in a garden center in Watertown. He was a wizard with plants. A very shy man, he seemed to have no family at all. He took Ethan under his wing, was very patient with him and became in a way a substitute parent."

"Do you know where Mr. Shevchenko is now?"

"I heard he went back to Garden's Bounty, the store where he was working when I first met him."

"One last question. Did you ever hear Ethan talk about a sixth or seventh grader who was his friend?"

She shook her head.

"Apparently the boy liked comics the way Ethan did."

She shook her head again. "My poor baby didn't have many friends his own age. We would suggest sleepovers, or pizza and movie nights, but he would get so nervous at the thought of having to entertain, we gave up trying. His father worked long hours, and I was trying to become a lawyer. I don't think we were good parents."

We sat and drank our coffee in silence. When I was finished, I stood up. Larry did the same. "Thank you for your time, Mrs. LeBrun," I said, and we left.

Chapter Sixteen

Question: How was Ethan LeBrun kidnapped from a street crowded with kids without anyone seeing the kidnapping?

Answer: Two boys lured him into a comic book store. Once inside the store the proprietor had an epileptic attack, and did not see the two boys force Ethan out the back door of the shop and into the woods where he later died.

Question: Did Ethan's father have any enemies who might have taken their revenge by kidnapping the son?

Answer: One of Sandy LeBrun's patients died during surgery before the LeBruns left New York City. Name: unknown.

Question: Why did the kidnappers demand such a low ransom amount, when they knew Sandy LeBrun was rich?

Answer: There might have been another reason for the kidnapping.

Question: Why does Evangeline Swindon dislike April LeBrun, her former employer?

Answer: the obvious one, because after the kidnapping, the LeBruns divorced and Evangeline lost her job. Other answers?

Question: Did April abuse her son?

Question: Who took the picture of Sandy and the girl?

Question: Who is lying and who is telling the truth?

Question: What have Larry and I have overlooked?

As Larry and I walked back to the car from April LeBrun's office I considered the questions that seemed to be multiplying uncontrollably like cells in a Petri dish. If I got a partial answer to one question, six more would spring up to taunt me.

We got in the car and drove to the address April had given me for Greg. The apartment was above a pizza parlor in a neighborhood of run-down buildings interspersed by a deli, laundromat, pawn shop and second hand store. All of it screamed poverty, but because it was within walking distance of an expensive university, it was genteel student poverty, and not the grinding, soul-destroying poverty of those with little education.

We rang the bell beside the name and waited. No answer. We rang again. Suddenly a young man appeared at the top of a staircase. "What the fuck?" he yelled. "I was trying to sleep."

It was one thirty in the afternoon; maybe this young man had a night job somewhere.

"We're looking for Greg LeBrun."

The young man nodded, acknowledging that he was Greg. The apartment into which we were ushered was cluttered with clothing and empty pizza cartons. Two expensive looking cameras were slung casually over a straight chair and a pile of colored photos occupied most of a wooden table. One part of the single room was curtained off and, from the smell of chemicals, I assumed that was the darkroom. A computer blinked on a desk and books were piled on the floor. An unmade bed took up most of the space along one wall. Greg pushed some papers off a chair and sat. It was the only chair, so I set myself on the bed. Larry did the same. It was then that I noticed the strong smell of marijuana floating in the air from a cigarette burning nearby.

"Don't worry," I said. "We're not here to bust you. We just have a few questions."

"About what?"

"The death of your brother, Ethan."

Greg stood up, walked to the joint and took a long drag. Then he dropped it into the sink and flushed it down. "All right," he said. "But don't forget. I was just a kid myself when it happened."

"Do you remember anything from that night? You came home from school and what did you find?"

"Crazyness. Dad was home. He was never home that early and Mom was out, which was just the reverse of the usual. Dad was calling all of Ethan's friends, trying to find out if little bro had gone home with anyone else, though he never did anything like that. Then Mom came home. She started crying. Dad started yelling at her. He found the note in the kitchen, told Vangie to go home and then he took off in his car."

"Where did he go?"

"He said he went to get money and try to get Ethan back."

"Do you believe that's what he did?"

"How the hell do I know? I was just a kid. Is that it?"

"No," Larry said. "Did your brother have any friends who were older?"

"Jimmy four-eyes. He was a seventh grader. I met him once, but I didn't think much of him. He was a suck-up, hanging with my brother 'cause Ethan had money."

"What did Jimmy look like?"

"Jesus, I don't remember. Short with dark hair, I think."

"Did Ethan spend much time with Jimmy?"

"I don't know. Once a week they'd go to the comic book store and then go have a coke together and read the comics. Ethan told my mom he was staying after school because of a chess club. He knew Mom wouldn't approve of Jimmy."

"What about your father? Did he know about Ethan's friend?"

"No," the answer was short and angry, more of a grunt.

"Do you get along with your Dad?"

"He pays the bills, stays out of my way and I stay out of his. That makes us both happy."

"Does he disapprove of your photography?"

"He doesn't even know I take pictures. Look, he was never around when I was growing up. When I was seven and eight I cared about that stuff, but I'm over it. He can be his 'wild man of the woods' in the Adirondacks. I don't give a shit. As long as he doesn't crowd me, I'm good."

He reached over and began fingering a manila envelope. A photograph had escaped and he was trying to push it back. "Just going through some old stuff," he said. "From when I was starting to take pictures."

I looked around at the photos on the wall. "These are very good," I said. I wasn't just greasing the wheels of communication, Greg had an artist's eye. "Is photography your major?"

"Nah. Dad wouldn't pay for anything like that. I'm supposed to be studying psychology, but really I don't know when I'll graduate." He got up suddenly. "Sorry, I got to take a whiz."

When he was gone I stood up and walked around the apartment, looking more closely at the framed black and white photos. If Greg had hopes of being a professional photographer, he was on his way.

"My Dad bought me a camera when we were still in New York City," Greg said, coming back into the room to stand beside me. "I was maybe nine or ten. I just started snapping things that were interesting. People on the street, buildings, dogs, that sort of thing. I might put together a book some day."

"Well, you have enough high quality work to do that," I said. Had I laid it on too thickly? But Greg only looked at me and smiled.

Larry leaned forward, open, friendly. "There was a picture of your father and a young woman in one of the tabloids. Do you know which one I'm talking about?"

Something passed swiftly across Greg's face almost like a twitch. He shook his head.

"I was asking because the quality of the picture is very good, like something you might have taken, and when you said you'd been snapping pictures since you were a kid, I wondered if the one in the paper might be yours?"

"Don't think so," Greg said. "What paper was it in?"

He was fiddling with the manila envelope, pushing the flap up and down.

"*The Star*. I'll bring it by and you can take a look." Larry looked at the envelope, and Greg immediately stopped fiddling. "Any chance we could borrow a few of your earlier pictures? I have a friend with a gallery and she might want to hang your work."

Greg shook his head. "Not ready for the public yet," he said. Larry nodded. He reached into his pocket and held out a card. "If you think of anything else, just give us a call." We stood up and took our leave.

"So you think Greg sold the picture to the tabloids?" Larry asked as we walked back to our car.

"I think so, but I don't know why. He can't have needed the money. He was only thirteen for Christ's sake."

"Even a rich boy has to explain why he needs money," Larry said.

"You think he was taking drugs when he was thirteen? He seems to like his pot, doesn't he?"

Larry nodded. "If Greg took the picture, he knows who the woman is."

"On the other hand, he could have been just taking pictures. There's his father with a strange woman who could be a patient, or just a casual friend. We need to get one of those pictures hanging on his wall, to see if Greg's digital signature matches that picture in the tabloids."

"We don't have the technology to match digital signatures," Larry said. Then he looked at me. "But Myra might be able to do some research for us."

It took me a minute to figure out what he was saying. "Your daughter would do this?"

"I think so. I've been encouraging her to find some paid work so she can save for college, and just to keep her busy."

"It's a big order," I said.

"Let's just ask her."

Chapter Seventeen

Amelia had been accepted into the play. Directions for a costume, a CD of the song she was learning and a rehearsal schedule were included with the letter. It was now almost the end of September. Rehearsals would be held once a week for the first few weeks, accelerating to twice and three times a week, until the week of the play, performed in mid November, when there would be rehearsal every night. It was an enormous commitment of my free evenings, but Amelia was so excited to be an actress in a real play that I couldn't say no.

I called Willi DeGrasse. We hadn't spoken since our date. but now I needed to know if she was still willing to sew a costume. "Of course," she said. "What's her part?"

"A dancing pumpkin. Have they recruited every kid in the school?"

"Pretty much," Willi said. "They could have added Easter and Halloween to the holidays and no kid in the school would be without a part. I volunteered to help, since Carey is on the set crew. Would you like me to come over tomorrow and pick up the pattern?"

"Let us feed you both dinner," I said on the spur of the moment. I love to cook, and even though hampered by my immobilized wing, I would manage.

"What can I bring?"

"Just yourself," I could rustle up a mean Chicken Parmesan and combine that with a fresh salad, some antipasto and a good wine and we'd be fine. Since tomorrow was Saturday, I'd have plenty of time to cook.

I spent Saturday cleaning the house and browning the chicken, then making the sauce and a special salad dressing. I took a shower and then put on a clean blue shirt and dress pants. I looked at the outfit, wondering if I should be less formal or more formal, blue jeans or dress pants. I finally realized that it really didn't matter. Either she liked me or she didn't.

At six, the doorbell rang. Willi handed me the bottle of wine, not a great vintage but a good one. I hung up her coat and ushered her into the kitchen. Carey immediately disappeared into the living room with Amelia.

Willi uncorked the wine and poured two glasses. I was cutting cheese into slices, pairing it with crackers and black olives.

"My husband never cooked," she said. "If I were going to be away during suppertime, I'd have to leave him something in the fridge. His favorite meal was tater tots and fish sticks."

Remembering Larry's lesson about the birds, I took a piece of the aged Asiago and gently held it to her mouth.

"Mmm, that is good. How did you learn to do that?"

"Do what?" I asked. I'd been thinking about the proficiencies I could demonstrate in places other than the kitchen.

"Cook. How did you learn to cook?"

"I spent a lot of time with my grandmother when I was a child. She loved to cook, and she taught me."

"So Italians all love to cook?"

"They love to eat," I said. "For an Italian, food is love and cooking food is making love."

Had I really said that? I looked at Willi to see her reaction. She didn't seem to be upset so I deftly changed the subject.

"When my father died my mother went to work, first cleaning people's houses and then baking pies for the local diner. I spent a lot of time in the kitchen with her. Then when I was in eighth grade, she went back to college and got a teaching degree."

Take My Hand

"A teaching degree? No kidding."

"I had three sisters, all of them older than I was, so after Mom went back to school and to avoid getting bossed around, I hung out with my Nonna."

"It must have been hard. Being the only boy with three sisters." I couldn't tell if she was serious or being ironic.

"It was tough. After my dad was killed, I had no man in my life. And when I married, we had a little girl, so I was again surrounded by women." I looked down at the plate of cheese and crackers. It was empty. I had violated the 'ping-pong' rule, which says if the other person is the only one eating, you are hogging the conversation.

"We should call the kids for supper," I said.

I thought she would move away, and get the girls. Instead she came closer and kissed me gently on the cheek. "You're a wonderful man." I kissed her back then, taking her into my arms. She didn't resist, and it was only when the two little girls came running into the room that we stopped. Then we had to endure the ribbing from our children.

Throughout the dinner I tried very hard to give Willi room to talk. She told us that she was a budding poet, hoping to publish a book if she could find an agent and promising to send me some of her poems. After supper, the kids went into Amelia's room to play a game and we cleaned up the kitchen.

We had moved to the couch and were talking, when I suddenly realized I could no longer hear the girls. Putting my hand on my lips, I rose and went up the stairs. When I opened the door, I saw the two children, their heads together, both fast asleep. I picked up the game which had fallen to the floor and put it away, while Willi covered up the kids.

"I hate to wake her up to take her home," Willi said.

"You could just leave her here."

She looked at me and nodded quietly. I shut the door. We went downstairs to the kitchen where I poured two glasses of a very nice Sauterne rumored to have aphrodisiacal properties, and set out some cheese. Taking our wine and cheese we went back to the living room and sat side by side on the couch.

"This has been a wonderful evening, thank you," Willi said. She had stretched her arm out and was toying with my hair.

In response I turned and pulled her toward me, kissing her hard. Her tongue found mine. She was as hungry for me as I was for her. I reached around behind and unhooked her bra, pushing her shirt up and feeling the softness of her delicious breasts. Her head was thrown back and she was breathing heavily, I was sucking nibbling, working my way down.

"Oh God, Chris," she moaned.

"We. Should. Go. To. The. Bedroom," I said. She was fumbling with my shirt, unfastening my belt unzipping my fly. We stumbled toward the bedroom, leaving a trail of clothing in our wake.

I closed the door behind me and pushed her onto the bed. She was naked now, her long slender body stretched out before me. Carefully I lowered myself onto her, kissed her lips, her neck, her breasts, working my way to her vagina. She moaned as I moved into her and then we came in one glorious moment of climax.

I was too quick of course. I should have taken my time, but I'd been out of practice for so long. She ran her fingers down my side. "My God, Chris," she said. I kissed her again, and again we began that long slow ascent toward climax.

I woke to sunlight filling the room. It was quiet, which meant that Willi and I still had a few wonderful moments together and if we were lucky, time to make love again. She was awake, watching me, her fingers running down the side of my body. I felt her hand stop. "What's that?" she asked.

"What's what?"

Take My Hand

"That scar?"

"Knife wound. I was called to a restaurant where a drunk had taken up residence in the doorway. When I tried to move him he knifed me."

"You have black and blue marks on your neck," she said. "What happened there?"

"Hedgewick beat me up. He's mad because all the stuff about his son is hurting business."

"And this is where you were shot," she said, her fingers touching the scar on my shoulder.

Enough of this trip down memory lane. I sat up and pulled her to me. "What do you have planned for today, beautiful lady?"

"Carey has a dentist appointment at ten, and we're going to the mall for new shoes."

"Damn," I said softly. "And I had other plans." I ran a hand over her breast, and then kissed it. Just at that moment there was a knock on the door.

"Poppi? Are you awake?"

"Yes, but stay out there."

With a rueful look toward Willi, I got out of bed, put on underwear and jeans. Buttoning my shirt, I stepped outside the bedroom, being careful to close it tight behind me.

"Carey's still asleep. Did her mom go home?"

"No, she's here too. Come on, let's make you some breakfast."

By nine thirty, Willi and her daughter had left. Amelia and I worked on her homework, practiced the songs she would sing in the play, and generally enjoyed a lazy Saturday. Part of me replayed the evening with Willi. I couldn't wait to see her again.

Chapter Eighteen

On Monday we sat in the office discussing the issue of Greg LeBrun's photography. We needed to confront Greg with the tabloid picture of his father and ask if he'd taken the photo. If he said no, it might still be possible to compare digital signatures, but that required some expertise we didn't have. If we found the original of the picture and took it without permission, whatever evidence it provided would be inadmissible in court. On the other hand, if Sandy LeBrun was fooling around with a younger woman, there was no obvious connection to his son's death, and if there was no connection, why were we wasting our time? The picture might explain Greg's bitterness toward his father but nothing more.

"Let's talk to Besom," Larry said. "He might have some insights we hadn't considered."

We called Gerald Besom. The phone was answered by a woman with a soft voice who, when I told her who we were, perked up. "He'd be happy to talk with you," she said. "He's out on the Lanai watching the woodpeckers eat oranges."

It didn't sound like an exciting retirement to me. In a minute Besom came on the phone. He was breathless as though he'd been running.

I told him again who we were and why we were calling. I asked if he had a computer and whether we could Skype him. "Sorry, I'm too old for that newfangled stuff," he said. "But I'll answer any of your questions." I put him on the speaker phone, introduced Larry and began.

"We're coming to a dead end," I said. "Did you and Gunther come up with any conclusions you'd be willing to share."

"Gunther thought that Dr. LeBrun wasn't telling us everything. When something like this happens, statistically it's the parent who's guilty. Gunther really believed that. We grilled those two over and over, but nothing ever popped up. But then what parent would take a little boy, tie him up and leave him in the woods to die? It's unconscionable."

"Is there any truth to what the tabloids printed?"

"Who knows? If you wave enough dollars in someone's face, he'll say anything. I think some of that crap came from Swindon, the maid. She was pretty angry at the LeBruns."

"Still is," Larry said.

"The gardener, Shevchenko is an interesting case. Did you know that his mother died on Dr. LeBrun's operating table. Heart attack. I understand there was an inquiry, but no charges were made. I guess when you get to be a doctor, you can kill without punishment."

"You think Shevchenko wanted to get even with Sandy LeBrun?" I considered a scenario I'd never thought about. A man set on revenge takes a job with the family of the person who killed his mother, befriends the man's little boy and kills him.

"Shevchenko said he was in New York City that night looking for his ex-wife. We tried to double-check the story, but we couldn't locate the wife, so we couldn't ironclad his alibi."

"He could have hired some kids to do the kidnapping."

"Yeah, I know. That's the other thing. The boy 'Jimmy' disappeared from town the night of the kidnapping, It was as though he'd never lived there. And the other young man, no one had ever seen him. I'm sorry I can't be of more help," he said.

I thanked Besom. He seemed unwilling to hang up, wanting to talk about the case and what we'd discovered. I wanted to keep him on our good side, in case we had more questions, but he wasn't technically on the investigating team. Finally, I managed to extricate myself and hung up.

"We need to talk to Shevchenko,' I said. "Where did April LeBrun say he worked?"

"Garden's Bounty in Watertown. That's where she found him and that's where he went when the LeBruns left Euclid."

"If April knew that Shevchenko's mother died on Sandy's table, why would she hire him?" Larry asked.

"Good question. Maybe April didn't know. Didn't she say the dead woman's name was...?" I looked at my notes. "Norris or Nordland?"

"Seems like too much of a coincidence. A woman goes looking for a gardener and ends up hiring the man whose mother has been killed by her husband."

"Did she really find him at that garden supply store?"

"She says she did, but if Shevchenko wanted to get close to the family, he'd have to make it a sure thing, like getting a friend to recommend him."

"He'd have to know the LeBruns needed a gardener."

We sat in silence for a moment, mulling over the various iterations the case could take, then Larry picked up the phone and dialed Garden's Bounty, learning that Mr. Shevchenko had taken some vacation days, but we could probably speak to him at his home. They gave us the number at an address in the Watertown area.

I called and when Shevchenko answered I asked if we could come and talk to him tomorrow about the LeBrun case.

"I already answered them questions ten years ago," Shevchenko said. "I ain't got nothing more to say."

"We won't take up much time. Give us twenty minutes. You knew Ethan; surely he deserves to have his kidnapper brought to justice."

"Yeah, OK," Shevchenko said finally. We set up an appointment for the next day, then we spent the rest of the afternoon going over the transcripts of the Shevchenko interview. At that time, the man had lived in a small mobile home, not far out of town. When the detectives interviewed him, they found numerous photos of a small boy, about the same age as Ethan and with the same pale hair and blue eyes. When questioned, Shevchenko said the child in the photos was his son, Nicholas. Was Shevchenko's attachment to Ethan LeBrun one of a man who missed his own boy, or had there been something else in the relationship? We would find out tomorrow.

Chapter Nineteen

The next day we drove to Watertown to interview Konstantyn Shevchenko at his home. Shevchenko was waiting at the door when we drove up. He was a skeletal man, with thick horn rimmed glasses and long hair which he'd pulled back into a pony tail.

"We can go in here," he said, leading us through the house into a small living room which looked as though it had been furnished from one of those low-cost furniture warehouses where every sofa and chair is dark plaid, and within weeks of the purchase the covering is wearing away and stuffing falling out. There was a strong smell of cooking cabbage.

A woman came out of the kitchen, wearing an apron. She was as tall as Shevchenko, with pale blue eyes and washed out hair. She was carrying a coffee pot. Shevchenko introduced her as his wife, Anna.

"Would you like coffee?" she asked in heavily accented English.

"Sure," Larry said. I shook my head. I'd already had two cups and my bladder had reached capacity.

While the woman served coffee, I watched Shevchenko and his wife, trying to gauge their relationship. She seemed deferential to him, but unafraid. If she knew something he wasn't telling would she be willing to talk to us alone? Finally, I settled back in the chair and looked at my notes.

"Thank you for seeing us, Mr. Shevchenko," I said. "When did you first meet the LeBruns?"

"About eleven years ago, I was working at Garden's Bounty. The lady come in with her little boy. They were building a house and were looking for gardener."

"Did you know at the time that April LeBrun was the wife of the man who'd killed your mother?" Larry said.

"Ya. 'Cause I know the name. He don't know me though, cause my mother, her name is different."

"Your mother's name was what?"

"Nordeen. My father died when I was small and she remarried."

"Did you ever confront Dr. LeBrun about your mother's death?"

"Nah."

"Why not. She died under his care. Surely that must have weighed on your mind when you were working for him? I think it would be hard for me to forget someone who had done that. I might find a way to get revenge."

"I had no money. Hospitals they got all the power. It wasn't his fault that she died; she had a bad heart."

"Why did you decide to take the job with the LeBruns?"

"It was November. After Christmas they lay people off because not many people buy plants."

"So the LeBruns hired you even though it was nearing winter and you wouldn't be able to work on their garden for several months?"

He shrugged. "They were building a new house. They wanted ideas on the landscaping. They put me on salary; I was lucky to have the job."

"Mrs. LeBrun said she found you when she'd gone shopping in the garden center. Is that how it happened?"

He shifted in the chair, glanced at his wife who sat on the edge of her seat watching us.

"It wasn't like that."

"What was it like?"

"One of my regular customers told me that a new doctor and his wife were building house in Euclid and looking for a gardener. I wrote letter and mailed it to doctor. The lady called me up the next week, then she came up to where I worked and we talked."

"Was this the only gardening job you could find locally?"

"No. I could have worked for one of them big box stores, but in those places no one really wants to talk about gardens, they just buy their stuff and leave."

"Working for the LeBruns would give you a better salary."

"Ya. And it give me a chance to design a garden and watch plants grow. And I met the little boy, Etan."

"Ethan?"

Shevchenko ran his fingers through his hair and stared at the coffee cup on the table. "I wasn't going to take the job. I knew who the LeBruns were. But then I saw the little boy."

"What was it about Ethan LeBrun that made you want to work for the LeBruns?"

"He reminded me of Nikki, blonde hair and blue eyes. And he even talked like my Nikki."

"Nikki is Nicholas, your son?"

"Ya. When my wife and I split up, she took him to New York City. Etan was like him, gentle, curious, smart. My son was very smart. Was reading even before he went to school."

"Do you see your son often?"

A wave of raw sadness crossed Shevchenko's face. "My wife Elle took him. I don't see him now for many years."

"So you haven't located him?"

He shook his head. "When Elle took my son, I think about how when I see her I will kill her." He looked at both of us. "Yes, shooting her with a gun, stabbing, poisoning, running her over with car. All of that. And then one day, I thought. 'This is no good. I am wasting my time on something that may never happen.' So I decided to forgive her. And I forgive Dr. LeBrun too."

"Admirable," Larry said dryly.

"No, no. Not for them, for me. So I could sleep at night; so I could find another woman and start a new life. And when Mrs. LeBrun showed up, I saw a little boy that needed a man in his life. I wanted to be that man."

"But Ethan had a father."

"What father is never at home because he is always at work, or pretending to be at work?"

"Pretending?"

"I knew how he chased after the nurses at the hospital. I got friends who work there."

"What friends?"

"Trena James, Helen Kolinski."

I put the names in my notebook.

"Mr. Shevchenko, did Dr. LeBrun ever figure out who you were? Maybe he came out to the garden one day while you were working to tell you how sorry he was?"

"Dr. LeBrun was never at home when I was working and I was just the gardener, hired by his wife to keep grounds looking nice."

"Tell us again, what you were doing the night of the kidnapping? You told the other detectives that you were in New York City. Is that right?"

"A friend of mine said that he'd seen my wife and son on the subway. The friend followed them to an apartment in the Bronx, so as soon as I got my day off, I went to the apartment to find them. The woman looked like Elle but it wasn't her. When I got back two days later, they told me that Etan had died."

"Who told you?"

"The cops what interviewed me. It was very sad for me. I liked that little boy."

I looked down at my notes. "When you were interviewed by the other detectives, you had a lot of pictures of a child in your home. Were those pictures of your son, or of Ethan?"

He twisted in his chair. "Most of them were of Etan. I had some pictures of Nicholas, but from when he was younger."

"Why did you have pictures of Ethan? He wasn't your child."

"Yah. I know. He reminded me of Nicholas. I liked him."

This line of questioning seemed to be going nowhere, though I was getting a creepy feeling about the relationship between Shevchenko and Ethan. I had been looking around the room as Shevchenko was talking. On the wall was a photograph of a young man, posing in a boxer's stance. "Mr. Shevchenko," I asked. "Were you ever a boxer?"

"Yeah. I was boxer in Ukraine when I was sixteen."

"Were you as tall then as you are now?"

He nodded. "Yah, I shot up early."

"How long did you box?"

"Couple years. I made some good money at it."

"Did you ever have any problems? Boxing?"

Shevchenko's wife had left the room. He got up and moved toward the kitchen where he poked his head inside and looked around.

"My wife does not know this story," he said quietly. "She knows I was a boxer but not that the man died."

"Tell us what happened."

"It was in the seventh round. It was amateur boxing, no locker rooms, nothing, just a square of ropes set out in a field. If someone got hurt, they took him in car to the hospital, thirty miles away. I hit the man, Brunhoffer, very hard in the seventh round, and he just folded. I was happy I had won. It was money for me, nothing more. But then Brunhoffer didn't get up, and two of his friends came and took him away. Later I heard that he died. That was when I decided to give up boxing."

"Were you ever charged with a crime?"

"There was an investigation, but when they did the autopsy, they found Brunhoffer had a brain aneurism that had burst. It was already there, just waiting for the right blow. They said I wasn't responsible."

"Mr. Shevchenko," Larry said. "Did anyone ever approach you about Sandy LeBrun, asking you, to hurt him or his family?"

"No, why would they do that?"

"They might have had a grudge against him. They might be someone like you, who'd lost a loved one on his operating table. Or someone who just wanted revenge. The LeBruns were rich, and they'd had a lot of power when they lived in New York City."

Shevchenko shifted in his seat. "I never do nothing like that," he said, but he wouldn't meet our eyes.

"Mr. Shevchenko did you spend a lot of time with Ethan LeBrun?"

"No, not much. Sometime he come to the garden where I am working and ask to help and I give him little job. He was a nice boy, worked hard when I gave him job, but wasn't very strong."

"Did he ever talk to you about a friend of his, a boy named Jimmy?"

Shevchenko shook his head.

"Did he ever talk about liking comic books?"

"Ya, that. He had lotsa books. His parents let him buy many. I saw his bedroom once; it was crammed with comic books. He talks to me about some of the characters in the comic books. The ones he liked were men who were scientists who discovered a cure for sickness, that sort of thing."

"Not Superman, Batman, Spiderman?"

"Ya, some of them, but others I never heard of : *General Brownwell, The Silver Sword, Ben Rathwell and the Poison of Doom.*"

It was getting late and we really hadn't gotten anywhere. I looked at Larry to ask if he had any more questions. He gave a little shake of the head. We stood. "Thank you very much, Mr. Shevchenko." I handed him my card. "Call us if you think of anything."

"You think he had a motive to kill Ethan?" Larry asked when we were in the car.

"He had more of a motive to kill the doctor," I said. "I think he genuinely like the kid."

"Do you believe the crap about forgiving LeBrun? I'll bet someone else whose relative died on Sandy's table got to Shevchenko and talked him into getting revenge. Possibly paid Shevchenko to do it."

"We need to double check his alibi. Besom said they couldn't find the wife. Maybe we'll have better luck."

Take My Hand

It was too late to go back to the station, so we said good-bye at my house, where Mrs. Gentile was putting a casserole in the oven for our supper. I asked if she could stay and eat with us but she begged off. She was going to the movies with a friend.

"Male or Female?"

She blushed coyly, but offered no more information. When she'd left the house, I sorted through the mail. There were too many ads, too many requests for money, some legitimate bills and an envelope with my name hand written on the front, and a return address of someone vaguely familiar. When I opened the envelope, I learned that in two weeks there would be a reunion of my high school class in a fancy hotel in Watertown, seventy miles away. I would need a hotel room, if I were going to stay and drink with my classmates. And this was happening in two weeks? I looked at the date of the letter and then the envelope. It had been mailed a month ago to the wrong address, returned and re-mailed. God bless the U.S. postal service.

I held the invitation in my hands, remembering the small group of kids I'd hung around with in high school: Buzz Tildon, Will Green, Lorna Smith, Tansy Marcher. Buzz had an old car, the only kid with parents rich enough to afford one, and we'd drive out to the lake to go fishing or swimming. In the winter, we'd go cross-country skiing or just drive around town. I had lost touch with all of these people, and I would love to see who was still alive. Lorna Smith had come to our wedding, and then we'd seen her about four years after that. Cecile was a baby and Lorna had seemed happy as she walked beside the good-looking, tall drink of water that was her new husband. What was his name, again? I took out my phone and called the number given on the invitation and said, yes, I would like to come. Since I'd just received my invitation, was it too late to sign up? The woman, who was someone I vaguely remembered from junior year English class said sure. And how was I doing? She said, she remembered Claire, who'd been in her class. Would we both be coming?

"No," I said. "I'll be coming alone." To prevent further questions, I gave her my credit card and she said there would be a ticket for the banquet waiting for me at the door.

That night I dreamed of our group, especially Lorna Smith. She was working in a factory that made guns, and when I stopped to say hello, she aimed the gun at my head and pretended to fire.

Chapter Twenty

Lorna Smith Watson

The high grey walls of Greenville Maximum Security Prison loomed over the street, throwing their shadow over Lorna Watson as she entered. Sometimes Lorna thought of the prison as one of those medieval castles whose presence dominated not only the town, but the whole countryside. Greenville drew most of its employees from the towns around it, but it also cast a long dark shadow over the life of the community. What person, riding down Main Street, with the wall of the prison towering over him, would not feel the darkness that seemed to encompass everything?

She took a deep breath and went in through the gate. On a normal day, she would have stepped through the metal detector, said hello to whoever was on duty at the front desk, collected her keys and gone in. But this morning the man at the desk simply pointed to the right.

Damn, she hated surprise inspections. She knew they were necessary to ferret out contraband, but the casual humiliation of the whole thing unsettled her.

She walked into the room and stood behind a line of men and women, reminding herself that this was necessary to her teaching job, something like going through airport security. A person spoke and she looked up. She was at the sorting table, and a Corrections Officer who seemed barely out of his teens was telling her to hand over her belongings. Lorna gave him her purse and he dumped it unceremoniously on the table. He began picking through her personal objects: lipstick, hand cream, a wallet, a small notepad, a pen, two tampons, a calendar, a bottle of Tums, a nail file and three dusty life savers. As his hands touched the tampons, a faint smile crossed his lips. Lorna wanted to smack him and say "Just do your job, you've seen these before." Instead she repeated her own personal mantra "I need this job. I need this job." She was forty years old, too old to go looking for another teaching job, and too young to retire.

The C.O. put the lipstick, hand cream, tampons, Tums, and calendar in a paper bag. He picked up the wallet, took out the bills and counted them slowly in front of her. "Sixteen dollars," he said. No more than twenty five dollars was allowed to come into the prison. If there were more in your wallet, the guards confiscated it, and you might never get it back. He put the wallet in the paper bag. He picked up the small notebook and rifled through it, stopping at a page.

"You a poet?"

Lorna nodded.

"I write poetry too. Got a piece published in the *Daily Bugle* last week." The *Bugle* was what remained of two dailies that had served adjacent communities for years. Now the editor had to scramble to fill its few poorly-written pages. His solution was more material written by locals; the one from Greenlawn Assisted Living Facility, often filled two full columns.

"Mabel Artmore has just returned from a two week trip to Minneapolis to see her daughter and new grand-baby. Brought back lots of pictures. That child is sooo cute." and on and on in the same vein.

The other filler was poetry. Lorna realized that she might have seen this young man's opus, which could have gone something like:

"Blood can't lie

How do you see the man?

Leave it to the Street

Cry Little Stone

When I can't sleep

I feel queasy

I feel misty

Cry Little Stone."

Take My Hand

The C.O. poet was smiling at Lorna as though, because they were both poets, they were best buds. He dropped Lorna's nail file into the "confiscated" bin. "You can pick it up from Security tonight," he said. He did a quick search of her lunch bag and then she was done with this part of the inspection.

Grabbing her stuff, Lorna took a seat to wait for the drug- detecting dog to come around. When she'd started working here, she'd made the mistake of trying to pat the creature and was sharply rebuked for it. Now she sat and waited, watching her class preparation time slip away.

Hank Walters, a fellow teacher, was two seats away, looking glum. They'd taken his newspaper, his only lunchtime recreation. *You ought to take up poetry, Hank*, she thought. The dog came around, gave Lorna a cursory nosing and she was free to go.

She walked through the Sallyport, hearing the heavy metal gate close behind her. She collected her keys, remembering to turn the disk with her number, in case there was a hostage situation and they needed to know where she was. The second gate opened and she walked between the two rows of chain link fence topped by razor wire, then into the prison itself. She could see her classroom building on the far end of the compound. Taking a deep breath, she started across the yard.

She walked past the greenhouse, the vocational building, the mess hall, gym, and dormitories. A few inmates were outside, tossing hoops or running the track. She could see the distant guard tower and the man inside. An inmate called "Yo teach," but Lorna ignored him. Until she was actually standing in front of her students, this was her time.

She entered the classroom building which had once been part of a psychiatric center. There were still hand-holds bolted into the walls to steady those with too much medication. She walked up the stairs to the second floor where C.O. Abrahamson, who provided security for four classrooms, sat at his station. His feet were on the desk, he had a cup of coffee in one hand and was deep into Playboy, probably a magazine confiscated this morning. He nodded at Lorna and she nodded back.

She didn't like Abrahamson and he didn't like her. She knew he resented the fact that inmates got a "free education," and she'd overheard him referring to her as "that cunt who coddles criminals". Abrahamson was prone to taking long breaks away from his desk, meaning that if anything happened in her classroom, she would first have to get herself to the room's only exit, and then race down the hallway to try and find the C.O.

In spite of this, Abrahamson was all she and three other teachers had for security. In her years of teaching, she'd already had one inmate expose himself to her and another with mental health issues pound on the desk and scream. She'd never been threatened with a shiv, but that didn't mean it couldn't happen. She'd learned to dress conservatively, to ask for respect and to handle discipline her own way. Now she moved past Abrahamson and went around the corner to her classroom. She unlocked door, put her purse and coat in her locker, locked it, and then set out the books, paper and pencils the students would use this morning.

This morning's GED class would focus on writing, since that was now part of the test. Most inmates hated to write, but Lorna enjoyed teaching writing, since it was the only way she got any glimpse into the minds and hearts of the prisoners who sat in her room.

At eight o'clock they filed in. She'd had these eighteen men since early September and it was now the twenty-fifth, so most were familiar. Her roster changed from week to week as inmates were paroled, went into isolation or the infirmary and new men come in. Lorna took attendance, counting heads twice to make sure she'd got it right. Once, after the men had been dismissed for lunch, she'd found an inmate sleeping behind a book locker and had to shamefacedly tell the C.O. she hadn't done an exit count.

When the inmates had settled into their seats, she talked a bit about the writing process, encouraging the men to write anything they wanted. They would do other exercises later that 'wrote to the question' but writing for this group was still something they were embarrassed to do.

Take My Hand

"I'm not going to correct for spelling or grammar," she said. "I just want you to write."

She passed out paper and pencils and there was five minutes of groaning, then twenty minutes of pencils scratching on paper. She collected the papers and then they went on to the math lesson.

At eleven thirty, the inmates were dismissed for lunch. The new group would come in at one, so Lorna had a lovely hour and a half to herself. She picked up the writing assignments and began to work her way through them.

Most of them were mundane stories, full of spelling and grammar mistakes, but Lorna tried to write something encouraging on each. But one bit of writing stopped her.

"He wuz just a kid, maybe six or sevn, younger en me, but Wright tole me to make friends with him and since he likked comics, I said I likked them too. It took me a while, but then he got to trusting me. On the day we waz going to take him, I seen him near to his school. My homey says, don't scare him none, just tell him we got something speshal at the comic book store. I done it, taked real nice, got him to go wit me to the store and got him inside.

He got skeered, but we had him by the arm. The kid was havin some problem brethin. I says to Wright, I don like what we doing, what if somethin happen, but Wright tells me shut my face or I get nothin, plus he go to the poleese. I do what Wright said, but I ain't hapy."

Lorna stared at the paper. Once in a while inmates shared personal information, but most of their talk was about the unfairness of the system, or the stupidity of their lawyer. Very seldom did an inmate talk directly about his crime.

Had this really happened? If so, how long ago? And had the child been rescued? A shiver of horror ran through her. She needed to report this to her boss, Sarah Callahan. She took the essay and went downstairs to Sarah's office, but Sarah's door was locked. "She's gone to lunch with the Superintendant," the C.O. said. "Won't be back until two."

At two, Lorna would be in class. She went back upstairs, and put the paper into her purse in the locker. If she had a chance to see Sarah today, they would talk.

At the end of her teaching day, she was standing in the doorway to her classroom, waiting for the inmates to move past her on their way back to the dorms. She had learned through hard experience that if she got into the crowd of men while they were in the hallway she was likely to be pinched, prodded or fondled. She waited. Suddenly a man detached himself from the crowd and came closer. He was from someone else's class, a stranger. She started to retreat into her room but not before the inmate reached her. "Don't show that writing to nobody," he hissed and then he was gone.

She almost said, "What writing?" but she knew what he meant. Fear coiled in her gut. How did this inmate know what another inmate had written? And what was she getting herself into the middle of?

Chapter Twenty One

Lorna Smith Watson

After the inmates had gone, Lorna went downstairs and spent a fruitless half hour trying to convince her boss, the Educational Supervisor that the inmate's essay reflected something serious. Sarah seemed distracted, dismissive of the danger and Lorna had to conclude that something else was going on. Did the lunchtime meeting mean that Sarah was being promoted, or possibly fired? Lorna liked her boss, but she knew that there was criticism about the way Sarah ran the department. Finally, she made two copies of the essay, one for Sarah, one for herself and tucked the original in her purse. She would return it to the inmate on Monday and then all of it would be someone else's problem.

That evening as she made supper for herself and her dog, Peaches, she began to consider her personal safety. She worked in an unsafe environment, where she could be stabbed by a shank, raped in a dark corner, have her head slammed against the wall, or as had already happened, sat beside an inmate to help him and looked down at his naked penis. If Abrahamson weren't down the hall in his break room she might survive, otherwise she could die. Every morning when she walked into the prison, there was the possibility that a riot could break out and she might be taken hostage. In 1971 prisoners at Attica Correctional Facility rioted and took civilian staff hostage, dressing them in the prisoner's greens. When the prison was retaken nine days later, the hostages, thinking they were being freed, stood up, and because they were in greens like the inmates, were shot. Twenty inmates and nine hostages died that day.

She accepted personal danger as part of the territory. When she'd been hired seven years ago, the job had been one of the few in the area that paid well, offered good benefits and a good retirement. Now she wondered if she'd been too naive in assuming she was safe.

Peaches gave a soft woof, and Lorna realized that she'd gotten lost in thought. The dog's dinner dish was still on the counter, only half full.

"Sorry, Peaches," she said, filling the dish and putting it down. She nuked a supper for herself, poured herself a glass of wine and sat down in front of the television set. She picked up the letters that had arrived that day. Most of them were bills, with a few requests for money thrown in. She tossed the requests for money in the trash. She put the bills up on the bulletin board beside the invitation to her high school reunion. When the invitation had come a month ago, seeing old classmates had seemed like a nice idea. She needed to get out more, to talk to people who weren't inmates or nursing home staff. Now she was having second thoughts about being away. If she missed seeing her husband on the weekend of the reunion, would he even miss her? It was always a crap shoot whether he would recognize her. Some days she made the visit without Harold giving the smallest indication that she was his wife.

She thought of the reunion. Maybe Claire Baxter, would be there. Claire had been her best friend in high school, and had married Chris Bellini. She'd been to their wedding and had met their little girl. How many years ago was that? They'd lost touch. She shook off the memories, went to the bedroom and put on a blue sweater and jeans, taking some time with her hair, so she would look nice for Harold. The nursing home was less than twenty minutes away and that had been a consideration for her when she'd chosen it. She also knew that they took good care of their patients, especially those with Alzheimer's.

The home was a sprawling single story building made of brick that sat at the end of a one-way street. The building was surrounded by lawn, and backed up to a patch of woods, through which a stream flowed. In the spring and summer, the gardens were filled with flowers, and the patients who were still ambulatory would sit on benches and enjoy the air. But at this time of year, late September, many of the flowers were already gone. There were still Cardinals, Chickadees and some hardy Goldfinches, moving back and forth to the bird feeders, but no one was outside. It was just too cold.

Take My Hand

Lorna punched in the code for the front door and opened it, then walked down the hallway toward Harold's room. In the beginning, the hospital smell would hit her square in the gut as soon as she entered. And she would be bothered by the men and women just sitting in their wheel chairs staring out into space. She knew the staff here did everything they could to bring the patients back to the present. A crafts workshop was offered once a week, mostly getting patients to glue paper cutouts onto a background. A man came twice weekly to play his guitar, encouraging residents to sing along. But most of the time the patients sat staring at a TV, with no interest or understanding. It broke her heart to think of her husband who'd once had such a lively intelligence, sitting in front of something he called the "box for idiots." It had taken her all of the three years that Harold had been here, to accustom herself to the place.

She walked into Harold's room where he was sitting with a magazine on his lap, thumbing through the pictures. Harold had been a ferocious reader, devouring novels at the rate of six a week and when he was first diagnosed, one of his major complaints was that he couldn't remember what he read. Now all he could do was look at the pictures, and even those sometimes produced anxiety and confusion.

She walked up slowly and touched his shoulder. "Harold, it's Lorna." She knew from hard experience that she shouldn't startle him. He might see her as a stranger and lash out.

He turned and looked at her. "Lorna, my best girl." He stood up, the magazine falling to the floor and put his arms around her. For a moment, she leaned into him, feeling the comfort of his touch. This was the man she'd fallen in love with when they were twenty one and twenty-two, whom she'd noticed because he asked such smart questions. This was the man she had lived with for close to eighteen years, with whom she'd had spirited conversations and who could make her laugh until her sides ached. All of that was gone. All of it. Most of all she missed his touch. He gave her another short squeeze and released her. "You'll never know who came to visit this afternoon," he said.

Harold had fantasies about his former students coming to visit. Some of these people were now in their forties, but he always imagined them as twenty somethings, coming to ask for his advice. Lorna waited.

"William came to see me."

"William who?"

"William, our son. You remember him, don't you?"

Of course she remembered him, but their son had been dead for many years. He'd been playing by the river, and fallen in and drowned. Their only child, dead.

"He told me he's working at a diner and…" Harold's voice ran down. He looked at his knees. "I forgot the name."

Lorna stared at her husband. He'd never had this particular fantasy before. Her hands went cold.

"It was nice to see him," Harold continued. "I told him, working in a diner is not a good career path."

How could they be having a conversation about the career choice of their long dead son? "What did he look like?" she asked.

"What do you mean 'what did he look like?' He looked like William, our son. He was thin and I told him if he was working in a diner, he should eat more." Harold glared at her. He was getting angry, as he often did when anyone disagreed with him.

"Of course," Lorna said. "William should eat more."

"Yeah." He looked up at her smiling, all traces of his ill humor gone. "It was nice of you to come Agnes."

Agnes, who was Agnes? She had abruptly ceased to be Lorna, his wife, and had become some phantom woman from his past. Lorna stood up and kissed him gently on the top of the head. "I'll see you tomorrow," she said and left.

On her way out, she stopped at the front desk where a young woman in a uniform imprinted with teddy bears was talking on the phone. When the woman had finished, Lorna said "Could we talk about my husband Harold Watson?"

The woman nodded.

"Did he have any visitors today?"

"This afternoon? Just one. A nice young man. He said he was your son, William. I was surprised since I've never heard you mention a son. He told me that he'd been on the West Coast and just dropped by to see his Dad."

"We don't have a son," Lorna said. "We had a son, but he died when he was a child. He would have been eighteen. How old did you say this young man was?"

"A little older, maybe twenty five. You said you don't have a son?"

"That's right."

"I am so sorry," the young woman said. "He was so nice and friendly, I just assumed..."

"Please give me a call before you let anyone in to see my husband," Lorna said. At the woman's stricken look, she reached out and touched her hand. "It's not your fault. But check with me in the future."

The young woman nodded.

Lorna walked to her car feeling the net of fear tightening around her. Someone knew that her husband was in a nursing home. Not any nursing home, but this one. Someone knew that she'd had a son named William. They might not know that William was dead, or maybe they did know and had counted on the nursing home staff to be ignorant. All this time, working in the prison, she had told herself that even though her job exposed her to danger, her private life was sacred. Now, her private life had been violated. Their lives would never again be secure.

Chapter Twenty Two

Chris

It was Monday. Larry and I sat staring at the bulletin board where we'd posted all the pictures of the suspects. We needed to contact Shevchenko's first wife, but had no information in the files.

"I've got a great idea," Larry said. "Why don't we call information for New York City?"

Could it really be that easy? People moved around. Shevchenko's first wife could be AWOL in another country, the reason the first two detectives hadn't been able to find her or she could have changed her name. And what about Shevchenko's son, Nicholas? He would be a teenager now. Was he living at home? In college somewhere? Touring the country with a rock band called 'Nick and the Shevs'? I picked up my cell phone and on a whim dialed Shevchenko's number at home. His second wife answered.

"Mrs. Shevchenko," I began. "When we were visiting you the other day, I forgot to ask about your husband's ex-wife. Do you know where she is?"

"Of course," she said. "Just a minute."

Quickly, she came back on the line. "She's in Brooklyn. I'll give you the address."

"Why did Mr. Shevchenko tell us he had no idea where his wife was?"

"I don't think he said that," she responded. "He said he hadn't seen his son in years. That is true."

"The first detectives Gunther and Besom tried to find Mr. Shevchenko's first wife, but they had no luck."

"Konstantyn told me she'd gone back to the Ukraine. He didn't know where, but five years ago she returned to U.S. She wrote to us, something about insurance money. I don't know. She still won't let Konstantyn see Nicholas."

I had copied the address and phone number on a piece of paper. I thanked Mrs. Shevchenko and hung up. I pushed the paper over toward Larry. He studied it.

"Why did Shevchenko's first wife flee to Europe? Was he abusive? Drinking, drugging, running around?"

Just at that moment Chief O'Malley popped his head into our office. "Can I see you boys?"

We followed him dutifully into his office, where he settled himself into the oversized desk chair. "Got some great news," he said.

He'd located the kidnapper and the man had confessed? I looked at my boss, waiting.

"*Upstate Monthly* called," he said. "They want an interview. Apparently this bullying thing has touched a nerve with a lot of school districts and they've had calls." He leaned back in the chair and I swear he preened. "They want to ask us some questions about how we inspired young people to tackle the bullying question."

"Count me out," Larry said quickly.

"This town has had a black eye for years because of the LeBrun case and now's our chance to shine," the Chief went on as if Larry hadn't spoken.

"We could shine more if we actually solved the case," I said.

"True," the Chief said. "But bullying is here in the present. That kid's been dead for nine years."

"Ten," I said. Had O'Malley really forgotten why he'd asked us to investigate? I wish I'd had a tape recorder of his dressing us down, when the bullying thing went viral. Had all of that been pushed away under the glare of magazine fame?

"Speaking of the case," I said. "We've been interviewing a man who worked as the LeBrun's gardener, Konstantyn Shevchenko. There are some interesting things that have come up that we'd like to discuss."

"Shoot."

We told him about Shevchenko's mother dying on Sandy's table, and what seemed to be his unnatural interest in Ethan LeBrun. O'Malley listened.

"Good, good," he said enthusiastically. "This is a real breakthrough. What's your next move?"

"We need to talk with the ex-wife. She lives in Brooklyn. Elle Shevchenko fled the country about the time of Ethan's death and has refused to let Shevchenko see his son. The first detectives, Gunther and Besom found lots of pictures of Ethan in Shevchenko's home and he had a relationship with Ethan. I need to see if there is more here."

O' Malley nodded.

"One more thing. I need access to Shevchenko's computer to see if he has pictures of Ethan there and whether he might have had contact with the kidnappers? I know it means getting a warrant..."

"I don't think that's a problem," O'Malley said, standing to tell us the interview was over. "When you've talked with the ex-wife, let me know." He looked at me, "You sure you don't want to sit in on this magazine thing. She's coming on Thursday at two."

We shook our heads in unison, pleading mountains of work. I think the Chief was pleased. Now he could have all the glory to himself.

When we got back to our hole, I made the call to Elle Shevchenko. She answered on the third ring, and I put her on speaker, so we could both be part of it.

I introduced myself and Larry and said we were calling about the death of Ethan LeBrun. "Your ex-husband worked for the family. On the night of the kidnapping, Konstantyn said he was in New York City searching for you and your son. Did detectives Blake Gunther or Gerald Besom ever interview you about that night?"

"No I was out of the country, visiting relatives when the kidnapping happened. But Konstantyn knew where I was. I don't know why he would lie about it."

"Why did you and your son run away from your husband?"

There was silence on the line and then Elle said. "I ran away to protect Nicholas. I got an order of protection against my husband."

"Why was that?"

Again a long silence. "I believe he sexually abused my son. When Nicholas was four he went from being a bright, happy child to one who was withdrawn and angry. He began hitting other kids in kindergarten, even trying to bite me. He never wanted to sit near Konstantyn or have his father read to him. And this was a boy who had loved his Dad. I took him to a doctor, who confirmed that there might be sexual abuse going on."

"Could you prove that it was your husband who did it?"

"Who else could it be? All his teachers, all his caretakers were women? I did try and talk to Konstantyn about it, but he refused to say anything."

The man we had interviewed didn't seem the type, but what man who abuses children is? I knew that unless you could prove without doubt that something happened, an innocent man could be unfairly judged, even jailed.

"Thank you for your time, Mrs. Shevchenko," I said, giving her my phone number. "Can we call you again if we have more questions?"

"Of course," she said.

I had one more question. "How is Nicholas doing now?"

"He's fine. He's working in a daycare center in Brooklyn. I'm very proud of him."

When I hung up, Larry said. "Time for lunch?"

"Why not." I patted my middle. "No doughnuts though."

We walked downtown to a diner that specializes in Italian dishes. I ordered my meal and a box, cut the meal in halves and put the uneaten half in the box.

"You still on that diet?"

"Let's just say, I'm hoping to lose a few pounds."

Larry looked at me, but asked no further questions.

Chapter Twenty Three

We ate in silence while I tried to digest what we'd learned about Shevchenko.

"I'd like to call Besom," I said. "And get his take on this. How could he have missed something this important?"

"Gunther and Besom were under a lot of pressure. The child of a famous New York surgeon dies in a small town. You have the notoriety of the father, and the fact that this is a place where we all know each other's business. They had the press all over their asses, and a Chief putting on his own pressure to get it solved. I could see how they might focus on suspects close to hand."

"Mrs. Shevchenko said she was out of town. Why did Shevchenko lie about his relationship with his wife and son?"

"You think he did it, Larry?"

"I don't know. A man has a 'special relationship' with his child and then the boy is taken away. Maybe he's looking for someone to replace the son he lost?"

I made a face.

"Didn't he say he took the job because of Ethan? He still has this need. When a kid appears within reach, he can't control his lust."

"God, I hate this," I said, looking down at my meal which had suddenly lost its appeal. "I can't understand why men abuse children. It turns my stomach."

"Children are vulnerable. They won't complain because they're scared."

I nodded and shoveled the remainder of my meal into the takeout box and paid the bill. Then we went back to the station and called Besom.

With the speed that he answered, he must have been sitting right next to the phone. I described what we'd learned from Mrs. Shevchenko.

"Christ, and we missed all that?" he said.

"You were under a lot of pressure, and she was out of the country," I said. "Is it possible Shevchenko did it?"

"Shevchenko was around the kid a lot, and from what I learned, Ethan was often unsupervised at home. Damn," he said. "I wish we'd known about the wife."

"Thanks for your help, Gerald," I said. "We'll keep you informed."

"I wish I were there," Besom said. "I thought I'd enjoy retirement, but I've never been so bored in my life."

We said good-bye and hung up. We needed to talk to Konstantyn Shevchenko again.

"Let's run this by the Chief," I said. "I'd like to get a look at Shevchenko's computer. If he's a pedophile, there might be evidence there."

Luckily the Chief was available. We laid out our case for bringing Shevchenko in for questioning and getting access to his computer. O'Malley agreed to contact a judge who would give us a warrant. It would take a couple of hours, but in the meantime, we could drive to Watertown and question Shevchenko again.

Shevchenko was at work, so we had to interview him in a covered area crowded with plants. We squeezed ourselves around a Rattan table, part of a set of garden furniture. In spite of plastic sheeting covering the openings, it was cold.

"Mr. Shevchenko, tell us about your ex-wife Elle," Larry began.

"Elle is gone. She takes my son, Nikki and runs away. I don't know where she is."

"You're lying. We made contact with her. She's in Brooklyn. Do you know what the penalty for lying in a police investigation is, Mr. Shevchenko?"

He looked stricken. "She don't want me to be with my boy. That's why she run away. I love my son, but she don't want me to see him."

"Why did you and your wife separate?"

Shevchenko hesitated. "We argued a lot about Nikki. She thought I was too hard on him. I wanted to teach him to box, he needed to learn how to defend himself against bullies. He wanted to be a dancer. A dancer is a sissy."

"Mr. Shevchenko, why did you go to New York City on the day Ethan died? "

There was a long silence. Shevchenko looked down at the table top, and fidgeted with his hands. "I was meeting someone," he said, finally.

"Someone? Like a date?"

"Yeah. A date."

I took out my notebook. "We need to confirm that you were where you said you were. What is the date's name?"

"I can't do that. The person don't like publicity."

"You can give us the name right now, or we can take you with us to the station. You have already lied to investigators once, don't do it again."

"His name is Randy Hillyard."

"Do you have an address for Randy Hillyard?"

"It was ten years ago," he said. Then he took out a small book and gave us an address and phone number in Manhattan. "He's probably not there anymore," he said.

I wondered why a man would travel all the way to New York City to have a date. There seemed to be only one answer. He didn't want anyone to know.

At that moment Shevchenko's supervisor appeared. He looked at Larry and me. "Listen, fellows," he said. "If you keep my employee here much longer, you'll have to start paying his wages."

I stood up. "We're conducting a criminal investigation," I said. "Your employee may or may not be involved."

"I'm just the messenger," the man said. "We're short staffed here."

"Give us ten more minutes," I said. "And you can have him back."

I went to the back of the store where I dialed the number Shevchenko had given me.

A woman answered. "May I speak to Randy Hillyard?" I asked.

"He's not here, he's at work?"

"Are you Mrs. Hillyard?"

"Yes. And I'm about to hang up unless you can tell me what you want with my son."

"I'm Detective Chris Bellini investigating the death of a little boy on April 5, ten years ago. One of our suspects Konstantyn Shevchenko said he was in New York City visiting your son on that date. Was he there?"

"How old is Mr. Shev….whatever."

"Late forties, maybe early fifties."

"Mr. Bellini my son is twenty years old. Ten years ago, he was a child. Why would a man I'd never met be visiting him?"

"Did your son have access to the internet ten years ago?"

"Sure, he e-mails a lot of his friends that way. He's always on the computer."

"Did you keep an eye on what he was doing?"

"Now you are scaring me detective. I don't pry into my son's life. He was a good child who has grown up to be a fine young man. I've never had a bit of trouble with him."

"I'm going to tell you something that you may not believe, but I think you should ask your son about it. The man we're investigating, Konstantyn Shevchenko is accused of molesting his son, and perhaps a boy who was later murdered. I think he enjoys sex with children. It is possible he met your son for that reason. On the other hand, your son may have gotten smart at the last minute and refused to meet him. I would appreciate it if you would ask him. This is my phone number." I gave her the number, said good-bye and hung up.

I returned to where Larry and Konstantyn were sitting. "Mr. Shevchenko," I asked. "Do you like having sex with little boys?"

He gave me a startled look. "No, of course not. I am married now, and I love my wife."

"You liked Ethan LeBrun. He was a little boy. Did you have sex with Ethan LeBrun?"

"No, no. We was just friends."

"Your wife, Elle says she separated from you because she felt you were sexually abusing your son. Did you want to be with Ethan because he was like your son? Did you like him because you could have a sexual relationship with him?"

"No. Is not true." Shevchenko got up from his seat. "This is all lies. I was friends with Etan, nothing more. My wife says these things to keep me from my son, is all."

"You knew that Ethan liked comic books. It would have been easy to hire some boys to take him to the store and kidnap him from there."

"Why would I do that? I loved that little boy."

"Maybe Ethan was going to tell his parents what was going on between the two of you. You would be arrested for child abuse; you'd be branded as a child molester and never be able to work again. You decided to scare Ethan into silence, so you hired a kid named 'Jimmy,' to kidnap him. What was Jimmy's last name?"

A strange look crossed Shevchenko's face. For a moment I thought we had him. Then he put his head down on the table and began to cry.

"Do you know what they do to child predators in jail, Shevchenko? Think about it. And when you get out of jail, if you get out, you'll always carry the stigma. Is that what you're worried about, Konstantyn? Is that why you killed Ethan?"

"I like women," he said weakly. "I did not do nothing to little Etan. He was like my own son. I loved him."

I stood up. "We're not letting this rest," I said. "We could have you arrested right now for lying to police during an investigation, but we're giving you a break. Don't go anywhere. We will be talking to you again."

On the way back to Euclid I called the Chief. He'd not been able to convince the judge to issue a warrant to seize Shevchenko's computer, and if we couldn't get the computer, or if there were nothing on it, we were screwed.

When we got to the station, we told the Chief everything we'd learned.

"OK," he said finally. "I'll go to the judge again. I'm putting my neck out here, and the judge is going to ask for a favor in return."

Three days later, we had the warrant and had assembled a couple of cops just to accompany us to Shevchenko's house. By the time we reached our destination it was five thirty, so we would be facing both Shevchenko and his wife. I did not look forward to that, but my job was to find a killer, and I had strong suspicions that Shevchenko might be our man.

Take My Hand

I knocked on the door with Larry and two patrolmen behind me. There was no response from the house so I knocked again. Finally the door slowly opened and Mrs. Shevchenko faced us. She was wearing a sweatshirt and jeans. Across the front of the sweatshirt was blood. Tears were running down her cheeks.

"Show us what happened," Larry said. Wordlessly she led us down the hallway to the bathroom.

She opened the door. There, lying in the bath was Shevchenko. In his hand was a gun. He had blown the top of his head off.

"He was going to take a bath," she began. "And then I heard the shot. Oh God." She burst into tears.

I put in a call to the station to tell them what had happened. Fifteen minutes later the Chief and two of his deputies were standing in the living room, taking charge. I watched as the tech guys did their thing. There was no other murderer here. Shevchenko had done this all by himself.

Someone who I recognized as a reporter from a local newspaper had pushed his way into the house and before we could get rid of him, he'd snapped a few pictures.

"Publish that, and I'll break your balls," O'Malley said. The reporter was undeterred. Turning to me, he said. "I heard this guy is a suspect in the LeBrun case."

I shook my head, trying to head off trouble.

"Let me handle this," O'Malley said. "Go sit with the widow."

So we sat with the widow, a woman we'd met only once before. He'd been depressed, she told us. They were going to fire him from the job, and then there were the police poking into his personal life. He missed his son; he said he loved the boy and hated his wife for taking Nicholas away. There was no confession. Whatever information we might find on Shevchenko's computer now was worthless.

The body was removed in a hearse and Larry and I made our way home. By now it was almost ten o'clock. Amelia was in bed, and Mrs. Gentile who'd stayed late to care for her, was stretched out on the couch, asleep. I woke her gently, telling her I could walk her home, but she declined saying she was perfectly safe.

I poured myself a tumbler of Maker's Mark, the drink I save for extraordinary circumstances, hoping to use the booze to wash away the image of Shevchenko's body in the bathtub. I was sick of death, the death of a child, the death of a man who may have been just an innocent victim. I wondered idly whether I could go back to being a regular cop on the street. In my years on patrol, I'd dealt with lots of things, but I'd never confronted a bloody body in a bathtub like I had today. Maybe street work was safer than being a detective.

Tomorrow I would have to file a report at the station and there would be an inquest, at which I would have to testify. I turned on the TV and was assaulted by the late night news.

The reporter, a perky young thing named Sky Warner, was talking about Shevchenko's death. As I sat and listened, I recognized O'Malley's fingerprints all over the thing. He had spilled it all, probably first to Mr. Pushy, the reporter at the scene, and then to TV. God damn him. I poured myself another shot, feeling the liquor incinerate my throat. Since Shevchenko was dead, he was a convenient villain, but had he really done it? I'd seen his face when he said he'd forgiven LeBrun and I believed him. Was I just getting soft?

I needed someone to bounce things off of, but it was now almost eleven, too late to call Willi. Reluctantly, I put my glass on the counter and made my way to bed, but it was a long time before I fell asleep.

Chapter Twenty Four

On Saturday morning I padded downstairs to make coffee and read the paper, my only moments of solitude in the day. On the front page was a repeat of last night's TV report, complete with a photo of a much younger Shevchenko. There were also quotes from his current wife declaring the man to be innocent of all charges. I knew I had to talk to O'Malley, but the thought made my stomach acids churn. I wondered idly what Willi De Grasse and Carey would be doing this weekend. It was now mid October and though there was ample evidence that winter was on its way, we still had some stunning days. Should I call Willi up and suggest something?

I sat on the couch with my coffee and the vision of Shevchenko's dead body swam into view. I would probably have nightmares for weeks. One positive thing was that my arm was now out of its sling and I could use it with care. I looked up as Amelia came down the stairs. She sat down beside me on the couch. Like her grandmother and mother, she was slow to wake, and if you tried to hurry the process, it would only result in tears and an unpleasant morning.

"What would you like for breakfast?" I asked gently.

"I want a dog," she said.

"You want a dog for breakfast? Sorry, we're fresh out."

She gave me 'the look.' "Poppi, I want a real dog. Mary Sinclair has a puppy and I was dreaming he came to our house to live." She put her hand on my arm, her 'seductive temptress' move. "Can we have a dog, Poppi?"

"We'll see," I said.

"You always say that when you really mean no," she said rising and glaring at me. "You never get me the things I want."

The morning that had started so beautifully, now had storm clouds gathering. "I told you that I will think about it," I said rising and walking to the kitchen. "In the meantime, what would you like for breakfast? I could make some very nice scrambled eggs with cheese and broccoli."

"I hate broccoli."

"OK, just cheese."

She sat glumly at the table. "All right," she said finally.

I got out ingredients for breakfast and poured myself more coffee. When the eggs were scrambled and on the table, I sat.

"What would you like to do today?"

"Go to the pet store and look at dogs."

"I'm not sure they are open on Saturday," I said, hoping that they weren't. Just then the phone rang. It was Willi.

"I've got the costume made, can we bring it over? And then we're going to see Boldt Castle in the Thousand Islands," she said. "Would you like to come?"

"We'd love to," I said. "Let me tell Amelia."

The thought of an outing with her best friend, spurred Amelia to run up and get dressed, all thoughts of dogs conveniently gone. She was waiting by the front window, when Willi and Carey pulled up. Carey bounded in, followed by Willi, who was wearing a bright red parka and a red hat, which only seemed to accentuate the blue of her eyes and the color of her hair. She put a bag on the floor and pulled out a round orange costume in the shape of a pumpkin. With it was a little cap, with a green 'stem' poking out the top.

"Oh, I love it," Amelia said. "Can I try it on?"

"It's wonderful," I said. "I couldn't have done anything like this, even if a seamstress were standing over me with a rubber whip."

She smiled. "It's fun sewing for kids."

In a few minutes, Amelia was back wearing her costume. She threw her arms around Willi and hugged her hard. "Thank you. Thank you," she squealed, and did a quick turn. Her movements were somewhat restricted by the costume, but nothing could impede her enthusiasm.

"These go with it," Willi said, holding up a pair of orange tights. Amelia grabbed the tights and dashed off to change back into street clothes.

Fifteen minutes later we were dressed and ready. We piled into Willi's car and headed south toward the Thousand Islands. On the way, I told the story of how George Boldt had built the castle for his wife Louise, but ceased construction when she died suddenly.

"He musta had lots of money," Carey said.

"He did." The girls were squirming around in the back seat. "The castle has six stories and one hundred twenty rooms, though I don't know if we'll see all of them."

"Thanks for inviting us," I said to Willi. I leaned toward her. Her closeness was so intoxicating that I almost forgot what I was going to say.

"Amelia wants a puppy," I whispered. "You saved me from a trip to the pet store."

She nodded and smiled. "At least not today."

"What are you talking about?" Amelia asked from the back seat.

"Cherry pie. I hate making pies. I'm terrible at the crust," Willi said. I had to admit she was a better at fibbing on the spur of the moment than I could have been. To change the subject, I said. "Why don't you two sing us one of your songs from the play."

"Sure," Amelia said, and started in. She got most of the notes correctly, though she was very loud. I looked out the window, watching the St. Lawrence River roll by us, sparkling under the fall sky. A Saltie made its way majestically up the river. It would carry grains from

Saskatchewan through the Great Lakes System and out into the Atlantic.

We got to the boat landing with about twenty minute to spare before the next boat left. In spite of the sun, the wind was fierce and I was glad I'd insisted on warm clothing. We ran into a shop more to keep warm than to do any real shopping, and then the blast of the boat's whistle reminded us that it was time to go. Just as the boat was ready to leave the dock, a man with two small boys jumped aboard.

"Brad?" Willi cried. "I didn't think you were coming."

"You asked if I'd be interested, and it turned out to be good weather." They hugged briefly.

He looked at me and at Amelia, and I knew we were both asking the same question. "Who is this joker?"

"This is Chris Bellini and his granddaughter Amelia," Willi said. My mind was churning through this change in scene. Fading into the background was the lonely widow being rescued by her knight in shining armor (me) and in its place was what? A woman with a lover she hadn't bothered to mention? I took another look at Brad, trying not to be too obvious in assessing his boyfriend-worthiness. He was reasonably handsome, not overweight, and damn, she seemed to be paying more attention to him than to me.

Brad, Willi and the three children had moved to the rail where they clustered together admiring the scene. Amelia put her hand in mine. "I wish he hadn't come," she said. "I thought it would only be the four of us."

"We can't control who gets on the boat," I said, but the trip had lost its luster for me too.

By the end of the day we had explored Boldt Castle, and then, without Brad, had gone on to Fineview. When we stopped for pizza and ice cream, I got Willi aside privately.

"This Brad fellow, he's a friend?"

She looked at me sharply. "He's not a boyfriend if that's what you mean. He's just someone I know. Sometimes Carey and I spend time with him and his boys. This summer we went to baseball games together, and we saw Johnny Cash in Syracuse."

Sounded like a boyfriend-in-waiting to me.

"I got the impression that you didn't have many close friends."

"I don't. Not really." She looked at me again. "You're not jealous, are you?"

"No," I lied. Willi might not consider Brad to be someone special, but I had seen how he'd put his arm around her shoulders, their heads together whispering. It might not be a platonic friendship now, but Brad was working on it being something more.

It was almost five o'clock when we got back to my house. Both kids were fast asleep in the back. "Thank you for a wonderful day," I said, reaching across to give Willi a quick kiss on the cheek. Instead she turned her face and kissed me full on. I returned her kiss, realizing in that instant that this was a woman, I'd already fallen for.

"I'll call you," I said. She nodded. I got my sleepy girl out of the car and together we went up the front walk into the house. I heated up macaroni and cheese in the microwave and we ate it in front of the TV.

"You like Mrs. DeGrasse, don't you," Amelia said.

I nodded. "I had a good time."

"You should ask her out again, Poppi. She's single and you're single. I saw you kiss her."

She looked at me pointedly. Here I was a middle aged man, getting dating advice from a six year old.

She put her almost empty plate on the table. It was eight o'clock but we were both tired.

"I think I'll go to bed early, how about you?"

"Can I stay up and read?"

"If you do it in your room."

At nine, I climbed into bed. I remembered Willi's lips against mine, the smell of her perfume, the way her body fitted against my own. Lust was one thing, but was I ready to have a woman permanently in my life? And what about this Brad fellow who was "just a friend?" I was still wrestling with this worrisome combination when I drifted off to sleep.

Chapter Twenty Five

Lorna Smith Watson

On Saturday Lorna went to visit Harold, still troubled by how easily someone could come into the nursing home without anyone's knowing it. She brought a small photo album, and a book of poetry. Harold especially liked John Donne. Before his illness, they would spend evenings reading the poems together. At the beginning, Harold would do the reading while Lorna quilted or painted, but as his Alzheimer's grew worse, he found it hard to follow the words on the page. He would get frustrated, throw the book on the floor and stomp out of the room in anger. It broke Lorna's heart to see that happen. Harold had always been a voracious reader and a writer. Some of his works were love poems to her.

When she got to his room, he was sitting in the chair, his hands folded in his lap, just staring out the window. Was this one of the days when he would remember her?"

"Harold?" she asked.

He looked up and smiled. Maybe it would be a good day. "Hello Sweetheart," he said. He stood up and enfolded her in his arms, and they stood for a moment in the embrace. She had missed those embraces, more than anything else. That, more than sex, had been the touchstone of their relationship. They'd never gone to bed angry with each other, sometimes sitting up in the living room arguing out their various points of view until one convinced the other or one of them gave in. Then they would hug and go to bed. But on the days when she was a stranger, there were no embraces, and it left her feeling adrift with loneliness. She loved her husband, but most of the time, the man in whose arms she now stood, wasn't anyone she knew.

"How are you, dear?"

"Not good," she said. She began to relate the story of the inmate essay, when Harold interrupted. "William's wife came to see me today. Did you know he was married? A very nice little girl."

William's wife? Their dead son William's wife? What was going on?

"I told her that she ought to take better care of our little boy. He's all we have."

It was time to nip this in the bud. "Harold," she said. "Our son William is dead. He died when he was nine years old. He can't have a wife."

"But she came to see me today. She said they just got married and …" he paused. "I don't remember the rest, but she showed me pictures."

This must be the new aide, they'd told Lorna about. Was the woman saying she was William's wife, or was this a fantasy generated by Harold?

She reached for his hand and held it. He was becoming agitated and she needed to try and reason with him. "Harold, darling. Listen to me. Our son drowned when he was a child. Don't you remember? He went swimming with some friends, there was fast current that he got pulled into..." Her voice broke. If William hadn't died, he might be here now, trying to reason with his father. He might be a man whom she could lean on, not exactly a substitute for her husband, but someone she could trust.

"You don't believe I met William's wife," he said.

It would do no good to dispute this with him. Instead she pulled out the small photo album and opened it to the first picture, the one taken at their wedding. She laid the album on his lap. "Do you remember these two people? Weren't they good looking?"

Harold peered at the photos. "Me and you," he said.

"Right after college. You had a contract for a teaching job. I was going to look for work as a secretary or something. Instead I got hired by the local school to teach GED." She flipped the page to a picture of herself and Harold cradling an infant. "William was two months old in this picture. Remember how proud we were of him? We would dress him up in funny costumes, one for each holiday and take his picture." She flipped the album. There was William, looking unhappy, dressed as a miniature Santa Claus, and propped up beside a Christmas tree. "He hated those pictures. Said it made him look like a toy, not a real baby."

Harold was smiling now. Lorna wasn't sure whether it was because he remembered the people in the pictures, or because they weren't arguing.

She flipped to the next picture in the album. This album was a concentrated story of their lives, as much as Harold would be able to remember. This one featured Lorna sitting on a sled holding William, who was about four, with Harold about to push them down the hill. It had been one of those sunny, cold days that happens in February, and the hill where they went sledding had received a dusting of snow so it wasn't too icy. They'd sledded for almost three hours, coming back to the house for popcorn, hot chocolate and a game of Monopoly. She remembered it as one of the perfect days of her life, the others being the day she married Harold, and the day William was born. Why was it, when you were living those days that you didn't see them for what they were, precious objects that would never come again? After William's death, she'd berated herself for nagging at the kid, or even yelling at him. He wasn't perfect but if she'd known what a short time he would be in their lives, she would she have acted differently.

Harold reached out and touched William's face in the picture. "He was a good kid."

"Yes, he was. We were very lucky," Lorna said.

"I've got to get to my job," Harold said. "They'll be expecting me at the college." Those words were often his signal that their visit was over. She wasn't sure if Harold really believed that he still worked as a college teacher, but she could take a hint. She rose and kissed him gently on the lips. "I'll be away this coming weekend," she said. "My high school is having a reunion but I'll tell you all about it on Monday."

She walked down the hall, stopping at the nurse's station. She wanted to get more information about this new aide. But no one was at the station. So she took a sheet of paper and wrote out instructions, telling the staff that only people with whom Harold was familiar should be admitted to his room.

She drove back to the house and let herself in. Peaches heaved herself up laboriously from her dog bed and came padding over. Lorna patted her head, feeling the silky softness of the hair under her fingers. She went into the kitchen and poured herself a glass of wine and then she sat on the couch. Peaches climbed up beside her.

"Do you like John Donne?" she asked the dog. Peaches looked at her with those deep, sympathetic brown eyes. "I'll read you some," Lorna said.

Chapter Twenty Six

Chris

On Thursday evening I stood in front of the mirror trying to decide what I should wear to my high school reunion. The blue suit made me look like a Midwestern car salesman, and the grey suit made me look like a banker. The tie, which I had chosen because it was bright and colorful, only seemed to accentuate my belly, and it had been so long since I'd worn a suit that the jacket didn't really button.

I rummaged through my drawers, looking for a sweater. Maybe aging college professor was the look I wanted.

"Whatcha doin?" Amelia stood in the doorway, a bag of potato chips in one hand and a bottle of juice in the other.

"Trying to find something to wear." I turned toward her. "Amelia, I've told you not to eat in the bedroom. You'll get crumbs on the floor and then we'll have mice. Go eat in the kitchen." When she didn't move I said "Do it now, please."

"I don't know why you're so grumpy," she said as she turned and began to stomp away. "You used to be nice, now you're all grumpy."

I sighed and pulled off the jacket. Walking downstairs to the kitchen I found Amelia sitting at the table reading a book and eating her chips.

"That's enough chips," I said, taking the bag away. "We're going to eat in half an hour, and you won't be hungry if you eat all that junk."

"But I'm hungry now," Amelia wailed.

"I'm going to start cooking in a minute." I walked toward the refrigerator and took out some frozen chicken breasts, and then pulled a container of rice from the cupboard.

"You know that Mrs. Gentile is going to be here tomorrow night and all day Saturday," I said. "I'll be back some time Sunday afternoon."

"I don't know why I can't come," Amelia said. "I've never been to a re-oon-yun."

"This is for grown-ups," I said. I went over and kissed her gently on the head. "When you are a grownup and have gone to high school and then to college, you can go to a reunion and see the friends you went to school with too."

"Did you have lots of friends, Poppi?"

"Some," I said. "I was on the track team, and the yearbook committee, and I helped plan the Senior Prom."

"What's a yearbook?"

"I'll show you." I went to the bedroom and reached up to the shelf above the clothes, being careful that things didn't tumble onto my head. My fingers found the book and I gently worked it out. I sat on the bed and got Amelia to sit beside me. "This was my high school yearbook." I flipped a page. "And this was me."

"Poppi, that was you?"

I looked at the picture of myself. Underneath were the words, "Most likely to run for public office." Well, that part hadn't come true.

I flipped to another page. "These were my best friends Buzz Tildon, Will Green and Lorna Smith. We hung around together."

"Were you and Lorna boyfriend and girlfriend."

"No, I liked your grandmother. She was the cutest girl in school."

"Why isn't she in this book?"

"She's here," I said, flipping through more pages. I pointed to the picture of Claire looking incredibly young in her dark sweater, white lace collar and poodle skirt. "She was a cheerleader, and on the debate team."

"Did Grammy get a picture by herself?" Amelia asked.

"Not in this book. She was a year behind me, so she got her own book."

"Can I see?"

"After supper," I said, standing up. "I'll find Grammy's book and we can look at it then."

The next day was Friday, so I worked an abbreviated shift, mostly looking through material developed by Gunther and Besom, hoping for some clues. Larry had taken the day off and the Chief was at some conference, so I was mostly alone. Finally, at two I gave up and went home. The opening banquet for the reunion was due to start at six thirty. I showered, shaved and put on the blue suit with the bright tie. Then I drove to the hotel.

When I walked into the room, and gazed at all the grey hair and sagging middles, my first thought was *where have all these middle-aged people come from*? Some of my classmates now wore glasses and a few were losing hair. I recognized a boy who'd always been a loner, now surrounded by people, who was now CEO of a large corporation and was describing his month cycling in Crete. I moved past the knot of admirers toward the bar. And then I saw Lorna Smith, sitting at the bar, talking to another woman. At least I thought it was Lorna, we hadn't seen each other in years. I stepped up to the bar and turned toward her. "Lorna," I said. "I was hoping you'd be here."

She turned and gave me a wide smile. "Chris Bellini." Turning toward the woman beside her, she said. "Do you remember Pam Atkinson? She was a year behind us."

I shook my head.

"Of course you wouldn't remember Pam." Lorna said. "You only had eyes for Claire Baxter. Is she here?"

"Claire died three years ago," I said. "Cancer."

"Oh Chris, I'm so sorry. You had a daughter, didn't you?"

"Cecile," I said. "I don't have much contact with her. I'm raising my granddaughter, Amelia."

"That's tough," Pam said. "Raising a child while you're still working is hard at our age."

I don't know how old Pam thought I was. I didn't feel that I had reached 'our' age.

A man came over to join us, and Pam introduced him as her husband. The two seemed more intent on their own conversation and eventually they drifted away. I gestured toward a table in the corner; Lorna followed me to it and we sat.

"It's so nice to see you, Chris," Lorna said. "I would say you haven't changed much, but of course we've all changed."

"How is your family?" I asked.

"Harold has Alzheimer's. He's is in a nursing home."

"I'm sorry. You had a son, didn't you?"

"William. He died many years ago now. Drowned when he was nine."

I reached forward and took her hand. "I didn't know."

We sat in silence for a moment.

"Are you still a policeman?" Lorna asked.

"Detective," I said pointing to my shoulder. "I got wounded about a month ago and now I'm working on the case of a little boy who was kidnapped in Euclid ten years ago."

Take My Hand

"Kidnapped?"

"You may have heard of the case. The boy's father, Sanford LeBrun was a well-known plastic surgeon who moved to Euclid from New York City. He'd been there less than two years, when his son died."

She was leaning forward, her face fixed on mine with the same curiosity that lots of people feel about public tragedy. I suppose it's what impels people to gather on the sidewalk when there's a fire, or when a killer is led out of a building in handcuffs. "Who kidnapped him, Chris?" she asked.

"Two boys, one of them was named Jimmy. They took him to a patch of woods and he died there."

She looked down at her lap and then slowly opened her purse. "I work as a teacher at Greenville Correctional Facility. It's a maximum security prison."

I watched as she unfolded a piece of paper she'd taken from her purse. "Eight days ago, my class was doing writing exercises for the GED and one of my students handed this in." She passed the paper over to me.

I glanced at the writing, feeling my heart race. I looked at Lorna. "Was the man who wrote this telling the truth?"

"I don't know, Chris. But after I got this, a couple of strange things happened. This was written on Friday, in my morning class, and at the end of the day an inmate I didn't know came up and warned me not to share the writing with anyone."

"On Monday when I tried to return the essay, I was told that the inmate who wrote it had been beaten up and was in the infirmary."

"Did you show this essay to anyone else?"

"My supervisor. But she didn't think it was serious."

"I think it's serious," I said, studying the essay again. "How old would you say this L. Grainger is?"

"Early twenties. He seemed pretty immature."

"Do you know why he's incarcerated?"

"The prison doesn't give us that information, Chris. I only know what the inmates tell me."

"Will you give me the name of your superintendant? I'd like to contact him."

"There's one thing more, Chris. It doesn't have anything to do with the prison, but I think it's related." She took a deep breath. "Someone visited Harold in the nursing home, pretending to be our son. When Harold first told me, I thought it was just one of his fantasies, like his telling me that his college students are visiting him." Her voice broke.

"Sorry, I'm very worried about him. If someone knows that my husband is in a nursing home and that we had a son, it means that he or I could be a target."

I reached out and took her hand. "Lorna," I said. "My partner, Larry Grindon and I are working as hard as we can to solve this case. If you feel you need police protection, I will contact the station in your area and tell them your concern. I'm sure they can help."

She wiped tears from her eyes. "Thank you, Chris. You were always such a nice guy. I have to tell you I had this huge crush on you when we were in high school, but of course you were already Claire's steady. Thank you for being here."

I looked at the essay. "Can I keep this?"

"Of course," she said. "I made a copy."

I looked at my watch. We still had twenty minutes before the banquet would start and my glass was empty. "Would you like another drink?"

"Sure," she said. I went to the bar and bought two glasses of wine. When I got back to the table, Lorna was standing up, her coat on. "I just got a call from the nursing home," she said. "Harold has disappeared."

Chapter Twenty Seven

Lorna Smith Watson

It took her only a little time to re-pack her suitcase. She'd hardly opened it, just hung up a few things, but returning the key and having the hotel agree to refund her money took an age. All she wanted to do was get on the road. Twice she tried calling the nursing home, but the line was always busy. Hopefully they'd called the police and everyone was out scouring the neighborhood. What kind of clothes would Harold be wearing? A warm jacket, she hoped, but if no-one had supervised him when he left, he wouldn't think to put one on. Of course he would be confused, not knowing where he was, and if he were outside, he wouldn't know how to get past the locked front door in order to return to his room. And it was now full darkness. She tried not to think of her husband, cold and confused, huddled somewhere in the dark. *Let Harold be all right*, she prayed silently. *Please, let him be all right.*

By the time she got on the road, it was close to nine. It would be almost ten by the time she got to the nursing home. She tried dialing again and this time someone picked up. Thank God.

"Hello," she said. "Who is this?"

"Gabriella Sanchez."

Gabriella was a woman in her late fifties, one who had been with the institution for a long time. "This is Laura Watson. Do you know what's happening with Harold?"

"Mrs. Watson. I am so sorry. We have been trying to understand how he got out."

"Have they found him, Gabriella?"

Take My Hand

"No. I am sorry. The police are here, and some folks from the neighborhood, just in case he might be hiding in someone's back yard or a garage. Can you think of anywhere he might go?"

"Our home, but that's more than ten miles away, too far for him to walk, and anyone seeing an old man alone beside the road would have picked him up and notified the police don't you think?"

"Yes, they would have. What about the university where he worked?"

"That is the same distance away. I don't think there is anything close to the nursing home that would be familiar. Do you know what he was wearing?

There was a pause on the other end of the line. "We found his jacket hanging in the closet. I think he was wearing just a light sweater and slippers."

Oh God, Laura thought. *Let him be all right.*

"Have the police focused their search on any particular area?" Laura asked.

"The river," Gabriella said.

Harold didn't swim. She tried to block the image of Harold, cold and confused, standing by the edge of the river, but it came any way. Would he be thinking of William?

"We will find him, Mrs. Watson. We have been looking since we found him missing this afternoon. Please don't worry."

But of course she did worry. She could not protect her husband from the disease which was destroying his brain. She could not protect him from the cold, or from his confusion. Just as she and Harold had not been able to protect their child from drowning, so she could not protect herself from the heartbreak of losing him. On the rest of the trip, she tried to think of other things. Maybe Chris Bellini would be able to find the truth about the essay. Maybe the local police would help find her husband. And maybe, in a better world, pigs would become airborne.

She pulled into the parking lot of the nursing home and saw four police cars lined up beside an ambulance. Did that mean that Harold was dead? Just at that moment a door opened and two EMT's pushing a gurney emerged. She recognized the person on the gurney as Harold.

She rushed over and looked down. Harold was pale and his eyes were closed, but he was breathing shallowly. She touched his hand. Ice cold.

"Where did you find him?"

"In a tool shed about a quarter mile from here. Apparently it was open and he got in there to keep warm. We're taking him to the hospital. You can follow us."

At the hospital, they wheeled him into the emergency room and she had to wait, while they did the exam. Finally a doctor came out and found her.

"We'd like to keep him overnight for observation Mrs. Watson. He's been badly chilled and we want to prevent pneumonia. Would you like to talk with him?"

"He's awake?"

"He's somewhat agitated. You might be able to calm him down."

She followed the doctor into the room. Harold was sitting up in bed, wearing a hospital gown. A tube ran from an IV drip hanging beside him into his arm.

"You've had quite an adventure, I see," she said.

"An adventure," he echoed.

She sat beside him and took his hand, feeling pleased that it was warmer. His breathing was still labored. "Why did you go outside?" she asked.

She didn't really expect an answer, but sometimes her husband surprised her.

"She told me she would show me something special."

"Who told you that?"

"William's wife."

"Do you remember her name?"

He shrugged, and then put his head back against the pillow. She watched as his eyes closed and he began to snore gently. She stood up, kissed him on the cheek and left the room. Outside in the corridor were two policemen. Laura walked up to them.

"Thank you for what you did," she said. "I don't know how you found him, but you saved his life."

One of the policemen nodded. They both seemed very young, probably their late twenties. It was possible they might even be in their thirties; everyone seemed young to her these days.

"The dog was barking," one of the men said.

"It was tied up behind the house, and the owner went to check on it."

"How did Harold find his way to the shed?" Lorna asked.

"Don't know," the older of the two policemen said. "My question would be how he got out of the nursing home? Those places are pretty secure, aren't they?"

"He's been talking about our dead son coming to visit. And last week he mentioned that our son's wife dropped in. Our son never had a wife. He was young when he drowned. When I asked Harold why he went outside, he said that William's wife was going to show him something."

Both men looked at her thoughtfully. "Does he get confused often? Or talk about seeing people who aren't real?"

She nodded. "The people he used to talk about were his former students or his colleagues. Only recently has he mentioned our son coming to visit. Then the last time I saw him, he talked about William's wife. I'm sure a man's fantasy can't unlock the door to a nursing home and lead him outside."

One of the policemen had taken out a notebook and was scribbling in it. "Do you remember what the person posing as William's wife was called?"

She shook her head.

"Did the nursing home hire any female staff recently?"

"I think they did, but I don't remember the woman's name. I left strict instructions at the desk that they should call me before they let any visitors see him, but I was away for the weekend." She felt the tears starting "I shouldn't have gone away. I never do things like this, but I thought he would be OK." She started to sob, embarrassed to be seen breaking down in front of strangers. She struggled to pull herself together and one of the policemen put his hand on her shoulder. "Don't worry, ma'am. We're on this."

Lorna nodded and turned back to the room. Harold was sleeping peacefully, so she could go home and sleep in her own bed, rather than try and catch some rest on one of the chairs. She walked to the window and looked out into the dark. Somewhere, out there was a stranger who had lured Harold to what could have been his death. Was this her punishment for talking to her boss about the essay and would it get worse, now that she'd given the writing to Chris Bellini? If someone could do this to Harold, what might they do to her?

Chapter Twenty Eight

Chris

It took a lot of talking for me to get into the infirmary to see LeRoy Grainger, the man who'd written the essay about the kidnapped child. He lay in the bed, one arm in a cast and bandages around his head. The bruises on his face were turning purple and one IV tube pumped liquids into his arm while another snaked from under the covers to a collection jar on the floor. Whoever had beaten him up had done a pretty good job.

"Good morning," I said. I'd been given fifteen minutes to talk with the prisoner, and I didn't want to waste time.

"My name is Chris Bellini and I'm investigating the death of Ethan LeBrun," I said, watching as Grainger's eyes began to travel the length of the room, looking everywhere except my face.

"The boy was kidnapped ten years ago by two young men. One was about twelve and the other about eighteen. The younger boy's name was Jimmy." I looked at the information I'd been given. "LeRoy James Grainger. Twenty-two. You're the right age. You ever been called Jimmy?"

The prisoner nodded and mumbled something. I think it was "but I didn't kidnap no one."

"So Jimmy," I continued, pulling out the copy of the essay and holding it up in front of his face. "Tell me what this is all about?"

"Just playing myself," Jimmy answered. I could understand him better now.

"This was a joke?"

"Didn't have nothing else to write about."

"This is pretty detailed for something you made up," I said. I put the essay on the bed in front of me and started to read.

"He was just a kid, maybe six or seven. They told me to make friends with him and since he liked comics, I said I liked them too. On the day we was going to take him, I seen him near to his school. He dint see me or my homey 'cause we were back near the wall. Wright says, don't scare him none, just tell him we got something special at the comic book store. I done it, talked real nice, got him to go with me to the store and got him inside."

"Then he got scared, but we had him by the arm. Wright twist the kids arm, but then he was havin some problem breathing. I says to Wright, I don like this, what we doing, what if something happen, but Wright tells me shut my face or I get nothin, plus he go to the police. I do what Wright said, but I ain't happy."

"How did you know the boy was six or seven? Had you talked to him before?"

Leroy blinked. His face reddened, and tears began to form in his eyes.

"Mr. Grainger. I must remind you are a witness and possibly an accessory to a crime. You can cooperate with me here and now, or things can get a whole lot harder for you. How did you know Ethan LeBrun's age?"

"He tole me."

"When did he tell you this?"

"When we was talkin' about comic books."

"Did you pretend that you liked comic books, so you could get close to him?"

A nod.

"Did you help to kidnap Ethan LeBrun?"

A long pause and then a very slight nod of the head.

"Why did you kidnap him?"

A pause and then with difficulty, LeRoy said. "Big Boy said we'd get paid. All we had to do was get him into the woods and leave him there. Big Boy says, 'tie him up, but not too tight.' The kid was fighting and hollering, so we put tape over his mouth."

"Who is Big Boy? A friend?"

A nod.

"Where is Big Boy now?"

LeRoy shrugged.

"Is Big Boy the one who beat you up?"

A nod. "He had his homies do it. He dint like me writing the story."

"Did you tell the authorities this?"

A shake of the head.

"Why not?"

"Big Boy is my brother. We got different names 'cause we got different daddies."

"Thank you," I said. I went out into the corridor and asked one of the nurses to direct me to the Administration building. The Superintendant was in a meeting so I waited for fifteen minutes outside his office.

When I finally got in to see him, he was sitting behind his desk, reading. He looked up. "How did the interview go?"

"OK" I said. "Thank you for letting me see Grainger." I paused. "I believe he and his half brother Big Boy Wright, were involved in the kidnapping of Ethan LeBrun ten years ago. Is Wright incarcerated here?"

"He was. We released him three weeks ago. He was sent by bus to New York City, and from there to a half-way house, or to whoever has agreed to take him in. Unfortunately, an inmate can skip out on any part of that journey. Once he's released from prison, it's up to the parole system to keep tabs on him."

"I think Wright was the one who planned the kidnapping," I said. "They were going to get money for the job. Grainger befriended the kidnapped boy by pretending to like comic books and the two lured him into a comic book store and kidnapped him. They took him through a wooded path to an area behind the LeBrun home and left him there. That's where the child died."

The Superintendant was shaking his head. "Grainger was incarcerated for breaking and entering. It was his third offense and New York State has a 'three-strikes-you're-out' law. Wright was here on an involuntary manslaughter charge. He was burgling an old man's house; the man woke and had a heart attack. Wright should have got more time. Before the I.M. charge, he raped and knifed his girlfriend. Fortunately she lived, but she declined to testify against him. I'd look out for this guy. He's a mean customer."

"I saw what he did to his brother."

"Let me get you the name of his parole officer. He'll know where Wright is."

The Superintendant picked up the phone and said something and a few minutes later a secretary came in with a file folder. He copied an address from the folder and gave it to me. "This is the number of his parole officer in the Bronx."

"If he's not there, I will call you."

"If he's not there, he's in a lot of trouble. Don't worry, we'll find him."

I walked out into the chilly fall afternoon. Soft white clouds scudded across a blue sky, but the sunshine was deceptive, I could feel snow in the air. I glanced around, half expecting to see someone with a knife or gun charging toward me. Wright would not be here on the prison grounds, but as the Superintendant had said, he could be anywhere, waiting.

Chapter Twenty Nine

The next morning I made a call to Wright's probation officer who told me that Wright had made contact within twenty four hours of his release. He was living with his sister in the Bronx and looking for work. So far he was behaving. Had Wright actually turned over a new leaf or was he just biding his time, waiting for the right moment to strike? I told the parole officer that I would come down the next day and meet with Wright, but I would appreciate the officer's not mentioning my visit. I got the address of Wright's sister's place. It would take me all day to get to New York City, and if I were lucky, I might catch Wright at home. I was prepared to wait all day and all night to talk with him.

I wished Larry were here so we could talk about things, but the limited budget for this case only allowed one officer to travel to the city. I called Larry's number, but it rang without anyone picking up.

It was three o'clock when I got home. I tried Larry again, but with no luck. I sat at the kitchen table and made a list of questions I would ask Wright? Then I poured myself a beer. OK, I know. Drinking at three o'clock in the afternoon was not a good idea, but I would limit myself to one.

At three thirty I heard Mrs. Gentile's key in the lock. She was surprised to see me.

"I'm taking the train to New York City tomorrow," I said. "Can you stay overnight tomorrow night?"

She nodded.

"I'll be home some time on Wednesday," I said, writing a list of the things Amelia needed for the play rehearsal in the afternoon. "I'll call Willi DeGrasse. Her daughter's working on the set, so she can drive Amelia home."

Just at that moment, the door slammed and Amelia burst into the room.

"Poppi," she cried, and ran to hug me.

"Well that's nice," I said. "Is it because I'm home early?"

Instead of answering she went to the refrigerator and got the milk jug and poured herself a glass of milk. Mrs. Gentile put out some cookies. We sat companionably at the table.

"Poppi," Amelia asked. "What do they call those guys with ear plugs who walk around with the President?"

"Ear plugs?"

"You know? They walk around when the President is outdoors with lots of people around." She mimicked a man looking quickly right and left and then talking into a hidden microphone. "They protect him."

"Secret Service," I said. "They're bodyguards for the President."

"Bodyguarders. That's them. " She took a sip of her milk. "You don't need to have a bodyguarder for me, Poppi. I'm a big girl."

"Have you seen a bodyguard around the school, Amelia?"

"Sure," she said, taking a bite of cookie. "He was there this morning, and then this afternoon. I saw him standing across the street, watching me. I waved to him, but he didn't wave back. I was the only kid he was looking at. When I got on the bus, he got in his car. I didn't see him no more after that."

I felt dread rise up in the pit of my stomach. "What did the bodyguard look like?

She shrugged. "He had sunglasses on, and a dark coat, like a man who goes to the office."

"Shit," I said aloud.

"Poppi, you said a bad word."

"So I did, sweetie. I did." I went to the living room and dialed Larry on my cell. I told him that I thought Amelia was being watched at school. I needed to go to New York City tomorrow and could he take some time and go over to the school when the kids were getting out of rehearsal and keep an eye on Amelia. Willi probably would take her home, but I needed him to watch her just the same. I filled him in on why I was concerned about Amelia, and then we talked about the case. I told him about my interview with Grainger and my upcoming interview with Wright.

"The boss has taken me off the case," Larry said.

"Taken you off the case? But we were getting close."

"He says we've run out of money, Chris. I tried to argue with him, but he wouldn't listen. He's starting up a drug task force and put me on it."

I felt my anger rise. How could O'Malley do this? Did he assume because Shevchenko was dead that the case was closed. Damn him.

I said goodbye to Larry and dialed O'Malley's number but no one was answering. The hell with him. I'd finish this by myself. I called Willi and asked if she could take Amelia home after play practice tomorrow. I briefly explained my trip, saying that if I were home earlier, I could do it myself, but I didn't know when I'd return. I toyed with the idea of telling her about the 'bodyguarder' but I didn't want to alarm her. If Larry could keep an eye on Amelia when she was going into the school and coming out after rehearsal, my granddaughter should be all right.

The next morning, I took the bus to Hudson, where I changed to the train for New York City. As I was riding in the train, I tried to imagine Wright's motive for kidnapping Ethan. Grainger had said they were going to get money. Had Sandy LeBrun actually paid the ransom? I didn't think so. Had Wright written the ransom note? If so, how had he gotten it onto the LeBrun's kitchen counter, when Evangeline Swindon had been there all afternoon?

I pulled the ransom note in its plastic sleeve out of my case and glanced over it. It had been written in a neat hand, with no salutation, no signature and no misspellings. I knew from Grainger's GED essay that spelling wasn't his strong suit. Maybe Wright was smarter. Nevertheless, I needed a sample of Big Boy's handwriting to prove whether he was the author or not.

When I got to Grand Central Station, I grabbed a sandwich, and then took a cab out to the Bronx where Wright's sister lived.

The house was an ordinary two story job with peeling paint and a lawn littered with children's toys. I had no idea why a young mother would take an ex-con under her roof? But then I didn't know the relationship between these siblings. I paid the driver and exited the cab, shivering in the chilly air. It would have been nice to have my own vehicle, but then parking in the city could be a bitch. As I walked up to the front door, I could hear rock music coming from inside. Someone was home. I hoped it was Wright.

I banged on the door, and it slammed open. A man stood before me, blonde, heavy set, wearing pajama bottoms and no top. "What the hell?" he bellowed. He started to close the door, but I shoved my foot into the space, and then muscled my way into the house. It smelled of cooking grease and cigarettes.

"Get the fuck out," Wright bellowed. He took a swing at me, but I ducked, leaving him off balance. I spun him around and grabbed his arm, pushing it hard against his back, so the elbow was bent at an awkward angle. Wright howled.

"I assume that we're alone," I said. "I only see one car in the driveway, and at this time of day, the kids are in school."

"You can't just come in here like this," Wright whined.

I grabbed his other arm and pushing it back, snapped my handcuffs around his wrists, so he had both arms pinned behind his back. "Sit," I said, and shoved him into a chair.

"Get your fucking hands off me. I'm going to file a complaint."

"Be my guest," I said, breathing hard. If I were going to do more of this kind of thing, I needed to get in better shape.

"I'm investigating the death of a little boy, Ethan LeBrun. It happened ten years ago in a town called Euclid, New York."

He was squirming around in the seat, not looking at me.

"Look at me when we're talking."

"I don't know nothing about no kid," he said.

"I think you do," I said. "You and LeRoy Grainger kidnapped him and left him trussed up in the woods behind his house."

"Who told you that?"

"Grainger. He wrote it all out in an essay, and when you found out, you had your brother punished, didn't you?"

Wright scowled at me. "God damned perv. Can't keep his mouth shut. I told him, 'don't tell no one,' but he wants to brag on it like he's a somebody."

"You might have killed him. I saw the bruises."

"He's alive, ain't he?"

"If he dies, you'll come up against a manslaughter charge."

"You can't prove nothing."

"Grainger told me all of it; I have it on tape," I lied. I sat back in the chair. "Why did you decide to kidnap Ethan LeBrun?"

"His daddy was rich. I read how he was a fancy doctor in New York and he moved to that town so he could help people. Help people, my ass, those rich guys only want to help theirselves."

"So you got the idea to kidnap the boy because of a newspaper article?"

"Kinda,"

Take My Hand

"What do you mean 'kinda?'"

"It was actually her idea."

"Her idea?"

"Chrissy's. She was a little older 'n me and one day she shows me this newspaper article and says she's got an idea how to make money. She wanted to move somewhere warmer, like California or Hawaii."

"Where did you meet Chrissy?"

"In a bar in Watertown. She was working there, and I was a frequent customer. We hit it off, went to bed a few times, then she says she wants me to be her boyfriend. I mean, I'd had some girls before her, but never as classy as her."

"How old would you say Chrissy was?"

"Twenty-two, maybe. A few years older 'n me."

"Was it Chrissy's idea that you use your brother, LeRoy to befriend Ethan and lure him into the comic book store?"

Wright nodded. "LeRoy was thirteen. He was still living with my ma, going to school. I was seventeen and on my own. We drove into Euclid one day, scoped the town out. We saw that the store had a back door leading into the woods. Chrissy even figured out that the owner, Archer, sometimes had fits, so he didn't remember nothing."

"This took a lot of planning."

"Yeah," Wright said with a touch of pride. "Chrissy was smart, she was."

"What did Chrissy look like?"

"F've six. Blonde, blue eyes, great figure."

"Do you remember any identifying marks on her body? Did she speak with an accent?"

"No marks that I remember. Sometimes she did drugs that made her crazy. I tried to stay away when she was like that."

"Did she ever tell you where she had come from?"

"New York City. She was hot to get the money so she could move on."

I took out my copy of the ransom note. "You left handed or right handed?" I asked.

Big Boy looked at me puzzled. I moved closer to his face. "Answer me when I talk to you."

"Right handed," he said.

"I need a paper and a pencil, where can I find them?" He pointed to a desk in the corner of the room. I went over and pulled out a drawer. There, in a jumble of stuff, were a couple of pencils and some sheets of paper.

"OK, I'm going to take the cuffs off one hand," I said. "Don't try anything, or believe me I'll have you back in prison before you can blink."

I undid the cuff on one hand so it dangled free. I knew I was taking a chance with Wright, but I needed answers. I gave him the pencil and paper and picked up the ransom note. "I want you to write what I dictate," I said.

"I have something that is very dear to you."

"How do you spell dear? Is it deer like the animal or dear like I love you?"

"Just write," I said. When he was finished I grabbed the paper and looked at it. Big Boy had misspelled 'something' as somting, and the deer was the animal. The handwriting was very different. "So who wrote the ransom note?" I asked.

He shrugged. "That was Chrissy's job. She was going to collect the money, tell them where the kid was and then we would scoot. Only after we'd left the kid in the woods, she never showed."

"Did you try and track her down?"

"Hell yes. I went back to the bar where she worked; they said she'd quit two days before. I went to her apartment but she'd cleaned it out and didn't leave no address. She fucked us for sure."

"So what did you do when you realized there would be no money coming?"

"Leroy and I split. We took a train to Texas, and from there we bummed around for a while. Kept looking over our shoulder, keeping an eye peeled for the bitch, Chrissy. Eventually we got back to New York where we got arrested a few times."

"Didn't your mother come looking? You were both pretty young."

"I knew ma would miss us, but I couldn't tell her what happened. I said we'd both got job offers. Even though LeRoy was still a kid, he was tall for his age. My mom was never that bright. She believed us."

I looked at my notebook. "One more question. When you left Ethan LeBrun in the woods that afternoon, was he still alive?"

"Course he was. Thrashing around, kicking and hollering. That's why we put the tape over his mouth. But we covered him with a blanket 'cause it was cold. We didn't kill him."

"But you were the last people to see him alive, and he died that night. You could be facing manslaughter for this."

"Look man, I'm trying to go straight," Wright said. "I've been in and out of jail since I was twenty and I'd like to stay out for a while. Could you just keep this on the down low for a while? I promise I won't tell no-one."

I guess he was serious. I wanted to give him a break, but I kept thinking of how Ethan LeBrun had died, and the girlfriend Wright had knifed who had feared him enough not to press charges. I leaned forward. "Listen to me," I said. "And listen good. If I hear a whisper about your doing drugs, B & E's even lifting a pack of chewing gum from a Mom & Pop operation, your parole officer will hear from me. If you are even fifteen minutes late for an appointment, we'll start proceedings to have you returned to jail on kidnapping charges. Do you understand me, Wright?"

The sweat had beaded on his forehead. He wasn't fidgeting any more. "Stand up," I said.

I undid the cuff. At that point he could have slugged me; he was still bigger than I was. Instead he turned and walked toward the back of the house where I assumed the bedroom was. I used his telephone to call a cab and when it came I asked them to take me to Big Boy's parole officer.

The parole officer and I had a long chat about Big Boy. I had no clear evidence that Wright had been part of the kidnapping of Ethan LeBrun, only Grainger's written essay, which he could deny, and Wright's admission which I did not have on tape. We agreed that parole would keep a tight rein on the man and if anything changed, I would be called. With that I got a cab to the train station, and started the long journey back home.

On the train, I called Lorna Watson. It was now seven o'clock so I was pretty sure she'd still be up. Her phone rang three times before she picked up.

"Chris," she said. "I'm sorry it took so long for me to pick up. I'm at the hospital with Harold."

"That's what I was calling about. They found him then?"

"Yeah. He was hiding in a garden shed, near the nursing home." Her voice broke. "Oh Chris, he's got pneumonia. They don't expect him to make it."

"Lorna I'm so sorry. Is there anything I can do?"

"Pray for him, Chris. He's only in his forties, but the disease has left him vulnerable."

"Did he tell you any more about the man who was pretending to be your son William?"

"It wasn't just a man, Chris. There was a woman too. She told Harold she was William's wife. The woman got him out of the nursing home by telling him she was going to show him something special."

"What did the woman look like?"

"No idea. But the nursing home has a new staff member who started work not long ago. Now she's gone."

"Could you give me the name of someone on the staff who might have met this woman?"

"Sure, Alana Anderson is the staff director. She does the hiring."

I wrote down the number and hung up. Was the woman who lured Harold Watson out of the nursing home, the same Chrissy that Big Boy Wright had known? But what had been her motive then, and what was her motive now?

Shortly after we left New York City I fell asleep on the train and dreamed that I was walking toward the elementary school where Amelia was a student. As I got close, I saw Amelia just in front of me. She was walking away, her hand in the hand of a man wearing a long dark coat. I called her name and she turned. She saw me and started crying. The man was pulling at her now, dragging her faster and faster away from me. I started to run, but as fast as I could travel, Amelia and the man were faster. I woke with a start. I was sweating, and my neck ached from the odd angle I'd been resting. Was I dreaming something that was going to happen? Or was it just stress? I couldn't wait to get home and hold my little girl in my arms.

Chapter Thirty

I woke the next morning to the phone ringing. I'd arrived home at three o'clock in the morning and had fallen into bed and now, glancing at the clock, I saw it was eight. Who the hell was calling at this hour? I reached over and picked up the phone.

"Bellini."

It was the Chief. "In my office right now."

I hung up the phone and pulled myself up out of bed and staggered to the kitchen to make coffee. *The hell with this*, I thought. *He can wait.* By the time I got to the station, it was nine thirty. I knocked on the Chief's door and then opened it. He was sitting at his desk, poring over papers. Was he preparing to fire me? I sat.

"What time did you get in last night?"

"Three."

"I guess you deserve a little rest. So, what did you learn?"

I filled him in on what I had learned from Wright. O'Malley cut me off before I'd finished, waving his hand in the air as though brushing away flies. "How close are you to finishing this thing, Bellini?"

"I don't know," I answered. "I thought I had it wrapped up when we had Shevchenko, but that went bust. Wright admitted that he and his half brother were the kidnappers, but they talk about a woman being the one who got them into it. If I can find her…"

"Bellini, I'm running out of money. The grant was for a limited amount, and was never intended to cover two men. I'm not even sure I can fully cover your recent trip to New York."

"You're going to drop the investigation?" I thought of all the hours I'd put in, just gone.

"Listen to me. I've got cocaine coming into the North Country. And pharmaceuticals. We're assembling a task force to try and deal with it, and you're one of our most senior men. I need you on this."

"You've already taken Larry from me. If I drop the investigation now, we'll never know who killed that little boy," I said. "This is our last chance."

O'Malley got up out of the chair and turned so he was facing the window behind his desk. "Don't you want to find out what happened?" I asked.

"We've had four investigators working on this, Chris," O'Malley said, still facing the window. "I'm not a man who gives up on something, but I have no choice. I can't do anything for the LeBrun boy. He's dead Chris." He turned to face me. "He's dead."

"I'm not trying to bring him back to life, just find out who killed him."

O'Malley nodded. "OK, here's what I'll do. You get a week more. A week. That actually exceeds the money that's left in the fund, but I can find cash somewhere. If you haven't located a viable suspect by the end of that time, we'll drop the investigation."

I wondered briefly, if either of the LeBruns would pay me as a private investigator. Is that what I really wanted? To work as a private dick for someone else? I missed the camaraderie of the force. I already missed being able to bounce things back and forth with Larry. But there was a larger question. What kind of man would I be if I let a little boy down? Money or no money, I had to finish this thing. I looked up. The Chief was watching me, and I realized that he was waiting for me to make a decision.

"All right," I said. "I'll do my best to wrap this up, but if I don't, I'll finish it on my own time."

The Chief glanced at the papers on his desk. "Tomorrow morning there will be a meeting of the task force," he said. "I want you there."

I shook my head. If I had only a week, then I was going to use every bit of that time. "I'm going to Saranac Lake tomorrow," I said.

"Why?"

"I need to talk to Sandy LeBrun again."

"What do you have on the agenda today?" he asked.

"I'm going to talk to Greg. He knows something about this girl." I passed the tabloid across the desk to O'Malley and he studied it.

"OK," he said finally. "You get a little more time, but then you're on my team."

I went back to my office and dialed the college, but I was told that Greg had left, and no one knew where he'd gone. I asked to speak to Greg's roommate and after a long pause, a young man came on the phone.

"Who's this?" he asked.

"I'm Chris Bellini, a police detective. I'm investigating the death of his brother, Ethan and I was hoping to talk with Greg. Do you know where he is?"

"Sorry, no. He packed up and left two days ago."

"Why did he leave?"

"His dad pulled the money. Said Greg was just farting around, not going to classes and he wasn't going to support laziness."

"Do you know how I can reach Greg?"

"He has a cell, but he isn't answering. I tried. He left some stuff here that I packed up, but it's a small place. I wish he'd come and get it."

"Can you give me his number?"

"Sure." He read off some numbers and I copied them down. "Did Greg say what he was going to do now?"

"Yeah. He wanted to kill his Dad. I don't know if he really meant it, but he was pretty angry."

I hoped that wouldn't be the case. I couldn't see Greg as the killing kind, but then people surprise you. I thanked the roommate and hung up. When I visited Sandy LeBrun tomorrow, I might get some answers. Just at that moment, O'Malley poked his head into my office. "You've seen this?" he asked.

It was a copy of *Upstate Monthly* the page bent back to the article about the war against bullying. Chief O'Malley's picture filled most of the first page of the article. I flipped to the second page, there was a small shot of me, one taken several years ago when I was younger and thinner. I closed the magazine and gave it back to O'Malley, trying to look impressed. He smiled proudly.

I left work early and went to pick up Amelia at school. When we got home, a young woman who was vaguely familiar was sitting at the kitchen table talking with Mrs. Gentile. She rose when I came into the room.

"Mr. Bellini, Myra Grindon," she said. "Remember you asked me about the picture in the newspaper?"

It had been almost a month since we'd asked her to do the research and with all that had happened in the meantime, I'd forgotten.

"You said you'd pay me for this, didn't you?"

I nodded, aware that Mrs. Gentile and Amelia were watching the two of us. "Let's go into the basement where I have an office," I said. She followed me down.

"What did I say I would pay you?"

"Thirty five, but I think it's worth forty."

It seemed like an outrageous price. As if reading my mind, she said "I'm saving for college."

"What did you find?"

She pulled out a large manila envelope with Greg's name and address on the front, and drew out an eight by ten glossy photo of a student sitting on a grassy lawn, looking up at the photographer.

She pointed to the corner of the picture, where a clear image of a dancing bear was visible. "If you look at the newspaper picture, it's the same image," she said.

"How did you get this?" I asked, studying the digital signature.

"There was a photography show two weeks ago at Greg's campus in Vermont," Myra said. "Greg had a couple of pieces in it."

"You didn't steal this picture, did you?"

She slouched back in her chair. "Don't worry Mr. Bellini. My dad's a cop. We've had it drilled into us every day since we were little kids." She lowered her voice in an imitation of her father's "'If I have to go down to the station and bail you out, believe me, you'll get it ten times worse at home."

"So how did you get the picture?"

"It was a juried show. The students submit five pictures each and the jury decides which ones to show. Greg didn't pick up his rejects by the deadline, and they were going to mail them. I offered to do it for them."

"How did you know all of this? You're a high school kid."

"Screw the money," she said rising from her chair. "I'm out of here."

"No, Myra wait," I said. "I didn't mean to sound so dismissive..."

"Offensive, you mean. You think because I'm still in high school, I don't have a brain? You think because I'm female, that I can't figure things out? Someday I'm going to be a detective and I'll solve crimes as well as any man."

I had no doubt about it. I put my hand on her arm. "I'm impressed," I said. "Tell me what you did to get this picture."

"I read in the paper about the student photography show at the college. I had a friend drive me to Vermont. You owe me gas money by the way. I thought about lifting one of Greg's pictures, but I remembered my dad's words, so I took a close up with my cell. Then when I told the girl at the desk I was a friend of Greg's, she gave me the packet of photos to return to him. Anyway, his digital signature is pretty clear in this picture. We can compare it with the photo in the newspaper."

I went to get the newspaper. The image was blurry, but under magnification, it appeared to be the same.

"Bingo," Myra said.

"Why would he take this picture?" I asked.

"His father was fooling around with this girl. He was getting proof to confront his Dad."

"Sandy LeBrun said he didn't know who she was."

"If he said that, he's lying. Look at how Dr. LeBrun's got his arm around her, how his head is turned toward hers, like he's talking to her. You need to go back and ask him again. Now," she said rising. "I got school tomorrow."

I rose and peeled off two twenties and a ten from my wallet. "Thanks Myra," I said. "When you come up for detective in ten years, I'll put in a recommendation."

"Make that eight years," she said.

The next morning I tucked the ten year old tabloid with the picture of Sandy and the mystery girl into my briefcase and headed toward Saranac Lake. I got about an hour out of town when I thought I probably should call the clinic where he worked, just to make sure he would be there. They told me that he hadn't arrived, but it was early, and he would probably show up at about eleven. Since he only worked two days a week, and had no telephone, I would have to hope he showed up in order for me to interview him.

It was a lovely fall day. In Euclid the leaves were turning, the huge oaks and maples glowing against the sky. As I traveled south toward the Adirondacks, I could feel the cold and see patches of snow beside the road. I had only my work shoes on and it occurred to me, that if Sandy LeBrun were not at work today, I would have to hike in through snow or even mud to reach him. I stopped at a Wal-Mart and bought a cheap pair of winter boots. Hopefully, they wouldn't fall apart before I'd had a chance to talk to the man.

I drove to downtown Saranac Lake and parked my car in front of the clinic where Sandy LeBrun volunteered his time. But when I went inside, the nurse administrator told me that he hadn't shown up, even though he had been due two hours ago.

"We have no way to reach him," she said. "And we can't spare anyone to hike in to his place. Since the snow two days ago, it's a mess in the woods. Are you planning to see him?"

I nodded.

"Tell him to give us a call. We have to reschedule these patients." She gave a sigh of frustration. "He's a good doctor. I just wish he hadn't decided to live way out there in the woods, with no way to reach him."

I thanked her and drove the twenty minutes to Sandy's road. I put on my new boots, realizing as I did so, that they might not be as comfortable as I had hoped. I tucked the newspaper picture into my jacket and headed down the path.

Take My Hand

From the ruts on either side of a central mound, I could see that the path had once been a roadway, maybe something once used for logging or used by snowmobilers in the winter. But the forest had encroached, the trees overhead almost touching each other with saplings in the center of the road, taunting the unwary driver. On either side of me, the woods held about two inches of snow, and it was cold. The boots pinched a little, but I was glad I'd purchased them. I wish I'd worn my warmest parka. At home, it was still fall. Here it was winter.

After fifteen minutes of walking, I began to perspire so I took off my jacket and tucked it under my arm. There was nothing else I could do with it. It was too bulky to wrap around my waist. As I walked, I went over in my mind the details of the case. Larry and I had interviewed everyone we could think of. Once I had done this second interview with Sandy, I couldn't think of another person I should talk to. Maybe the Chief was right and I should call it quits. I struggled with that thought for a while. I hated to give up ; in all my years of police work, I'd never done it. Even if I had to work the case evenings and weekends, I would do what I could to finish this.

I was coming in sight of the cabin now. I expected the dog, to come bounding out to greet me, but everything was quiet. It was deer season. Maybe LeBrun had decided to take the day off and go hunting.

I moved closer to the cabin, walked around to the porch and stepped up onto it. The door was unlocked, so I went in. Everything was neat. The dishes were washed, and drying on the counter, a heavy coat hung on a peg by the door. I pushed open a door to what I imagined was the bedroom, and in spite of the cold I could smell it. Blood. There, lying on his back half off the bed was the body of Sandy LeBrun. He was wearing a sweater and pajama bottoms, and appeared to have been shot squarely in the chest. On the floor, just a few feet away was the body of the dog, who'd been shot too.

Damn, I thought. And then with a chill, I realized that since I was the first one to find the body, I might be considered a suspect. I tried to remember what I'd touched when I'd come in. The door, of course, I'd had to open it. What else? I looked down at my feet and back at the tracks my boots had made from the door, to the kitchen and now to the bedroom. Other than my wet prints the floor was clean.

I stared at the body stretched out at that awkward angle. If I felt for a pulse, I would get the victim's blood on my hands, which could make my situation worse. The victim wasn't making a sound, and I couldn't see him breathing. Better for me just to leave. Slowly I turned and retraced my steps, being careful to keep to the same tracks. When I got outside, I took out my cell phone and looked for coverage. Damn. Nothing. I would have to hike out and call the police from the road.

Several questions assailed me as I walked back toward the main road. Greg LeBrun's roommate said that Greg had threatened to kill his father. Had he actually done it? At twenty two, Greg was still a kid, but he was old enough to have bought a gun, gotten to the Adirondacks and killed Sandy. And why had the dog been shot? It was possible that the dog had tried to defend Sandy against Greg, but to me the animal had never been vicious. Maybe the dog had been surprised and threatened to bite, and Greg had shot to protect himself.

When I got to the road, my cell found a tower and I called the police. After explaining the situation to the dispatcher, a growly voice came on the line. I identified myself and said that I was at the cabin of Dr. Sandy LeBrun and that he'd been shot

"Are you there now?" the voice asked.

"No, I'm at the road. There was no cell service near the cabin. Who am I talking to?"

"Gerard Angleton, I'm the Chief," the man said. "What did you say your name was?"

"Detective Chris Bellini. I'm investigating the murder of Ethan LeBrun. Sandy was his father."

"What's your Chief's name?"

I gave him O'Malley's number. I wasn't upset that Angleton was going to corroborate my story. Criminals like to hang around after they've committed a crime, sometimes even phoning the police. But they rarely gave their true names.

"Stay right where you are," Angleton said. "We're sending two officers over there. We'll need you to show us where the body is."

"Bodies," I said. "The dog was shot too."

"Just stay the hell where you are," Angleton said, and hung up.

I tried to make the time go by walking back and forth on the pathway. *Think of it as exercise*, I told myself, though I'd always hated that sort of thing. I'd been trying to lose a few pounds, and maybe this would be the start of a new resolution. When I'd taken my third trip up the path and turned toward the road, I heard the noise of an engine. I looked up to see two ATV's, one behind the other. Both riders were dressed in dark blue parkas with helmets. They were not using the woods for recreation. They were police.

"You Bellini?" the first man asked, coming to a stop in front of me and flipping up the visor of his helmet.

"Yup." I pulled out my badge and showed it."

"Hop on. Unless you want to walk."

I'd had enough of walking. With two of us aboard, the machine strained and wobbled on the path that was more mud than snow. At last we reached the cabin. The first officer took off his helmet and goggles and I saw, up close, that he seemed to be about my age. He introduced himself as Jim Weims.

"Where did you find the body?"

I pointed toward the cabin and then followed Weims as we headed toward it. Weims stopped at the bottom of the steps to put on some paper booties. Then he turned and looked at my shoes.

"Did you go inside?"

I nodded.

"Touch anything?"

"Just the doorknob. Not the body."

"Waters will take you to the station," Weims said. "We need to get prints from your boots, and fingerprints."

I held up my gloved hands. "I never took these off."

"Just the same, we need prints." He looked at me hard. "Tell me again why you're here?"

I explained everything about the investigation and that I'd come hoping to get LeBrun to answer some questions.

"Did you think LeBrun had any enemies?"

"He has a son, Greg, who's a student at the University of Vermont in Burlington. Yesterday when I tried to contact Greg, I was told that LeBrun had withdrawn the boy's funds. Greg left the college three days ago. His roommate said he'd threatened to kill his father."

"Do you have any way to reach Greg LeBrun?"

I pulled out my cell and gave Weims the number. At that moment the man on the second machine came up to stand beside Weims. I assumed Weims was the lead detective, so this man could have been a partner. Since no one was giving me anything more than a name, it was hard to tell.

"Did LeBrun have any other relatives? We have to notify next of kin."

"An ex-wife, April. She's a lawyer in Burlington." I gave him that phone number. I looked at Jim Weims. "I think our two cases are related, Jim. I'd like you to keep me in the loop with what you find."

Weims was silent. He wasn't ready to trust me yet.

"I'd like to get going," I said. "I still have a two hours' drive to get home."

Weims gestured toward the man standing beside him. "You'll have to go back to the station with Waters. Just to rule you out as a suspect."

I was being dismissed. I followed Waters to his ATV and for the umpteenth time that morning I made the trip over the rutted, mushy ground to the highway.

At the station, I was fingerprinted and prints made of my boots. I didn't complain; our two cases might just be related, and I might need some future help from these guys. When the process was over, I gave Waters my card. Waters nodded. I'm not sure if the nod was just to get me off his back or if he genuinely intended to help. We wished each other good luck and I left and drove home.

Chapter Thirty One

The next day was Friday. If O'Malley was going to cut off my funding I had only a short time to make any headway on the case. I didn't even want to go into the office for fear that I would be pressed into service. It wasn't that I didn't want to bring down scumbag drug dealers. My own daughter had taught me what drugs could do to a person, but I knew if I stopped the investigation, I might never pick it up again. It would mean that I, personally, had let a child down. Sometimes at night, I would dream of Ethan LeBrun. What would his life have been like, had he not died so young? He might have become a doctor like his father, a lawyer like his mother. He might have been an artist, or scientist. He would be a teenager today, a boy ready to make his mark on the world.

So I sat at home, trying to think where to go next. I dialed the number Greg's roommate had given me. The phone rang and rang and I was just about to hang up, when a young woman answered.

"Lo?"

"I'm looking for Greg LeBrun. Is he there?"

The woman mumbled something. I think she was speaking to someone else in the room and my hopes rose.

"He ain't here," she said and hung up.

I dialed the number again. This time it rang more than ten times. When the young woman answered, I said. "Please don't hang up. My name is Chris Bellini and it is very important that I talk to Greg about his father. Is he there?"

"He went out," the young woman said. "I don't know where he is."

"Where are you?"

"Molly's house."

"And where is that?"

She hung up the phone. I dialed again.

"Listen," I said, as soon as she picked up. "I'm a detective investigating the death of Greg's brother, Ethan. I need to talk to him about his father."

"He's not talking to his dad," she said sullenly.

"I need to talk with him. Please tell me where he is."

There was a long silence on the phone. "OK," she said, and she gave me an address in Springdale, a hamlet about ten miles away.

"I'm coming over," I said. "Please don't go anywhere. And if Greg comes back, don't tell him I'm coming."

"Listen mister…" she began, but I'd already hung up.

Springdale is nobody's dream community. It was originally settled when a paper mill occupied land next to the Little River, but that was a hundred years ago, when paper mills were thriving. After the mill closed, Springdale became a bedroom community for the more prosperous communities of Euclid and Langdon Falls. As I drove down the main street I could see at least one boarded up business interspersed between a tiny grocery store, and a restaurant featuring ribs and home-baked pies. The Post Office was closed. There was a church, but its paint was crumbling and the sign board advertised a long ago Easter celebration. I turned down the street toward the address, past large brick houses that in their day had been magnificent, but now had broken windows and peeling paint. There were plenty of trailers, the poor man's housing tucked in between the homes. The address I had been given was a two story wood structure with the typical tall windows that had once graced turn of the century homes. In spite of its lack of care, the home had once been a beauty, maybe the residence of a mill owner or merchant. I walked up the steps, trying to avoid scattered children's toys, and rang the bell. No one came to the door. I rang again and then turned the knob and pushed open the door.

I was assailed immediately by the smell of cooking meat overlaid with marijuana smoke.

"Just leave it by the door, Hank," someone called from the interior of the house. "On the table."

"Hello," I called.

"If we owe you money we'll catch you next week," the same voice.

I moved toward the sound. A woman was standing in the kitchen, stirring something on the stove. A joint lay in an ashtray near her, beside two empty beer bottles. It was ten o'clock in the morning. Pretty early to party.

"Who are you?"

"Obviously not Hank," I said. "I'm looking for Greg LeBrun."

"Don't know him," she said. She glanced at the joint. "You're not a cop, are you?"

"No," I lied. "Just a friend looking for Greg."

"What does Greg look like?"

"Tall, with blonde hair. College kid."

"Samantha's new boyfriend," the woman said. "Never did catch his name. They're up on the second floor."

"Do you know if they are at home?"

She put one hand on her hip. "Look mister. They pay their rent, that's all I care about. I don't control what they do, or when they go in and out. If your friend is there, he's there. If not, you'll have to come back later."

Take My Hand

With that she reached for the joint and took a long toke. I could have busted her right then, and one tiny angry part of me wanted to do that, but it wouldn't connect me with Greg. Instead, I turned back to the front hallway and followed the stairway up to the second floor.

Someone was home, judging from the loud music that was floating out into the hallway. I followed the sound through an open door into a room where two kids were lounging on a beat up sofa, drinking beer. I recognized one of them as Greg.

"Bellini the cop," he said seeing me.

"A cop?" the girl said. "You didn't say you were a cop. Shit, Greg, I didn't know." Giving me an angry look, she stood and marched toward me. She was so small she came up only to my shoulder and I probably outweighed her by a hundred pounds. "You tricked me," she said.

"Sam, cool it," Greg said, moving to stand beside her, then pulling her back to the couch where they both sat.

"What can I do for you, cop?"

I could feel my anger rising. "It's Detective Bellini," I said. I looked at Greg. "Do you know your father has been killed?"

"Killed?" All of Greg's attention was now on me. "When did it happen?"

"I don't know for sure. I went down to Saranac Lake to visit him yesterday, and he'd been shot."

I watched Greg's reaction. Sometimes people who are trying to fake grief go overboard: loud lamentation, protestations that the dead person was someone they loved above anyone on earth. But Greg was silent. "Shit," he said.

"When was the last time you saw him?"

"A week ago, at the college. He came to tell me that he was withdrawing his support. He wasn't going to pay for me 'to laze around drinking beer and screwing girls.' We had a bit of an argument then. I'm sure the whole floor heard us. A couple of days later I packed up my things and came here."

"Greg didn't do anything wrong," Sam said loyally. "He's a good photographer, and someday he'll be famous. His father wanted to push him into science, which he hates."

Greg put a hand on her arm to quiet her. I wondered how old Samantha was. Seventeen, eighteen? Had she been attending the same college, and did her parents know that she wasn't there now?

"The Saranac Lake police might be calling you," I said. "My recommendation is that you call them back. Tell them that you were here and that you can prove you weren't anywhere near your father's house. I expect they will want you to go down there and be fingerprinted, just so they can rule you out as a suspect."

"I did threaten to kill him," Greg said. "Everyone heard me say it."

"You didn't mean it, sweetie," Samantha said. "You were angry. I mean who wouldn't be, getting thrown out of college like that."

Greg was ignoring her. "I hated him," he said. "I hated his guts. I hated him for dragging us from New York to that godforsaken little town. We had lives in New York. We had people we hung out with who were interesting and then *he* makes the decision, without ever asking what we wanted."

I nodded. I had one more thing on my agenda and I didn't want to let it slip away. I pulled out the copy of the tabloid with the picture of Sandy LeBrun and the girl on the cover. I put it on the coffee table in front of us.

"Who is she?"

He shrugged. "How should I know?"

I looked at him. "You know who she is, Greg. Do you know how I know? Because you took this picture." I pointed to the image in the lower left hand corner. "This is your digital signature."

He was silent. He looked at his shoes and then at Samantha. He reached forward and took a swig of the beer. "OK," he said finally. "I was mad at my dad because he was fooling around with her and I wanted to get even, so I contacted that guy who was writing the stuff about us in the paper and offered to sell him the picture."

"Did the paper pay you?"

"Yeah, sure. I told them to put it in cash and mail it to a friend of mine. They did. Five hundred dollars. I'm sure it wasn't what they paid other people for their pictures, but I was just a kid. It was a fortune to me."

"Greg, what's the girl's name?"

"CiCi Swindon. Her real name's Celestine. She used to work as our nanny when we lived in New York."

"Swindon? Is she related to your housekeeper, Evangeline?"

"Her daughter. CiCi came to work for us when Ethan was about four. She was like a teenager then. I don't know when she and my dad hooked up. It was maybe a year before we moved from the city. I didn't ever talk to her. I hated that she was sleeping with my dad. I saw them once, kissing on the balcony of our apartment in New York City when my Mom was away. That's when I started following them, taking pictures."

"Did your mother know this was happening?"

"Not right away. When she found out what was going on, she fired CiCi on the spot."

"Where is CiCi now?"

A shrug.

"When was the last time you saw her?"

"About two weeks before Ethan died. I came home from school and she was sitting at the kitchen table with her mom, sobbing. When she saw me, she jumped up, said good-bye and left."

"So you haven't heard from her or talked to her since?"

"Isn't that what I just told you? If you want to find her, you should ask her mother."

"OK," I said. "Do you have a picture of CiCi?"

"Yeah, I think so." He got up from the couch and shambled over to a desk that was piled high with papers. He pulled a photo out of the pile and brought it back. The girl in the picture was probably sixteen or seventeen. She had long blonde hair and green eyes, but there was something about those eyes, that seemed to know more than a seventeen year old should.

I took out my notebook and scribbled the number of the police station in Saranac Lake. "Call them, Greg," I said. "It will be worse if they have to come after you."

He nodded.

Walking back to my car I pulled out my cell phone and dialed the Saranac Lake Police Department. I asked for Weims and was put on hold for a minute. When he came on the line, I identified myself and Weims said, "Yeah. You're the detective that found the body. What can we do for you, Bellini?"

Maybe being called by my name meant that we were on friendlier footing.

"I know where Greg LeBrun is. I've talked to him, and he denies killing his father."

"We'll need to interview him."

Take My Hand

"I've asked him to call you. He did threaten his father, but I don't think he killed him. Let me give you his number. If you call, I think he'll answer."

"OK," Weims said. "Thanks."

"Wait a minute," I said. "I need something in return. What have you found out at your end?"

There was a long silence. He could have hung up. Detectives are very protective of their turf and Weims might have been one of those men. "This is still a new investigation, Bellini," Weims said. "I'm not sure we can share...."

Translated, it meant, "We don't trust you. Not until we confirm that you are who you say you are." I hated his decision, but I knew I needed his help.

"OK," I said, "I'm guessing whoever killed Sandy LeBrun was not a native. Sandy gave his time freely at the clinic. Who would be angry enough to kill him? I'm guessing that his killer was someone from out of town who might have driven his own car to the Adirondacks, or flew in and rented a car nearby. Am I warm?"

"You're warm. So you don't think Greg LeBrun did it?"

"I saw Greg's reaction when I told him. He wasn't heartbroken, but he was genuinely surprised." There was silence on the other end. "I could call the local airports to see who flew in and out." I said. " There must be a rental car business in the area."

"Let me run this by my Chief," Weims said. He wasn't going to budge.

"Go ahead," I said. "You have my number. And Weims, if you get a description of the person who flew in, I might be able to match it with someone on this end. If you get a handwriting sample from the rental agreement, I could match it with the ransom note. We can help each other."

"Yup," was all he said.

I called the Adirondack Regional Airport and asked to speak to a supervisor. I explained that I was a detective with the Euclid Police Department and was looking for someone who had flown in either Monday or Tuesday of this week, and left Thursday morning or Friday. Those days were only guesses. I didn't know exactly when Sandy had been shot.

"I'm sorry sir," the supervisor said prissily. "We cannot reveal that information to anyone."

"This person may have committed a crime," I said. "We think he's from out of town and was only here for a few days."

"We have a great many people who use the airline," the supervisor said. "We have agreed, as part of our corporate policy to keep our records confidential."

"Have you given this information to any other law enforcement officers?"

There was silence. Of course, they'd told Weims. Damn Weims. Damn him. We could have helped each other. OK, I would go at it another way.

I needed to talk to Vangie Swindon about her daughter.

Chapter Thirty Two

After leaving Greg, I dialed the restaurant where Vangie Swindon worked, hoping that I could come in and see her. The boss came on, sounding a bit peeved.

"Listen," he said. "I ain't seen that bitch for a couple of days. She was supposed to open up for me on Thursday and she didn't show. When I called her house, no answer so I sent someone over to wake her up. Even though she'd screwed up my day, I was a little nervous about her. She's been acting kind of funny lately, skittish you know. But there was no one in the house."

"Did you go in?"

"Go in? No. I don't break into people's houses. But her car was gone. I figured she'd decided to can the job and skip town for a little R & R. I wondered why she didn't tell me herself. She's got a week's worth of back pay coming."

Minutes after I'd hung up, my phone rang. I answered it.

"Bellini, it's Weims."

"Weims, how are you?"

"Listen, I want to tell you something. We went back to the airport, and interviewed the clerk. Everyone who flew in on Saturday was local. At least they all had local addresses. But we do have something that might be of interest. On Wednesday night at about eleven o'clock a woman was stopped for doing seventy in a forty mile an hour zone. The name on her license was April LeBrun. She's the ex-wife of the victim, isn't she?"

"She is. She wasn't particularly fond of Sandy, but ..."

"You think she'd kill him? In this business you see a lot of strange things."

"Did the cop who stopped her get a description?"

"Nope. It was dark and he said she was wrapped up pretty well. Unless she'd been drinking, they wouldn't ask her to get out of the car. The report only says that it was a woman."

"Where was she stopped?"

"Uh, just a minute. Here it is. Elizabethtown." Elizabethtown was southeast of Saranac Lake.

"Can you give me the license plate number?"

Weims read me the number. "Are you sending someone to interview April?" I asked.

"We're a little short handed here, but yeah, we need to talk with her."

"Jim, one more thing. Did they find the murder weapon?"

"Not yet. LeBrun was shot at close range, with what we think was a small caliber hand gun."

"The dog too?"

"Yup. The killer could have ditched the weapon in the woods, or have it with him still."

"Thanks Jim," I said and hung up.

I took a deep breath, trying to process what Weims had said. Was April LeBrun Sandy's killer? I couldn't imagine it, but then, people have all kinds of reasons for shooting each other. I played out a scenario in my mind. On November sixth, April learns that Sandy has withdrawn Greg's tuition money, so she decides to drive from Burlington to Saranac Lake. If the roads were clear and she didn't hit a deer, April could be in Elizabethtown at eleven, which would put her in Saranac Lake at midnight. She would walk up the rough road into the cabin, wake Sandy up, and confront him about Greg. She would yell at Sandy, telling him he was a poor father, and that Greg was troubled. He doesn't need to have his tuition withdrawn, she would argue, he needs support. April and Sandy would get into a shouting match, someone would pull a gun and a shot would be fired. All of that was a possibility but it didn't explain the dog? Why would someone shoot the animal, unless the dog was trying to defend Sandy?

I took out my notebook and found the number for April and dialed. The phone rang five or six times, but there was no answer. Then I dialed her office and learned that she'd taken some personal days off and would be back at the beginning of next week.

"What was the first day of her vacation?" I asked.

"We try not to give out personal information on our employees."

"Look," I said, trying not to let my Italian temper get the better of me. "I am conducting a murder investigation regarding April's son, Ethan. Two days ago, her husband was shot in Saranac Lake and April was seen in the area."

"Her husband was shot? Oh my God, is he OK?"

"I'm afraid he's dead. Please, I need to know when was her first vacation day?"

"Wednesday, November seventh. She called me Wednesday night about nine and said she was taking some time off and she'd be back on the twelfth. I've had to reschedule all her clients."

"Did she say where she was going?"

"No, just that she needed to take a few days off."

"Thank you," I said and hung up.

If April had gone to Saranac Lake to confront Sandy about their son, why did she go so late at night? Why not wait for a more reasonable hour? Had she tried to call Sandy earlier, maybe as soon as Greg told her what happened? Or maybe there was some secret that April knew about the kidnapping and death of Ethan. Something for which Sandy had now paid the price.

It was now early-afternoon and I'd been sitting in my car in Springdale talking on the phone. I drove back to Euclid, making a detour to check on Evangeline Swindon's house. I could see newspaper piled up on the front step, and when I opened the mail box, there were at least ten pieces of mail inside. I walked around the house, hoping for a back door where I wouldn't be seen. But the door was locked securely and when I looked in the window everything seemed to be in order. I picked up my phone and dialed a number, taking the chance that Myra would be able to answer it.

"Lo?"

"Myra this is Chris Bellini. I have another assignment."

"Same payment? "

"Yeah. I'm looking for a woman named Cecilia Swindon. Can you help me find her?"

"What about her mother? Wasn't Mrs. Swindon one of your suspects?"

This girl knew too much. "Evangeline's not at home. I need to talk to her daughter about our investigation. Cecilia is also called CiCi and her last address was Williamstown, near Euclid. She left there ten years ago."

"Will do my best, Mr. B."

I'd had no lunch, and food always helped me think, so I drove to Euclid to my favorite restaurant, Jenny's On Main. Most of the usual lunch crowd had gone and there were only a few folks, sitting at tables eating a late lunch or enjoying coffee and Jenny's specialty, the pie. Spotting Larry at one of the tables, I slid in opposite him.

"How's it going?" I asked.

He made a face. "They've got me on this drug detail. Lots of meeting with local police, DEA, DEC, FBI, CBP even the Sheriff." He leaned forward and said softly. "They've got Hedgewick's dealership under surveillance. He's selling cocaine to college kids."

Remembering the brutal beatings Hedgewick had administered, I almost cheered. I hoped they would fry his ass.

"I miss working on the case, Chris. With this drug task force, I'm just part of a crowd. Half of us are clueless, and the other half are busy telling the rest of us how much they think they know. If they ever do a raid, it will be a free for all." He took a sip of coffee. "How's the case going?"

I ran the details of what I'd learned and then I said. "I called Myra to see if she could help me find a young woman named CiCi Swindon. Greg admitted that she's the girl in the tabloid picture. She was the family nanny, and Greg says his father was having an affair with her."

Larry whistled softly. "How could Besom and Gunther miss this?"

"People lie, especially if they feel guilty or they want to protect their own interests. And the detectives were under a lot of pressure to solve the case."

"Did you ask Evangeline Swindon about her daughter?"

"Larry, if Vangie were around, I wouldn't be asking Myra to help me find her daughter." I saw the hurt look on his face, and said, "Sorry, I didn't mean to bark. Evangeline hasn't shown up for her waitress job, and when I went to her house, no one was there. I've got to wrap this up soon," I said gloomily. "The Chief says there's no more money."

"Shit." Larry said. "I thought he would keep you on at least. He's just going to let it drop?"

I nodded. Larry shook his head in disgust. Just at that moment the waitress came with her order pad. I hadn't eaten yet, and Larry was done with his meal. We said good-bye with the promise that I would drop the photo of CiCi in his box and he would pass it on to his daughter.

It was now almost two o'clock. At two-thirty, Amelia would be getting out of school. Since the incident with the "bodyguarder," it would have been too easy for someone to snatch her as she was leaving the building. I tried to have Mrs. Gentile or myself meet her and walk her home. I ate my lunch and then set out for the elementary school, which like most things in Euclid is not very far away.

On the way to the school I had to pass the gutted remnant of the Morrissey Hotel. I was within sight of the school, and as I rounded the corner someone grabbed me by the shoulders and shoved me against the wall.

My assailant was wearing a dark ski mask which covered his head and face, so only his eyes and a pair of lips were exposed. "You should have left it alone, Bellini," he hissed. "The customers aren't coming around. They say I'm responsible for my kid being a bully."

I looked around me. We were in the shadows, away from the street. I could see parents on the sidewalk and if the fuckwad hadn't had his meaty fingers around my throat I would have called for help.

I was trying to figure out what my next move would be when the guy punched me hard in the gut. I doubled over. He cracked me on the back of the head. I saw lights and went down. "That's for my son," he said. He kicked me hard in the side, I felt a couple of ribs crack and then he kicked me hard in the side of the head. I blacked out."

I came to in what seemed like hours later. With difficulty I got myself to my feet. My ribs hurt, my head hurt, my gut hurt. I could scarcely stand upright. But I needed to get to Amelia, who would be waiting for me at school. I knew the asshole who'd beaten me. Was he the same 'bodyguarder' who'd been watching Amelia? My heart began to race and I moved as fast as my wounded body would let me. When I got to the school, to my relief, Amelia was standing there waiting.

"I waited for you, Poppi like you told me."

"Good girl," I said. I was moving at a kind of shuffle, trying unsuccessfully to seem normal.

"You have blood on your face. Did you fall down?"

"Something like that."

Take My Hand

She went to hug me, but I cried out.

"You got hurt," she said. "I'll take care of you."

We passed the hotel, the scene of my beating and moved on to the police station.

I ducked my head as I moved past the officer at the front desk. I hadn't decided what to do about Hedgewick. Filing a complaint would mean that I needed proof and all I had was a bully in a ski mask. I would find another way to get even. In the men's room, I washed the blood off my face and tried to do an assessment of my injuries.

When I returned to my desk, Amelia was sitting in the desk chair spinning it around. I found two aspirin in my desk and swallowed them without water. Then I put Greg's photo of CiCi in an envelope for Larry.

Just then the phone rang. It was Jim Weims, but the connection was poor and kept fading in and out. "Where are you, Jim?"

"At the murder site. We found a single bullet which we might be able to match to a gun, if we find the gun. We were able to pick up a single foot print which could be that of a woman. Did you get in touch with April LeBrun?"

"Nope. The law firm said she's gone on vacation. What about fingerprints, Jim?"

"Only yours and LeBrun's."

"Thanks for all this. Can I ask why you decided to share information?"

"Ah, well. It's personal, Chris. It was that show about bullying. My son is kind of a shy kid, and gets a lot of other kids picking on him. After your show, our local school system started a program like yours, the older kids filming bullies on their phones. For the first time, my son felt like someone had his back."

"I'm glad to hear that."

"My boss wasn't too happy about all this closeness, but he'll get over it. Keep me informed and I'll do the same for you."

I hung up. Amelia had taken a piece of paper from my desk and was drawing on it. She'd gotten a candy bar from the vending machine and bits of candy were on the desk, as well as a candy wrapper on the floor.

"Pick this up and then we'll go home," I said.

She swept the mess into the trash can. We put on our coats and headed for home. When we got home Amelia helped me tape my ribs. I knew I should go to the doctor, but he would only take time and money, and do essentially the same. That night, after Amelia was in bed, I sat with a glass of wine trying to dope out what was going on.

April LeBrun didn't seem the killer type to me. And if the shooting had been an accident, why hadn't April turned herself in? She was a lawyer ; she knew the penalties for first and second degree murder. Weims had found the bullet and footprints. But footprints were only good if you had a match, and Weims had none. Neither did he have a weapon as a match for the bullet. My head ached, not just from my recent beating, but because I couldn't get through to an answer. Finally, I went to bed.

Chapter Thirty Three

Saturday morning dawned wet and gloomy. From my bedroom window, I could see the garden, which still had not been cleaned up. The limp plants hung gloomily from the trellises, and the weeds, kept under control all summer, now crowded the pathway. I needed to do something, but I was still stiff and sore from my beating and I didn't think I had it in me to pull weeds. Besides, today was Amelia's day, hers and mine. I'd been spending so much time away from home recently, that I thought she deserved to have me to herself for the day.

I got dressed and went down to the kitchen and made coffee. Then I got out eggs and flour and other ingredients for waffle. Today we would have Amelia's favorite breakfast, waffles with strawberries and whipped cream.

I took the strawberries from the refrigerator, to let them warm up. They were, in truth, just for decoration. The label said Mexico, a place where strawberries grew in November, and where perhaps, given a chance to ripen, they might have had flavor. Unfortunately, by the time they reached northern New York, these fruits were strawberry shaped, and strawberry colored globes of cellulose. When my wife Claire was alive, we'd spend every June going to the U-Pick farms to spend a day picking the fruit. With the hot sun on our backs, and the bees buzzing around the flowers, we would pick for an hour, occasionally popping the warm sweet berry into our mouths just to taste summer.

And then we would cart the berries home by the quart, and the next day we would cook up a vat of the sweet, sticky jam. By the end of the day there would be a dozen or more pint jars, their glowing carmine contents lined up on the counter. No jam was ever as good as the stuff we made ourselves.

But then Claire got sick, and it was hard for her to spend the time on her knees picking, even harder for her to stand at the stove in the heat. Reluctantly we gave up our home-made jam.

"Whatcha doing?" It was Amelia, standing in her pajamas at the kitchen doorway.

"Making waffles, with strawberries and whipped cream."

She sat at the table, swinging her legs beneath her and watched me work. "Can I have some juice?"

I handed her a glass, and she got her juice. "I was just thinking about your grandmother's strawberry jam. Do you remember picking the strawberries. You might have been two at the time."

She shook her head. "I remember making the jam though," she said. "I miss her Poppi, don't you?"

"Every day," I said. After she'd been diagnosed, it was as though the world split in half. One half was the life we had known B.C. (before Cancer), a life I had assumed was going to be ours forever. That life had been taken over by doctor's appointments and chemotherapy and by my wife gradually becoming sicker and weaker, and hope growing dimmer. "Sometimes I don't feel like I remember her anymore," I said. "It used to be that if I saw a person on the street that looked like her, I would rush forward thinking it was her, before I remembered she was dead."

Amelia looked at me. "She used to take me for ice cream, after day care. Or sometimes we'd make cookies together when we got home."

I thought about how I still hadn't emptied her closet, and how I couldn't bear the smell of the perfume she used to wear. I looked over at Amelia's sad little face. "Well," I said. "We should do something fun today. What about the mall?" I had poured the first mix of batter onto the waffle maker and I could see the edges turning nice and brown.

I opened the top and pulled out a perfect waffle, added some maple syrup, a dab of whipped cream, a strawberry and set it in front of Amelia.

"The mall. The mall," she said and began talking about the things we could buy at the mall. "I need a new pair of shoes, and I want a poster of Justin Bieber, and a necklace."

"OK, OK," I said. "We have a limit on what we spend, so you won't get everything you want."

"Can I get an iPod?"

"An iPod? No. Maybe in a few years, but not right now. That's too expensive, Amelia."

"OK," she said. "What about a dog? I really want a dog."

"So you have said." I pulled my own waffle off the machine, added syrup and strawberries with just a tiny bit of whipped cream. I didn't need the extra calories.

"We can have lunch at Uncle Teddy's," I said. "You like that place."

"I'm gonna get a super big hot dog," Amelia said. "The mall and then Uncle Teddy's. Can we call Carey?"

"Why don't we do it later? I'd like to spend some time together, just the two of us."

"There's a pet store at the mall," she said, "Can we go?"

"We'll just look. We're not getting a dog right now, Amelia. A dog is a lot of work, and I don't have time to walk it every day."

"Mrs. Gentile can walk it."

"I'm not going to ask her to do that. She works hard enough taking care of us. She has to stay late on the nights when I'm working, and sometimes she comes in early. If we get a dog, you have to take care of it yourself."

Amelia looked at me. "Would I have to do it every day?"

"Every day. A dog can't just eat when you feel like feeding it. A dog needs to go for a walk so he can use the bathroom. Sometimes when it's a puppy, you have to walk him twice a day. Can you do that Amelia?"

She looked down at her almost empty plate. "I don't know if I can do it *every* day," she said.

"At least you're being honest. When you tell me that you can take care of a dog every day, feed it, give it water, take it for walks, then we'll talk about whether you can get a dog."

She nodded slowly.

"Now," I said. "I want you to take a bath and get dressed. Put on something warm, it's cold out there."

We were inside Target, debating whether to buy a red blouse with flowers on it, or a blue blouse with stripes when my phone rang. I looked at the number. It was a local area code, but a number I didn't recognize.

"Hello?"

"Detective Bellini? It's April LeBrun. I need to talk with you."

"April, just a minute." Amelia had begun to wander away down the aisle, unaware that I wasn't right behind her. I caught up with her and grabbed her by the hand. "Amelia, you need to stay where I can see you," I said.

I went back to the phone. "Where are you April?"

"At Greg's place in Springdale. Please, I have to talk with you."

"Does anyone else know where you are?"

"No, I just got here about half an hour ago. Greg told me what happened to Sandy." Her voice wavered and she broke into a sob.

"OK," I said. "Give me about forty five minutes to get there. I'm at the mall, shopping with my granddaughter."

"Sure," she said and hung up.

"Who's that?" Amelia asked.

"Someone that I have to go and talk to." I began steering her toward the checkout line, but she balked.

"We were going to look at puppies and then eat at Uncle Teddy's. You promised, Poppi."

"Look," I said, getting down so we were at eye level. "I know you are disappointed, but I have a job where sometimes I have to work on weekends."

"I hate your job," she said, pulling away from me and marching toward the checkout line.

I followed, paid for the blouses and we walked to the car in silence. When we were inside, and buckled up, I said. "Amelia, do you know what Poppi does?"

"Sure, you investigate people."

"Why do you think I do that?"

"I don't know," she said. "Cause people are bad?"

I started the car. "You are mostly right. I want to tell you about a case that I'm working on right now. A little boy about your age was kidnapped as he walked home from school. He was tied up and left in the woods all night long."

She looked at me horrified. "All night long? He must have been really scared."

"Yes, I think he was. He died all alone in the woods."

She looked down at her feet. As much as I can, I would like to protect my granddaughter from the evil in the world. But I also want her to know that what I do is important ; it's not just how I earn a paycheck.

"I'm trying to find out who let the little boy die," I said.

"OK," she said

"OK, what?"

"OK, I guess we won't look at puppies today and maybe we won't eat at Uncle Teddy's."

I wanted to reach over and kiss her. "I don't think this will take long," I said. "When it's over, we can still look at puppies. I'm not promising anything, we're just looking."

"And eat at Uncle Teddy's?"

"Sure."

We drove to Molly's. Molly herself, perhaps alerted to the fact that I was a cop, was standing in the doorway. This time there was no smell of marijuana on the air.

"Listen to me, Bellini," she said, hands on hips. "I don't like strangers coming and going like they own the place. I've rented the apartment to Samantha, and now I've got her boyfriend, her boyfriend's mother and you. Are you moving in too?"

"Nope," I said. "I'm just here to talk with Greg's mother."

She looked down at Amelia and smiled, her manner completely changed. "Hi, sweetie? Are you here with your daddy?"

"Her grandfather," I said. "Can we go up?"

"Sure," she said. We walked up to the second floor. I could hear voices behind the closed door but as soon as I knocked, there was silence. Greg answered the door.

"Come on in," he said. He looked down at Amelia. "Who's this?"

"My granddaughter, Amelia. Is your mother here?"

Greg moved away from the door and pointed toward April who was sitting on the sofa. She turned and stood up. It was then that I saw the bruises on her face.

"What happened to you?"

"It's a long story," she said. She turned to Samantha. "Would you make us some coffee?"

Sam nodded. "What about the kid?"

"Hot chocolate, please" Amelia said. She didn't like to be referred to as 'the kid.'

Samantha turned toward Amelia. "Want to come and help me make it?"

When they were out of the room, I sat beside April and took out my notebook. She took a deep breath and began. "I was at home alone on Wednesday evening, when I heard a knock on the door."

"What time was this?"

"About eight. I thought it would be a guy I've been dating, but he always calls first. I opened the door, and in waltzes CiCi Swindon. I was shocked. I asked what she wanted. She didn't say anything, just grabbed me by the hair and started slapping me on the face. She told me that Sandy had victimized her, and I had done nothing to stop it. All I had done was fire her. What she was saying had happened so long ago, I couldn't figure out why she was in my apartment now. I struggled to get free of her. We fell. I hit my head on a glass coffee table and blacked out. When I came to, I was sitting on the floor, with CiCi beside me holding a gun to my head and my hands duct taped behind my back. I asked why she was doing this. She told me to shut up. I was going to make a call to the office and leave a message that I was going on vacation. If I didn't do as she said, she would shoot me right there. She dialed the number and I talked to the secretary, telling her I was taking a few days' vacation. I thought she would just leave then, but she muscled me up from the floor and we walked out to the street. We went to my car which was in the parking garage. I think by then it was about nine-thirty. I kept complaining about the cold, because I had on only the sweatshirt I'd been wearing in the house. But she pushed me into the trunk of the car, jammed a needle into my arm and slammed the lid. I passed out. We must have traveled for miles. Then CiCi stopped the car and opened the trunk. She pointed the gun at me and told me to get out. I protested; we were in the middle of nowhere, and it was dark and freezing. She pulled me out of the trunk, got into the car and roared off. She'd kept my purse, so I had no money or identification. I was cold and hungry and miles from anywhere."

"And your hands were still bound by the tape?"

April held out her wrists so I could see the angry welts where the duct tape had irritated the skin.

"I managed to get the tape off by rubbing my wrists against a sharp stone. Then I started to walk.

I kept hoping that a car would come along, but there was nothing. I must have walked for miles. Finally I reached Tupper Lake, where there was a general store which was closed. I sat down on the ground with my back against the store. I was so tired, I must have fallen asleep. When the store opened, I went in and found a phone in the back, where I called Greg."

"Did the owners of the store see you make the call?"

"Sure. I asked them if I could do it. It's not a pay phone and I had no money, but they let me make the call anyway."

"When did you get the call, Greg?"

Take My Hand

"About nine on Thursday morning. I drove to the Adirondacks and picked up Mom. Then I took her back to Burlington."

"What was the name of the store where you made the call? " I asked.

"I don't remember," April said.

I looked at Greg. "Do you know?"

"Sally's something or other. The sign was almost worn away."

I turned to April. "What did you do when you got home?"

"I took a hot shower and went to bed where I slept until early Friday. Then I called on my land line to cancel the credit cards, and took a long run along the lake shore path. After lunch, I reported the stolen car to the police, and then I went to stay with a friend."

"What's the friend's name?"

"Larry Watkins. He's a teacher at the college. We've been dating on and off for about six months."

"What's his telephone number?"

"I don't think…."

"April, it's not enough that you're telling me these things. I need confirmation."

She nodded. "I'm sorry, I forgot to call the office to let them know I was home. I was shell-shocked, OK? Nothing like this has ever happened to me. On Friday, Greg called me to tell me that Sandy had been shot. I rented a car and drove up here."

"I need the phone number of Larry Watkins."

"Sure," she said reaching for her purse. She pulled out an address book. "Thank goodness, I had this at home, or I'd be really lost. As it is, I don't have my cell phone, my credit cards or driver's license. It's a nightmare." She read off the cell phone number.

Just at that moment Sam and Amelia came in from the kitchen carrying mugs of cocoa. From the splatters on Amelia's blouse, I guessed that they'd been having a lot of fun with the drink. Amelia sat next to me on the couch, swinging her legs back and forth. "Be careful with the cocoa," I cautioned, though a few more stains on this couch probably would not even be noticed.

"One more question, April. Why did you call me?"

"Greg said that the police were looking for me. I figured they thought I was a suspect. After all, Sandy and I didn't always get along. I guessed if I talked to you, you could help me work out an alibi?"

"An alibi? Don't you want to tell the truth?"

"Of course, that's what I mean. I need to tell them the truth. Do you think they will believe me?"

I might have said I wasn't sure whether *I* believed her? It was a story with so many holes, that only someone with a love of fiction would take it on face value. If April were stopped for speeding in Elizabethtown at eleven, she would still have plenty of time to shoot Sandy, drive back to Tupper Lake, ditch the car and be at Sally's store in the morning with her alibi. Except for the bruises, and the irritation on her wrists, which she could have administered herself, there was not a single person who could corroborate her story. The big question was, if she had murdered her ex-husband why fabricate this elaborate tale? Why not just flee?

Maybe she'd felt remorse? The man she'd shot was the father of her children. Maybe she'd had second thoughts about spending the rest of her life in prison and reasoned that if she were convincing enough, she could get away with murder. I had to find the store in Tupper Lake and locate the person who'd let her make the phone call. All of this was a long shot at best.

"I need to do some work," I said. "First we need to find the general store and see if anyone remembers you. Second, if you came southwest from Burlington, you may have crossed on the Lake Champlain ferry and it's possible they have a record of the car. That doesn't prove who was driving it, but it might confirm some of what you said. And there's the matter of the gun, which if it is found, might be traceable to the purchaser. And we need to locate your car, wherever the hell that is."

Amelia gave me a sharp look that said I had used a bad word. "Sorry," I said. "I'm not allowed to swear." I turned toward April. "You can see the devious route we need to take in order to get to the truth."

I put my coffee cup on the table and stood up. "I promised my granddaughter a day at the mall. Don't go anywhere, April. Jim Weims from the Saranac Lake Police Department will be trying to reach you." I wrote Jim's number on the back of my card. "It will look better for you, if you call him first."

"Sure," April said. She stood up and walked me to the door. "Thanks for coming, Mr. Bellini."

She closed the door, but not completely and I heard Greg's voice. "Look," he said. "I picked you up when you called, but that is the end of it. Once Dad's funeral is over, I'm having nothing more to do with you."

April's voice. "I don't know why you are so angry at me, Greg. I've done everything to support you. I pleaded with your father to keep you in college."

"It's just your guilty conscience, Mom. You were as bad as he was."

"What do you mean by that?"

"Where were you the night Ethan was kidnapped? You were supposed to pick him up. You said you were having a drink with a friend, but I went back to that bar and you weren't..."

The door was slammed shut. I looked down at the coat in my hand, suddenly realizing what I was supposed to be doing. "OK," I said. "It's almost one thirty. Let's go to lunch first."

"And then puppies, please?"

"OK, we'll just look."

As it turned out the pet store was closer, so we spent a half hour, with my stomach rumbling looking at a variety of very cute dogs. I tried to talk Amelia into a gerbil or a bird. Even a goldfish would be much less trouble, but she was firm. When we were sitting at our late lunch, she said.

"That little yellow dog was really cute, wasn't he Poppi?"

"Cute," I said. I'd been thinking about April LeBrun's motive for shooting her ex-husband. Had she been responsible for Ethan's death and Sandy learned about it and threatened to expose her? Greg's comments about where she'd been the night of the kidnapping, made me realize I'd never thought of her as a suspect. Had I overlooked one of the precepts that underlie all crimes against children? *Look at close relatives first.* Both parents had been questioned over and over by Gunther and Besom. Since those detectives had found nothing, I'd taken it for granted that the parents were innocent. But what if they weren't?

"Poppi," Amelia said. "You aren't listening"

I drew a breath and looked down at my hamburger, still only half eaten. Amelia had made short work of her supersized hot dog.

"You're right," I said. I took a sip of my coffee. "I wasn't listening. I have said you can't have a dog, but I will reconsider, with two conditions."

"Yes?"

"First, you need to promise that you will take care of this dog It's not going to be Mrs. Gentile's job or my job. It will be your job."

She nodded.

"Number two. We're not buying a dog from the pet store. Those puppies come from puppy mills, and I don't want to support those businesses."

"What's a puppy mill?"

"A place where the mother dog just has puppies and never has a chance to go out and play or have fun. I want to get a dog from the animal shelter."

"Can we still get a puppy?"

"I think we can. Sometimes a dog has puppies at the animal shelter and then the puppies are put up for adoption. Lots of people leave dogs at the shelter that they don't want."

"Why wouldn't someone want a dog? I want one Poppi."

I sighed. Could I withstand this emotional blackmail? "I know you do," I said. "Let's just think about it."

I needed to call Jim Weims and tell him about the interview with April LeBrun. She was his suspect as much as mine. "I need to make one call," I said.

Chapter Thirty Four

Jim Weims picked up the phone on the first ring. In the background I could hear a baby wailing.

"Jim," I said. "It's Chris Bellini. I just talked with April LeBrun. She's not in Burlington. She's with her son up here in Springdale."

"I've been trying to reach her," he said. "Why is she there?"

"She came up to make arrangements for Sandy's funeral," I said. "And there's more." I gave him the blow-by-blow of April's story. "She said she walked to a general store in Tupper Lake called Sally's. Do you know it?"

"Sure, Sally's Deli. It's run by a father and daughter team. I can talk to Sally and her father today. When was she there?"

"Early Thursday morning. She said the store was closed when she got there. She slept outside and called her son when it opened. Greg drove her back to Burlington and then she went to stay with a friend named Larry Watkins." I gave him Larry's number.

"If I drive up there on Monday can you get me to April?"

"No problem," I said. "It will be interesting to see if the story she tells you matches what she told me. Jim, I'd like to ask you a huge favor. I know Sandy LeBrun is your territory but I can't help feeling that April's story is related to the Ethan LeBrun kidnapping. If you come up on Monday, I'll show you where Greg is living, and then just sit in the car while you interview him and his mother. In exchange, I'd like to be with you when you interview Sally and her father on Tuesday."

There was a long silence. In the background, a dog barked and was shushed by a woman. Maybe the baby had finally gone to sleep.

"OK," he said finally. "What time do you want to meet?"

Take My Hand

"How about ten. That will give you time for breakfast with your family." I'll buy you coffee at Jenny's On Main."

"See you there."

"Who you talking to?" Amelia asked when I'd hung up.

"A man named Mr. Weims. He's a detective like me. He's going to come up here on Monday to talk to some people. Also I might have to go into the office tomorrow."

"Tomorrow is Sunday, Poppi. Why do you have to work on Sunday?"

"It will be just for a while. Tell you what, why don't you invite Carey DeGrasse for the day. The play is on Tuesday. You can practice your songs with Carey."

"Can we go to a movie?"

"Sure," I said. I'd have to double check what the movie was, but I wanted Amelia to be busy. I called Willi who said that Carey could come over, but she herself couldn't stay. I was disappointed. Willi and I needed to work out our relationship issues, but I had no other time.

On Monday, I waited in my car outside Molly's house, while Weims interviewed April and Greg. Today was a school holiday, so Mrs. Gentile would be taking care of Amelia and Carey. I would be home as soon as I could, but I needed to talk with Jim after he'd interviewed April and Greg. He came out of the house, opened the car door and got in beside me.

"Do you believe her story?" I asked.

He shook his head. "I don't know. If she was kidnapped and someone took her car, where is the vehicle? Has she ditched it somewhere? And where is this CiCi Swindon? The one she says kidnapped her?"

"No idea."

"The kid seems pretty angry at his father. When did he leave school?"

"Monday or Tuesday, November fifth or sixth.

"If Sandy was killed on the seventh, why did Greg wait so long?"

"He stewed on it, letting his anger rise? Plus, he had to find a gun."

"What else have you got?" Weims asked.

"I overheard Greg and his mother talking," I said. "Greg says his mother was drunk the afternoon, Ethan was kidnapped. He blames her for Ethan's death."

"If Greg was that angry, why would he have gone to the Adirondacks to rescue her?" Jim asked. "It looks to me like we've got two good suspects for Sandy's death. We need to find April's car and talk to the owners of Sally's Deli. If April is telling the truth, they can confirm or deny that she was there."

"What time do you want to meet tomorrow?"

"How about ten. I'll give you the address."

When I got home Mrs. Gentile was putting lunch on the table for the two girls. She looked frazzled.

"I'm so sorry to leave you with these two," I said. "I'll take over from here."

She grabbed her coat and hat and was out the door before I could change my mind. I went into the living room where two little girls were cutting up magazines. Pieces of paper were scattered all over the carpet.

"Come on," I said. "Lunch is ready." I looked at Carey. "What time is your mother coming to pick you up?"

"She said twelve." It was now ten of. "We have to go shop for clothes."

I looked out the window and watched as Willi's car pulled into the driveway. She'd been not answering my calls and I didn't know why.

"Give me a minute with her," I said. I went to the door and opened it, just as she reached for the handle.

"Willi, we need to talk," I said, pulling her into the kitchen. I parked myself in a chair at the table and she sat.

"What's going on with us? I thought we were friends." I lowered my voice. "I thought we were more than friends."

She took off her hat and gloves and laid them carefully on the table, not looking at me. "You're a great guy, Chris," she said. "Any woman would be lucky to have you."

"Any woman but you?"

She looked up, there were tears in her eyes. "I can't do this, Chris. I can't fall in love with a guy who is not going to be around. I did that once, I can't do it again."

"Who says I'm not going to be around?"

"You've been shot. You've been stabbed. You've been beat up. I'd say you have a good chance of not being around."

"That's my job, Willi. It's dangerous sometimes, but I can handle it."

"That's exactly what Jim said too. 'Don't worry about me, I can handle it.'" She reached forward and touched my hand. "You are the best thing that ever happened to me, Chris. I want to be with you, but I don't want to go through with you what I went through with Jim." The tears were running down her cheeks. She wiped them roughly away. She stood up. "I've got to go."

I watched her leave, feeling that my heart was cracking in two. Why did loving someone have to be so God-damned hard? How could you want to be with someone, and not want to be with them? Wasn't it one or the other? I went into the living room where Amelia was stretched out on the couch watching a movie, the cut paper mess still spread all over the room.

"Amelia, clean up this mess," I barked.

Chapter Thirty Five

On Tuesday I drove down to Tupper Lake. Tonight was Amelia's play and I needed to be back in Euclid in time to get dressed, so this would be a short visit.

Sally's Deli was right where Jim had told me, and Jim himself was standing outside with a cup of coffee waiting for me. It was an overcast day, with the feel of snow in the air. Global warming seemed to have brought winter earlier to northern New York, and especially to these small hamlets in the mountains.

I got out of the car and Jim raised his cup to me. "They make pretty good java here, Chris," he said. "I'll buy."

"Thanks," I said. "This is your territory so you take the lead."

He looked at me. "When I first met you, Chris, I thought you were some yahoo stomping around a crime scene, messing up evidence, but I think you're OK. If you have a question that I haven't answered, go ahead and ask."

We walked up a set of steps to a small open porch. In the summer, this would be where hikers, bikers and casual visitors would sit and eat an ice cream or sip a drink. I could see the plastic chairs piled up in the corner. I stepped up over a threshold into the store itself, a place that is a staple of many small towns. Here was everything anyone who was far from big boxes would ever want. Fishing poles and propane tanks were crammed into corners with winter boots, gloves, twelve packs of beer, and American flags. The shelves were crowded with dusty cans of stew and soup, boxes of cereal, even baby diapers. At one end of the store stood the coffee machines and behind a glass partition hot dogs roasted. The Deli part of the store stood in the back where huge hams sat in a glass fronted case. The only proprietor was a middle aged man with white hair and a beard.

"What can I do for you?" he inquired.

"My friend would like a coffee," Jim said. He turned to me. "Black?"

I nodded. When the man handed me the coffee, Jim took out his badge and showed it. "I'm Jim Weims, a detective from Saranac Lake. We'd like to talk with you about a woman who was here last Thursday morning. She said she spent the night outside your store, and when you opened, she asked if she could make a phone call. Do you remember her? Her name was April LeBrun."

"Last Thursday?"

"November eighth. She told us that both you and your daughter were here, and that you let her use the phone."

The man shook his head. "Don't remember no one here when we opened up on Thursday."

"Could we please speak to your daughter?" I asked.

"She's out in back. Just a minute," the man said. "Sally," he bellowed. "Some folks here to talk with you."

There was no answer. The man turned and walked toward the back of the store and disappeared through an open door. In a few minutes he came back with a plump girl of about twenty trailing behind him. She was wearing jeans, work boots and a flannel shirt, covered by a stained butcher's apron.

When she saw the two of us she said "Yeah?"

"We'd like to talk to you about the woman who was here last Thursday. She told you she'd spent part of the night outside, and wanted to make a phone call."

"Never saw her," the young woman said.

"Here," I said, pulling out April's picture from my pocket. "Take a look." I handed the picture to Sally and she glanced at it too quickly.

"Nope," she said.

"Who else comes in here early on Thursday morning?"

Take My Hand

"Jake Mackey comes in at nine for his coffee and newspaper. He was a little late. Then we had Millie from down the street wanting a few groceries."

"What time do you open?"

"Seven. Lots of folks stop by on their way to work. We get loggers or folks that work at the museum. And people picking up groceries to hold them over until they can get to a bigger grocery store."

"Where is your phone?" Jim asked.

The man pointed to the back of the store and we walked to the area close to the Deli where an ancient pale green wall phone was attached to the wall. It was not a pay phone. We returned to the counter where the proprietor was standing. "Do you ever have people who make calls without paying?"

"Sometimes, but not much. Most folks around here have cell phones. And the rest of the people who come here know us. They're honest."

It was possible that April had come into the store and used the phone without asking permission. But that meant that she had no alibi for the time she was supposedly being abducted.

"Thank you for your time," Jim said. We headed for the door. Just as we walked out, I turned back and saw the two, father and daughter with their heads together. The daughter seemed upset about something, and the father was talking to her in a low voice. When he saw me watching them, he stopped talking. I followed Jim out to the street and we got into his car. We needed to talk and it was too cold to sit on the porch. A few fat snowflakes were falling lazily from the sky, the gentle prelude to what could be a serious winter storm.

"How well do you know these people, Jim?" I asked.

"Not well. They've owned this place for about six years. I understand that the Dad is divorced from the mother, and the girl dropped out of college to help him run the store. But I rarely come into this part of the Adirondacks."

"So it's possible they might be lying."

"Possible. Is that your take on this?"

"I don't know. Why would they lie? They didn't do anything illegal, just let a woman in trouble make a phone call. It's possible that April might have made the call without asking."

"Yeah, my thought too," Weims said. Just then his cell phone rang. "Weims," he said. "Really? OK, we'll be right there."

He turned to me. "They found a prescription bottle on the road into Sandy LeBrun's place. It's medication for April LeBrun."

We drove to the police station, where one of the officers handed Jim a plastic bag. Inside was an orange prescription bottle made out to April LeBrun for Synthroid.

"It's prescribed for people with hypothyroidism," I said. "My wife took it."

"We've got April on record as speeding in Elizabethtown and now her prescription bottle shows up at the murder site. Do we have enough evidence to charge her?"

"What about her motive?" I said. "I don't think pulling a kid's college fund is a good enough reason to kill a man."

"It could be something else," Weims said. "Something April did on the day Ethan was kidnapped. The two of them could have argued and bam, she pulls out her gun and shoots him."

"Where did she get the gun? Was it her gun? Or his gun? Sandy might have been a hunter, but the gun that killed him wasn't a shotgun. Did he feel he needed some kind of protection out there in the woods?"

"It's hard to prove ownership of a gun without a bill of sale. If we have the serial number we can run the number, but that's a long process."

"So what do we have?" I asked.

"Let's go back and talk to the Arnstads," Weims said. "If April killed her ex-husband, I can't believe she would go north to Saranac Lake, then turn south to Tupper Lake, ditch the car and cook up this story about being kidnapped. She has the resources to run; criminals have done that before, and some of them don't get caught until years later. My money is on one or both of the Arnstads lying."

We drove back to Tupper Lake. By this time it was late afternoon and people were milling around the store, shopping and visiting with each other. I saw Sally Arnstad standing behind the deli counter, feeding ham into a meat slicer while a man waited for his sandwich to be made.

I looked at Jim. "Let's do this together, starting with the girl."

While Weims pushed himself behind the counter, I went to the customer and flashed my badge. "Excuse me," I said. "But we need to talk with this girl privately for a moment." Jim had taken Sally's arm and was guiding her toward the back room.

"You can't do this," she said, pointing to the customer. "He's been waiting for ten minutes."

I picked up the sliced ham that sat on the waxed paper and handed it to the customer. "Make your own sandwich," I said. Then Jim and I led Sally to a tiny storeroom in the rear of the store.

"Tell us what really happened," Jim said.

"I told you. We never saw the woman, or maybe she came in and made the call and didn't pay. It's busy in the morning. We don't keep track of who's here."

"Her son came and picked her up, later in the day. Tall boy with blonde hair. You're telling me you never saw either of these people. They swore to us they paid you for the call."

She was silent, her head down, picking at some skin on her fingernails. She was a pretty girl who might have had a life different than slicing meat and serving up coffee in a tiny store.

"Why didn't you finish college?" I asked.

She looked at me surprised. "My father was here all by himself. He has a heart problem and was doing a lot of heavy lifting. Cases of beer, cartons of canned goods. I was all he had, so I came to help him."

"Giving up your own life in the process?" Jim asked.

"It's not so bad," she said. "I've been taking classes on the internet. What I really want is to be a writer."

"I bet you miss your friends," I said. "Not much for a person your age to do around here, is there?"

I saw tears in her eyes, and I knew I'd hit a nerve. The tears spilled over and she started sobbing. Just at that moment, her father poked his head in the door. "Sally," he said. "What the hell is going on? People are waiting out there."

"I never lied to anyone in my life," Sally said. "But she said we'd be sorry if we said anything."

"She?"

"The woman who came into the store after the other one left with her son. She told us the police might be here asking questions, but we should say we never saw April LeBrun. If she learned we'd said anything she'd come back and shoot Dad."

Sally stood up and was immediately enfolded in her father's arms. I watched the two of them, my mind churning. Jim and I looked at each other. "I've got to get home," I said. "My granddaughter's in a play that starts in three hours. I've asked a friend to try and locate CiCi Swindon, but it could be a while."

Jim nodded, looking out at the snow which was now falling heavily. "Good luck," he said.

The snow not only made the roads slippery and hard to negotiate, but since it was the first serious storm of the season, no one knew how to drive in the stuff. Twice I narrowly missed drivers who had misjudged the stopping distance and almost spun off the road. Fifteen minutes out of Tupper Lake, I called Willi on my cell. She had promised to take Amelia home with her after school, since I didn't know when I would return.

"Hi, Chris," Willi said. "We're just going out the door. We're having an early supper of Pizza since the girls have to be at the school by six. Where are you?"

"A little north of Tupper Lake. It's starting to snow pretty heavily, so I have to take it slow."

"Want to say hi to Amelia?"

"Sure," I said. Amelia's voice came on, full of excitement. "Poppi," she said. "The play is tonight. Are you going to be there?"

"Of course. I'm on my way home; you know it's important to me."

"OK," she said. "We're going out the door. We'll save you a ticket."

I had slowed to a crawl because there was now zero visibility. In this part of the Adirondacks there was almost no cell phone coverage. I drove north to Childwold where I stopped at a gas station for coffee. Then my phone rang. I was so surprised to have cell service that it took me a minute to get it out of my pocket and answer it.

"Mr. Bellini, this is Myra Grindon. You asked me to find something about Cecelia Swindon. I'm sorry it's taken me so long. I've been busy with school and…"

"What did you find?"

"She works as a reporter for a small TV station near Chicago. WMSW. She's been there for about six years. She goes by Sissy."

"Did you get an address for her?"

"Oh, she's not there right now. She took personal leave to come east."

"When did she take the personal leave?"

"Just a minute, I've got it here in my notes. She flew into Boston on Tuesday, November third. She's due back at the TV station some time next week."

"Did she rent a car in Boston?"

"Yeah. From Hertz."

"What reason did CiCi give for taking personal leave?"

"Her mother died. She was going home to the funeral."

I hoped Vangie Swindon wasn't dead but I felt a drop in the pit of my stomach, like a pin ball falling into its slot in a machine, or a bullet dropping into the chamber. CiCi Swindon had flown to Boston, and rented a car. I was sure now that she'd then driven to Burlington and kidnapped April LeBrun. Sometime after she'd been stopped for speeding, she'd ditched April because CiCi feared if she were stopped again, April would be discovered. Then she'd gone north to Saranac Lake and shot Sandy LeBrun. I had no idea where CiCi was now, but if Evangeline Swindon weren't already dead, it was possible she would be soon. I glanced at my watch. It was five thirty. I had roughly an hour and a half to get to Euclid and the play.

I took out my phone and dialed Larry's number. When the answering machine picked up, I blurted out my message.

"Larry listen, it's important and I haven't got much time. I think CiCi Swindon killed Sandy LeBrun and may have been involved in Ethan's death. I need you to go to Vangie Swindon's house and make sure that she's all right. Break into the house if you have to. The other thing is, can you keep an eye on Amelia? She's in this play tonight, but I won't be there until right before it opens. Thanks buddy."

I called Jim Weims and told him what I'd learned. "Can you get someone to go to the parking garage attached to April LeBrun's apartment? I think a Hertz rental car in the name of Cecilia Swindon is parked there. I don't know what the license is, but if you call Hertz in

Boston, you can get the number. I'm sorry, I can't be there to help you. I'm trying to get home before seven."

I called Willi. The phone rang six times before it was picked up.

"Chris," she said. "Where are you?"

"Childwold. I'm amazed I'm getting any cell service at all. It's snowing like crazy. Tell Amelia I'm going to be there, even if I'm a little late. Is she there, Willi?"

There was a long sigh. "You don't know how crazy it is here, Chris. We've got kids all over the place, parents who want to come backstage and help their kids get dressed. Some woman from Chicago is here interviewing the children as part of a project, and half the kids have lost their costumes and forgotten their lines."

My blood froze. "Tell me about the woman from Chicago."

"She's tall and blonde. I don't remember her name. But she showed up forty minutes ago and set up this little interview corner right in the dressing room."

"Willi," I interrupted. "I need to talk to Amelia."

"She was right here just a minute ago. Let me go find her." The phone went quiet. I waited. Then the phone went dead. We'd been cut off.

Chapter Thirty Six

I dialed again, but there was no answer. Outside the wind was blowing and it was snowing heavily, but my hands were sweating and dread was lodged in my gut like a cannon ball. I grabbed my coffee and went to the car. I turned the key in the ignition, but there was only a click, no sound of the engine turning over. I turned the key again, once more. Finally, reluctantly the engine turned over and I drove away.

There are many ways to die on a wintery road. You can strike a deer or a moose that could crush the car, with you inside. You can hit an icy patch and spin out of control, ending upside down in a ditch where you lie, out of sight and immobilized hoping someone will rescue you before you die of your injuries. You can be struck by a plow or by another car. Your car can suddenly stop running and when you try to walk for help, you can die of hypothermia.

All of those things were running through my head as I drove north. But most of the worry that churned my insides concerned Amelia. CiCi hadn't taken personal leave to visit her mother. She had come east to kill.

It took me two and a half hours to drive what is normally an hour's ride. When I got close to Euclid, the snow had lessened to a small dusting on the road. I was rounding the corner to the school when my cell phone rang. I punched the button.

"Poppi?" It was Amelia and she was crying.

"What's wrong honey?" I looked at my watch. It was now almost eight. I'd missed the first hour of the play. "I'm sorry I missed part of the play," I said, "but I'm here now."

"Poppi, tell her to let me go."

My heart stopped. "Where are you Amelia?"

"In the hotel next to the school. I asked her why she was taking me to the hotel. It's cold here and dark. I don't like her, Poppi. I want to go home."

"Let me talk to the lady," I said.

There was silence on the line, the sound of something rustling and then a voice came on the line.

"Hello Chris. I bet you'd like to see your granddaughter wouldn't you? Better yet, you'd like to see her alive."

"I have to tell you that I'm a policeman," I said. "And if you do anything to hurt Amelia, I will bring the full force of the law against you."

"The way you've brought me to justice already? Come on, Chris. You're blowing smoke out your ass. I've got all the cards and you've got nothing."

"Where are you?"

"The old Morrissey Hotel, the one right next to the school."

The Morrissey was the hotel where Sandy LeBrun had gone to meet with the kidnappers. It stood near the school, and was being prepped for demolition, the windows and doors having been removed. I hadn't been inside but I remembered the rear of the hotel where Hedgewick had beaten me up. I parked my car in the crowded school parking lot and walked up the rough path to the hotel.

I stepped into the first floor. There was no furniture, only a vast dark space, lit faintly by the yard lights of the school next door. I could see the support columns that held up the ceiling and at the base of each bundles of dynamite. Through the empty windows, I could hear traffic from the street. No one came into this building because it was too dangerous, so no one would come to rescue me. I was on my own.

"Here," a voice called. I could see something that looked like a flashlight at the rear of the room. I walked carefully across the room trying not to trip on loose wires littering the floor.

The woman with the flashlight was tall and blonde and for a moment I thought it was April LeBrun. Someone had said that Sandy LeBrun liked young blondes, and now I realized that the woman he'd chosen for his affair had an uncanny resemblance to his wife. This was CiCi Swindon. In one hand she held a flashlight, in the other a gun. She was sitting in a plastic chair and at her feet was a yellow box that I realized must be the detonator. If she pressed the button, the whole structure would come down, crushing us.

"Where's my granddaughter?" I asked.

CiCi Swindon played the flashlight around and I saw Amelia. She was wearing her pumpkin costume and over that (thank goodness) her yellow winter coat. Her face was tear streaked and she was shaking. Attaching her to the support post was a strong rope and at the base was a bundle of dynamite.

"Tie him up," CiCi said.

Evangeline Swindon came forward from the shadows. She was trembling. "He's a cop, CiCi," she said. "What we're doing is illegal."

"I said to tie him the fuck up," CiCi said, moving forward to press the gun against her mother's head.

Vangie tied me to a column several feet from Amelia. Vangie's knots were loose and sloppy and before she'd even moved away, I'd begun to work myself free. I looked over at Amelia. If I could distract CiCi, I might be able to free her.

"Poppi," she said softly.

"I'm here honey. We're going to get out of this, don't worry."

"Shut the hell up," CiCi said.

"So, what happens next?" I asked.

"We wait for the play to end and people to come into the parking lot next door. I want an audience for this spectacle. Have you ever seen a building come down, Chris? It's amazing. First they fire the dynamite at the base of the columns, and then the whole place slowly collapses in on itself, a great edifice coming first to its knees and then to the ground until it is just a pile of rubble. It's too bad you won't enjoy the show because of course when the dynamite fires, you'll be blown up."

"It's not too late to give yourself up," Vangie said. "You can have a life CiCi, all you have to do is admit what you did."

"If you don't shut up mother, I'll kill you right here."

"What did I ever do to make you so angry with me?" Vangie Swindon cried. "I was a good mother. I had to do everything myself because I was raising you alone."

"When Sandy raped me, you pretended it didn't happen."

"I swear I didn't know, CiCi. He was a doctor, my employer. If I'd made a stink, I'd be without a job."

"That's it, wasn't it? A job was more precious to you than your own daughter. You didn't want to protect me, because that would mean sticking your neck out. I wish you'd gone to jail with my father, then I would have been an orphan."

"Your father wasn't a bad man," Vangie said. "Just sick. If he'd been able to take his medicine regularly, he might never have got in trouble. Just like you, CiCi. If you follow the doctor's orders, nothing bad will happen."

"Listen to her. Nothing bad will happen. It has already happened, Mother. I was barely a teenager when Sandy got me drunk, took me to a hotel and raped me. The first time, I tried to fight him off. I even told you what was happening, but you said I was making up stories. I had no one to turn to. Then when I got pregnant, Sandy took me to an abortionist, who bungled the job so badly I'll never have children."

"Is that why you killed him?" I asked.

CiCi was silent. "I made a life for myself in Chicago," she said. "I had a man who wanted to marry me, but he wanted his own children. When Mom called and said that you'd been asking questions about Ethan's death, I knew I'd never be free of this thing unless I finished it myself."

"So that's why you killed Sandy."

"I should have done it ten years ago," CiCi said.

There was silence in the building. Something creaked and I wondered, even without the dynamite, whether the building would just collapse around us. Outside I could hear the wind in the trees and a distant dog barking.

"Why did you kill Ethan LeBrun?" I asked.

"I wanted Sandy to suffer like I'd suffered. I found this hotel, because it was like the one in New York where he'd taken me, and I made friends with a kid who had a younger brother Ethan's age. All I wanted was for Sandy to know what it was like to lose something he loved. I hated him, but I wanted him to know I existed, that I hadn't been just a quick fuck in a hotel. My plan was to talk to him and then go back and free Ethan. I didn't care about the money. I just wanted to get even."

"Did you ever see Sandy?"

"When he came into the hotel, I was going to follow him and then I chickened out. Don't ask me why. I was young and scared. I left the hotel and ran back to the woods where the boys were going to leave Ethan, but he was already dead. They'd taped his mouth shut and he suffocated. That's when I panicked and ran."

During this exchange I had begun to work the loosened ropes against the rough surface of the support column. It was hard work, and I was often skinning my hands in the process, but this was my only choice. I finally got free. CiCi was looking over at her mother, so she didn't see me move toward Amelia and start undoing her ropes. "Stay quiet," I whispered. "When I tell you to run, you run fast."

"What the hell's going on," CiCi demanded, playing the flashlight over the column where I'd been tied. Seeing it empty, she pointed the flashlight at Amelia and me. "You two are dead," she said.

"Please don't," Vangie said, moving forward. I desperately needed a distraction. Just at that moment I heard voices, two people skirting the building as a shortcut to the street.

"Listen to me, you little fucker," the first voice said, "I told you to get your ass in gear twenty minutes ago. We've got business tonight and we're already late."

I recognized the voice.

"Hedgewick," I called. "Have you beaten up any kids lately?"

"Shut up," CiCi hissed. She flipped off the flashlight.

"Hedgewick," I called again. "I hear people aren't buying your cars. Why is that? Because you're an asshole?"

"Are you jerking off in there, Bellini?" Hedgewick called. "I should have known this is what you do for fun."

"I told you to SHUT UP," CiCi screamed. She moved toward where Amelia and I had been standing, but now we were free of the ropes, huddled in the dark against the wall.

"You want to teach me a lesson, Hedgewick," I called. "I'm right here. Why don't you bring your pansy-assed boy with you. I'll take you both on."

"Leave it, Dad," I heard Jason say. "We're already late."

"Not on your life. I'm going to finish this right now."

"We're right here," I called.

At that moment several things happened simultaneously. The first play-goers came out of the school and as cars were started, headlights went on, illuminating the open windows of the old Morrissey Hotel. Quickly

I moved Amelia to a darkened window at the back of the building and lifted her through the open space, urging to run as fast as she could. Then I went back to a window illuminated by the car headlights, and said to Hedgewick who was still outside, "Come and get me." As Hedgewick muscled himself over the window sill, CiCi cried "No," and fumbled with the flashlight.

I moved away from the window. "Come on you asshole," I called from the darkness. Hedgewick was in the room now, confused by the darkness. CiCi flicked on the flashlight, catching him full in the face. Hedgewick lunged forward. She fired and he went down.

"CiCi," Evangeline called and rushed toward her daughter. CiCi raised the gun and fired again.

At that moment I made a decision, I sometimes regret. Finding a window illuminated by the headlights, I jumped up onto the sill and was out. Breathing heavily I ran away from the building and stood on the frozen ground, waiting.

Someone was crying, I couldn't tell if it were CiCi or her mother. Then there was a pop, followed by several more pops in close succession. And then, the old Morrissey Hotel that had been part of this tragedy began to collapse. Watching a building topple is an awesome sight. The hotel which all its life had been a two- story upright structure, bent at the knees and then planted those knees on the ground. Then the top floors followed the same trajectory as the bottom, the whole structure folding in on itself in a cloud of ash and dust.

I was standing with my arms around Amelia, and I could hear people around me gasp in surprise as the building fell. I had no idea if the Wcked Witch of the West and her mother were buried under the building or had survived. Nor did I know if Hedgewick had made it. I could hear his son Jason, crying nearby. When the dust had cleared later tonight, dog handlers and paramedics would be looking for bodies. I was grateful to be alive.

I heard a noise and saw Willi and Carey running toward us. "Are you all right?" Willi asked. "When Amelia didn't show up for her part I was panicked, but I had no idea where she was. I tried to phone you, but no one was answering. Oh Chris, I was so worried."

I put my arm around her. It was nice to have someone worried about me. "Amelia and I are a little dusty but we're OK."

I heard sirens in the distance and an ambulance and two police cars pulled up. I detached myself from Amelia and went to speak to the cops, telling them about the people who might still be in the collapsed building. They wanted me to stay and help, but I'd had enough for the evening. I returned to my granddaughter. "Come on," I said. "Let's go home.

Chapter Thirty-Seven

The puppy's name was Buster, an unlikely name for a female Golden but that was the name Amelia had chosen. The dog was a goofy bundle of fur whose feet never touched the ground when Amelia was home. I guess the adoration was mutual, because the puppy spent all her time on Amelia's lap or on her bed.

On this day we were having a Christmas party and Willi and her daughter were there. Willi and I had cautiously rekindled our romance. I was trying hard not to get shot, stabbed or beaten up and Willi was trying to accept the realities of my job. Jim Weims had come with his wife and their two children. Mrs. Gentile had come with her new boyfriend, a man who never smiled, but whom she assured me was a treasure. Larry Grindon, his wife and daughter, Myra, were there. Even the Chief had come with his wife, a gentle grey-haired lady who seemed to be the real boss in the household. I had invited some of the neighbors and a few of the patrolmen.

I had not invited April or Greg LeBrun. Though we'd spent time together, I'd never considered them true friends.

We were half way through the party when the Chief said he'd like to talk with me alone in the kitchen. I wasn't sure what was on his mind, and I followed him with some anxiety.

"I got a call from a parole officer in New York City. He thought you might want to know that Big Boy Wright's been arrested. Apparently, he was in a car with a buddy who was driving erratically. When the cops tried to stop the car, Big Boy opened fire and fled. One of the cops died, so he'll be charged with murder one."

I nodded, not surprised.

"The officer wanted me to tell you that when LeRoy wrote the essay about the kidnapping, Big Boy called CiCi in Chicago. I think he was the one who got her the gun, too."

Take My Hand

"He told me he had no idea where she was," I said. "She owed him money."

The Chief shrugged. "So you believe all criminals tell the truth?"

I thought about the man who'd lured Harold Watson out of the nursing home by pretending to be his son, and the "bodyguarder" that had been watching Amelia. "There was a man," I said.

"Yeah, Wright had a friend, who might have been a sexual partner. He was arrested in this recent escapade. Is it worth our trouble to charge him with endangering an old man? That is if we can prove he was the one who was at the nursing home."

I shook my head. "Did you tell the parole officer that CiCi and her mother died when the Morrissey fell?"

"Nope. Didn't think it was relevant."

"I saw that Hedgewick's dealership is for sale."

"Yeah, he's looking for a way to raise money for a lawyer. Being indicted for drug trafficking isn't good for business."

"I'm sorry he lost his legs when building collapsed."

The Chief nodded. "Even though he was a bully, and raising a bully for a son, no one deserves that." He leaned back against a kitchen table and took a puff of a cigar. I hate cigarettes and cigars, especially in my kitchen where they stink things up, but I wanted to hear what the Chief said.

"April LeBrun contacted me two weeks ago. She and Greg would like to put up some kind of memorial to Ethen."

"What kind of memorial?"

"I have a little money left over from the fund. I could spend it on something like that."

"You have money left over? You told me that it was almost gone."

"I know, I know. I was too impatient to get you back to what I thought was your real job, helping to get rid of those drug dealers."

"Do the LeBruns have any suggestions?"

"Something for children," the Chief said.

"Is there enough for that?"

"April is willing to kick in whatever else we need."

"What about a playground, with his name on a plaque."

"The Ethan LeBrun playground," the Chief said. "It has a nice ring."

The End

If you enjoyed this book I would be grateful for an honest review on either Goodreads or Amazon. If you want to chat about it, you can e-mail me at funstories043@gmail.com or find me on my website: margueritemooers.com

Made in the USA
San Bernardino, CA
20 September 2017